Outrunning *the* Hunter

Book One

Kyona Jiles

ISBN (eBook): 979-8-9898052-0-4
ISBN (Paperback): 979-8-9898052-1-1
Library of Congress Control Number: 2024901669

Title Production by The Bookwhisperer

Cover Design by Sandy Robson

This book is dedicated to all the people who have ever tried to change their lives for the better.
You stepped outside your comfort zone and even if you think you failed, you didn't.
EVERYONE HAS A DREAM
FOLLOW YOURS

Chapter 1

Whoever said "What doesn't kill you will make you stronger" had obviously never been on the run for their life. The windshield wipers brushed away the raindrops sparkling from the streetlamps, and while it should have had a calming effect, Oakland at night was kind of scary. Chicago, Denver, and Tucson had seemed more cheerful than this. But maybe it wasn't the location as much as the *reason* she was here.

Kamielle wondered when she'd live somewhere that didn't seem scary. At the rate she was going, probably never. Her life was out of control and she was trying desperately to get it out of the hyper-drive tailspin. So far, it wasn't working out too well.

Pulling into her wet and dark driveway, Kamielle took a deep breath, trying not to think about the horrible day she'd had. Dark driveway? Had the porch light burnt out already?

Even though the large porch holding both entrances to the duplex had a small covering, the driveway did not. The rain was coming down hard and the neighbor's porch light wasn't on either, so no help there.

As Kami gathered her leather briefcase and laptop, she

thought she saw something move by the bushes next to the porch. Her breath caught in her throat and her heart threatened to beat out of her chest. She stared, unable to tell if anyone was there. A full grown man couldn't hide behind such short bushes, could he? She waited for a full minute just to be sure.

"Nothing to worry about," she said. "It's just the wind and rain. He doesn't know where you moved. And, if he finds you, just move again." Not that she *wanted* to move again.

She locked the doors and sprinted to the porch. The rustling in the bushes turned to a meow and purr and she sighed in relief. Her adopted tomcat trotted over and began rubbing against her legs.

"C'mon, kitty."

As she headed to the door, she cursed the dead porch light and fumbled for her keys.

"I hope your day was better than mine, Simon."

The cat was too busy trying to trip her to respond. She dropped her keys and they made a splashing sound as they hit the walkway. Leaning over, hair fell into her eyes and she almost dropped her laptop case.

"Seriously? Of all the lousy damn things to put an end to my perfectly shitty day!"

Bad language had never been allowed in the house while growing up with her parents. Swear words were only used by Frank, Kami's father. Now, she found cursing at certain times made her feel defiant toward the heartless man. He'd had a horrible drinking problem and a more horrible temper. Her mother, Evelyn, had paid the price. By the time Kami was fifteen, her mother was dead and Frank had gone to prison. Social Services placed her in a foster home. At eighteen she'd moved from Texas to Illinois, running from all the bad memories.

Now she was running again.

She felt the cool metal of the key ring on her fingers and lifted them from the puddle. Once inside her duplex she locked the two deadbolts.

Kami quickly put her stuff away and took off her wet jacket. She was on her way to her bedroom when loud pounding on the front door made her spin and slam her back against the hallway wall. Heart thundering, she stood frozen as the pounding became more insistent. Incoherent yelling followed. She moved silently down the stairs, toward the door, picking up a wooden baseball bat as she went.

"Open the fucking door, you bitch! I know she's in there! I'll break it down if I have to!" The voice was slurred. "Karen! If you don't come out here right now I'm going to come in and get you!"

Karen? Realization dawned on Kami as the voice screamed for Karen a few more times. It had to be a drunk, drugged up Stewart.

When Kami had moved her few items into the house, Stewart had sat on the steps drinking beer and eyeing her legs. The day after, a woman in a purple tube top and black leather mini-skirt came over. She'd introduced herself as Karen and said she lived next door with her boyfriend Stewart; aka: the leg watcher.

Karen had been nice enough and welcomed Kami to the neighborhood. Then she went into a big spiel about keeping doors locked at all times, never sleeping with the windows open, and always knowing who was knocking at the door before you answered it.

As Karen went on and on about how many cars had been stolen, Kami looked her over. You could see her ribs. The tube top was not the best outfit for her figure, or lack of. Not only that, she had healed track marks up both arms.

It's not that they had become good friends by any means, but in the last few weeks Karen had been coming over about every other day to visit with Kami, drink coffee, and smoke cigarettes. Well, Karen had smoked the cigarettes, a lot of them. She had seemed like she needed someone to talk to and Kami was a good listener. So, Stewart obviously thought Karen was there at ten o'clock at night and it was a good time to come looking for her.

"Karen isn't here," Kami said, hands shaking as she gripped the bat. "I don't know where she is." She hoped he would listen and go home to sleep it off.

No such luck.

"She's always over there with you. Talking 'bout things that are none of your business. Babbling on and on about shit she shouldn't. I'm gonna teach her a lesson. Then I'm gonna teach you a lesson." Stewart's voice made the hair on the back of Kami's neck stand up.

Her father's voice used to sound like that right before he hit Evelyn or her with one of his fists or beer bottles. Kami had also heard her husband Thomas's voice sound like that, once, and that was the day she had decided to leave him. She stood paralyzed next to the door, thinking of things in the past that were better forgotten.

The sound of metal hitting wood brought Kami back to the present. Stewart was beating on the door with something other than his fists.

Dropping the bat and running upstairs, Kami grabbed her car keys. She went out the back door and down the small set of stairs putting her into the grass of the backyard. Her cold and wet feet were the least of her problems as she snuck around the side of the house.

Stewart's porch light was on now, of course. Luckily for

Kami, Stewart was too high and dumb to realize he could get into the house faster by breaking the window instead of trying to hack open the front door with a crowbar. Who did he think he was? Jack Nicholson in *The Shining?*

Kami decided to try and get to her car and drive around until Stewart got tired of pounding on her door and went home to pass out. She hoped he wouldn't figure out how to break into the house, but she didn't want to be in there if he did. She couldn't call the police because then there would be an official report filed and someone could have access to her address.

Stewart stopped, resting his head on the door. Kami wished for the convenience of a new car with automatic door locks she would be able to access from her key chain.

She crept to the passenger side because it was the opposite side Stewart was on. She slipped the key into the door lock and slowly, carefully turned the key. The click was quiet. When she lifted the door handle and pulled the door open, the interior light of the car came on and Stewart spun around like someone had blown a whistle to get his attention.

He jumped off the porch, running at the car with the crowbar like he was getting ready to swing a baseball bat.

Baseball bat. Too bad I left it in the house. I'd at least have something to throw at him.

Kami opened the door the rest of the way and dove into the car. Her skirt made crawling across the center console difficult. She had one hand on the steering wheel, pulling herself into the driver's seat, while she put the key in the ignition with the other. Her knees were still in the passenger seat when she started the car and shards of glass shot into her face. Stewart reached through the newly broken driver's side window and grabbed her arm.

"Hi, baby," he slurred. His eyes were bloodshot and wild

looking. "Where's Karen? If you tell me right now, I might let you off without a really harsh punishment."

He dragged her partway through the window. The broken glass cut her arms and legs. Kami screamed while blindly trying to make contact with her fists to any part of Stewart's body.

"Let me go! I don't know where she is! I haven't seen her in two days!"

The yelling didn't do any good, especially as Stewart dragged her out the window the rest of the way. She landed on her face, bouncing slightly on the concrete of the driveway, tasting blood as the air was knocked out of her.

He rolled her over, sitting on her legs and stomach while covering her mouth and nose with one of his large hands. Kami froze as she tried to breathe and no air would fill her lungs. Her eyes met Stewart's. Tears ran down her face as the pain and severity of the situation registered.

As he looked down at her, Stewart narrowed his eyes. "You've been nothing but a bitch since you moved in. Flaunting that ass of yours in these tight clothes. Convincing my woman she needed to leave me. You're a meddling bitch and I'm gonna love teaching you a lesson."

Stewart moved his hand and Kami gulped in a much-needed breath. Then he backhanded her and blackness closed in as she struggled to stay conscious, white lights darting in front of her eyes. She could taste more blood as she took a deep breath and prepared to fight back.

Stewart leaned down and ground his mouth against hers in a sickening kiss. She bucked her hips off the concrete and since Stewart was leaning forward, he lost his balance and somersaulted over her. She jumped up, fighting a wave of nausea and started running across the street.

Unfortunately, she didn't see the car coming.

She froze as the lights blinded what little eyesight she had left.

The bumper hit her at the knees and sent her sliding over the hood into the windshield. The car stopped as she rolled like a rag doll and landed in the street.

Chapter 2

Carter stared at the windshield of his car for a moment until he got over the shock of what had happened. He dialed 911 on his cell as he set the emergency brake and switched on his hazard lights.

"This is Special Agent Michael Carter. I need an ambulance and police backup at 1401 Montgomery." He gave his badge number to dispatch, pocketed his phone, and walked to the body heaped on the ground.

"Jesus," he said. "You tryin' to be on that show Jackass? Because this would probably do it."

It was a woman and there was a lot of blood. Her knees were skinned, she wasn't wearing shoes, and her arms were cut up. He hadn't been driving that fast and his car wasn't damaged from the impact. The woman shouldn't have been this messed up.

He rolled her to her back and put his jacket under her head. Her face was bloody and bruised, both lips split open. Even through the blood, Carter could tell she was beautiful and was immediately enraged at whomever had hurt her.

Sensing someone behind him he spun on his heels, still

crouched, while drawing the 9mm from his shoulder holster. The man standing over him was almost six feet tall and holding a crowbar above his head, ready to strike.

"Carter," the man whispered. He backed up two steps, dropped the crowbar, and raised his hands. "I didn't have nothing to do with this, man. I came out to help when I heard the lady screaming. I thought you were the guy who hurt her, I was gonna knock him out." The words were slurred as he stumbled back.

"Sure, Stewart, that's why the skin on your knuckles is broken," he said. "Drop to your knees and put your hands behind your head."

Carter stood, holstered the pistol, and pulled a pair of handcuffs from the back of his belt. If Stewart was tall, Carter was a giant. Standing a good four inches over Stewart, Carter looked at him with cold, blue eyes and Stewart knew he had better listen to the agent.

He dropped to his knees. "I told you, man, I didn't do nothing! She's my neighbor. I heard her screaming for help. Being the outstanding citizen I am, I wanted to help her." He looked at Carter to see if he was buying the story. Arms behind his back, cuffs slapped on, Stewart knew it was useless to plead his case. Carter knew him too well.

With his foot between Stewart's shoulder blades, Carter gave a hard push and shoved him onto the street, face first.

"Fuck, Carter, that hurt. You don't have to beat me up. That's like citizen abuse, or something. I'm gonna file charges against you, you bastard!"

"Now you know how the lady felt when she hit the pavement. Quit using such bad language, I don't like it."

"Fuck you, Carter! You piece of shit! How's that for bad language? Does that piss you off? Cuz' I can go on and on, you know. I don't fucking like you anyway, I never have. You're the reason I was in prison for two years, you asshole! I'm gonna make you pay for—"

Carter planted a cowboy boot against Stewart's temple and Stewart slid to the ground unconscious.

Carter leaned down, picked the woman up, and put her in the backseat of his car. Brushing the hair off her face, he attempted to get her coherent. He needed to get her awake and see how much damage Stewart had done, and why.

"Ma'am, can you hear me? My name is Carter and I'm not going to hurt you. Can you open your eyes for me?" He spoke quietly, but insistently, rubbing her cold hand with his warm one.

Her eyes shot open and she tried to scramble over him and out the door.

"Whoa. You better slow down before you get hurt even more. I'm not going to hurt you. Stewart is out cold on the street. Do you see him?"

The woman stared at him for a moment. Then she stretched her neck to look over the driver's seat out the front windshield. She winced in pain as the muscles of her body protested. Sure enough, that asshole Stewart was face down in the street. She turned to Carter, looking at him with wide, green eyes.

Then she passed out.

"Shit." He caught her before she fell out of the vehicle.

The flashing lights and siren of the ambulance filled the night. The siren stopped and two EMTs ran over. Carter flashed the badge on his shoulder holster and told the men to take care of the woman first.

The men stared at each other, then back at the badge. FBI. They weren't going to argue with him. As the EMTs pulled the woman from the car to take her to the ambulance, Carter walked to Stewart.

Using the toe of his boot, he pushed against Stewart's shoulder. "Wake up, you piece of shit."

Stewart moaned and his eyes fluttered. Carter reached down and grabbed a handful of Stewart's soaked, slimy hair. Didn't the guy know mullets weren't in style anymore? At least it gave him something to grab on to.

"Damn it!" Stewart mumbled as he tried to get to his knees. "I'll get up faster if you stop pulling my fucking hair."

"I doubt it," Carter said.

With one more hard pull, Stewart was on his feet. Carter let go and Stewart fell back to his knees vomiting.

"I see you didn't really have anything to eat with your heroin. Or was it coke this time?"

Carter stepped back as Stewart continued to throw up. Out of the corner of his eye he saw the EMTs had the woman revived and were cleaning her injuries.

"You had better hope that woman's okay or you're going to find yourself up on attempted murder charges, not just assault and battery."

Stewart squinted and glared. "She won't press charges so you're just shit outta luck."

"Oh, she'll press charges all right. I'll see you back in prison before I'm going to let you beat up any more ladies. Speaking of, where's Karen and why did you guys move again? I don't like having to look for you when I need something."

Karen was supposed to get him some information about a case. She wasn't an official informant, but she and Carter had an agreement. She helped him out when he asked and she didn't go to jail. End of agreement. She had probably been a nice enough woman at some point, but she had hooked up with

Stewart and been in nothing but trouble since. Drug charges, prostitution, and in the hospital due to Stewart's temper.

Carter had been coming to this particular duplex, looking for Karen, when he hit a redhead in the street. Not exactly how the evening was supposed to go. Luckily the rain had almost stopped. At least one thing was looking up.

"Tell me about the woman. What's going on?"

Stewart wasn't going to tell him much. He was already coming down off the high and was dizzy from being kicked in the temple with a cowboy boot. Oops.

"Kami? Oh, she's been coming on to me and I thought she'd be an easy lay. We were just having a little fun. She likes it rough." Stewart flashed a sick smile, standing slowly.

"So, first you tell me you heard her screaming and you wanted to help. Now you're telling me you guys were having sex? I don't think so. I know you pay for your sex; you've been arrested for it before. Besides, no one that good looking would have any interest in you."

Caught in his lie—and insulted—Stewart lunged at Carter with his head down. Carter stepped to the side at the last second and Stewart tripped. He sprawled onto the street, again, and knocked himself out cold this time. The police cruiser pulled up just as Stewart hit the pavement and bounced a little. The officer driving got out of the car.

Flashing his badge, Carter laughed, "I give him a nine-point-oh for landing, but a four-point-five for style."

"I agree," the cop replied, also laughing.

His partner walked to where Stewart lay bleeding on the pavement. His face-first dive looked as though it had broken his nose. The male and female officers hauled Stewart into the back of the cruiser.

Carter quickly filled them in. He said the woman at the

ambulance seemed scared of him, so he thought the female officer should get her statement.

"She was beat up pretty badly and I think our boy was responsible. Why don't you go see if you can get her to talk, Officer Petty?" Carter read her silver name badge and gave the officer one of his dazzling smiles.

OFFICER DANA PETTY stared at Kami. "What do you mean you don't want to press charges? Ma'am, he hurt you and he should be punished for that."

Petty had seen a number of domestic violence cases in her seven years as a cop, but this woman didn't even seem to be fazed by the fact she had been beaten.

"It was a misunderstanding. I think he had a little too much to drink. I just want to go to bed. I've had a horrible day and I want it to be over." Kami poured on the sweet voice, keeping her hands tucked in her lap so no one would see them shaking.

She didn't know if she trusted her legs to hold her when she went to walk into her house, but she had to get these people to leave and not file any reports.

"Send me the bill for the ambulance." Kami hoped she sounded more convincing than she felt. After reciting her name and mailing address, she slowly stood.

Carter watched as the woman walked away. Officer Petty was standing at the ambulance with the two EMTs, faces slack. Carter went to them.

"What's going on? Why is she going in the house?" His voice getting louder with each word.

"She doesn't want to press charges, sir." Petty quickly repeated what Kami had said and Carter's eyes narrowed.

He caught up to Kami in three strides, hand shooting out to grab her elbow. She flinched and turned.

"Whoa!" Carter let go of her arm, putting his hands up in a non-threatening gesture. "Remember me? I hit you with my car?" He grinned to help her relax. It didn't work. "You were running from Stewart, weren't you? Help me out here, Kami, and let's put him in jail. You know he's beat up Karen before? You know Karen, don't you?"

Kami stared at him. How did he know her name? How did he know Stewart and Karen? She didn't trust him. He already knew too much about her and he'd only been here for... how long had he been here?

"He could have beaten you up more than he did or he could have done worse. Stewart has been arrested for a number of horrible things. He said you wouldn't press charges and now you're not. Why?"

"Because it's not worth the hassle." Kami was feeling dizzy again and wanted to get into the house before she passed out. "Now Mister, Mister..."

"Carter. Michael Carter." He kind of felt like James Bond when he said it that way.

"Mr. Carter. Thank you for not killing me when you hit me with your car and thank you for knocking out Stewart. I really want to take a shower and go to bed. I'm extremely tired." They had reached the front door.

"I'm assuming the car with the broken window idling in the driveway is yours."

Carter went to the car and got the keys. Kami reached for them, but he held on after he opened the door.

"You go in, lock the door, and take your shower. I'll finish up out here and then you and I are going to have a talk." He turned.

Kami watched him with her mouth hanging open. Finally,

she went in the house. She didn't like that he had her keys, but figured she didn't have much of a choice. Besides that, she was exhausted and too upset to argue.

She went upstairs, stripped off her ripped clothes, and threw them in the garbage. Making the water as hot as she could stand, she stepped into the shower and braced herself for the feeling of water running over all the cuts and scrapes.

It was painful but necessary. When the last of the blood and dirt ran down the drain, she sank down in the tub. She remembered the last time her body had hurt like this and the pain welled back up, threatening to suffocate her. She thought of the contagious smile of her best friend, Shelby.

"Shelby, who's dead because of me," she whispered.

It had been just over ten months since the car accident that claimed Shelby's life and Kami's freedom. Kami had woken up in the Chicago hospital with broken bones, a dislocated hip, and numerous cuts and bruises. Thomas stood by her bed and the first words out of his mouth were not in concern for her. He wanted to know why she hadn't told him she was three months pregnant. She honestly hadn't known, but he didn't believe her. He blamed her for killing his unborn son. She had pulled up the hospital gown and stared at the ugly bruises on her stomach. Thomas had needed to be removed from the room because he had begun throwing things.

They had been married for three years and lovers for almost three years before that. They had talked about having children, but decided to wait so they could travel the world and do all the things young married couples do. Even though Thomas was fifteen years older, he had a zest for life she used to find intoxicating. It was what had drawn her to him in a bar in Chicago where she had been a bartender and waitress.

Yet everything she had ever known about him, or thought she'd known, changed the day she woke up in the hospital.

She originally thought they would conceive another baby and everything would be fine. Kami spent sleepless nights thinking if they had a girl, they would name her Shelby, and if they had a boy, they would name him Thomas Jr.

Three weeks after the accident, Kami lay in bed with her eyes closed thinking about twins when she overheard a conversation never meant for her ears. Thomas had been sure she was sleeping and was careless in a discussion with one of his bodyguards stationed outside her door. She heard bits and pieces about the car accident, stupid mistakes, and taking care of the problem when she finally came home.

Thomas had said, "You screwed up the brake job. Kamielle is a liability and I have to make sure she disappears and no one wonders why."

Kami spent the entire night crying into her pillow, all her dreams washing away with her tears. Money didn't buy love or happiness, no matter how happy she thought she'd been for six years. It was time to get out.

Months in physical therapy had given her time to figure out how to get away. Because Thomas had money, she had demanded she live on-site at the rehabilitation center until her physical therapy was complete. This kept her away from the secluded mansion.

Finally, Thomas had been taking care of a business merger in New York, and Kami snuck away from the thugs who were supposed to be watching her. She went to their broker, withdrew three million dollars, bought the Accord, and drove off with a bag full of money and nowhere to go.

She had gotten on I-80, following it until she ended up in Colorado in the middle of December. After two months in Denver, she thought she noticed a car staking out her apartment. She ran southwest to Tucson and made it two more months until she got worried and left again.

That run brought her to Oakland and the end of April. Legally she was still married to Thomas. It was time to change that. Using her vast knowledge of computers and the Internet, she had managed to hack into some secure sites and change her last name to Johnson.

She got a new Social Security Card and with that, a new driver's license. She had also used the Internet to remove her previous name from phone and utility company lists so Thomas couldn't track her that way. Kami had convinced herself he would give up. In six weeks it would be her birthday and the anniversary of Shelby and the unborn baby's deaths.

Kami realized she'd never had an opportunity to mourn her best friend or lost baby. Between the memories, and the events of the day, it was all too much. Kami drew her legs up to her chest, wrapped her arms around her knees, and began to sob.

CARTER DEALT with the report for the local police department. The officers were taking Stewart to the station for resisting arrest. They had seen Stewart 'attack' an FBI agent. It didn't matter that he had been handcuffed, fallen on his face, broken his own nose, and knocked himself out. Carter smiled as he thought about the look that would be on Stewart's face when he woke up in a jail cell.

Putting Kamielle's name in the report, Carter noted she did not want to press charges. However, he believed the victim had a concussion and left the time frame open for twenty-four hours in case she had unknown injuries requiring additional medical treatment. In that case, he would allow her to press charges against Stewart Martin.

After signing his name, Carter turned to Officer Petty. "Did you sense she was hiding something?"

"I think we're all hiding something at some point in time," she said.

He smiled. Dana was the type of woman he usually dated. She was tall, quick tongued, and was good looking. Being a younger cop, she probably worked out to stay in shape and prove herself to a mostly male police force. She had shoulder length black hair and beautiful brown eyes.

"Don't look at me like that," she said. "You're cute, but I'm seeing someone right now. Not that I don't appreciate the offer." She smiled, then laughed at the look on his face.

Carter stuck out his hand so they could shake. "I knew I was going to like you. Dana, how would you like to be my local contact partner?"

"What do I get out of the deal?" She eyed him suspiciously when he lifted her hand and placed her palm flat on his chest.

"My honest to God promise I will never lie to you, lead you astray, shoot you, let you get shot, or use you without telling you first."

"Well, since you put it that way." She pulled out her notepad and wrote down the various numbers where he could contact her. "Don't ever call me before nine a.m. on my days off unless you're dying and need my help."

"You know, I already have a sister, but you're going to be the surrogate when I'm in town." He handed her his business card and hoped this partnership worked out. "When's your next day off?"

"Sunday."

"I'll call you for lunch. I have to introduce you to one of my colleagues and go over some of my ground rules."

"Okay. Thanks, Agent Carter."

"We have to get this straight right now," he put both of his hands on her shoulders. "If we're going to work together, you have to call me Michael or Carter. I'm not big on formality."

"Deal!" She flashed him a smile and he knew before he could introduce her to his partner, he would have to have the 'don't touch' talk.

As Tom and Dana got back in their cruiser, Carter pulled his car in the driveway behind the Honda. Kami's keys in hand, he went to find out what the lovely redhead was hiding or what she was hiding from.

Chapter 3

Carter unlocked the door and went inside. Except for a baseball bat laying by the front door, the house was tidy and had barely any furniture. He heard water running and decided to start a pot of coffee, figuring Ms. Johnson would need the caffeine jolt.

He waited ten more minutes. When she wasn't out, he went to the bathroom and knocked. "Ms. Johnson?" There was no answer but he could still hear water running. "Kamielle? Are you okay in there?" Worried she had passed out again, he opened the door.

A clear shower curtain distorted the view of her sitting in the bathtub. Her shoulders were slumped and she was shaking. No, she was crying. Carter cleared his throat and tried to get her attention, but she didn't notice.

"Ms. Johnson? Is there something I can do?"

She stared at him with unseeing eyes.

"If you won't be offended, I'll get your robe. I'll close my eyes and hand it to you." Carter walked to the bathtub. "I'm going to shut off the water." It was ice-cold.

Not nearly as worried about scaring her and more

concerned about her head, he pulled back the shower curtain and squatted down to eye level.

"You need to get out of the bathtub and dry off so you can get warm. I think you're in shock. Will you let me help you?"

Kami nodded once and that was all Carter needed. He grabbed a fluffy towel off the rack and draped it over her shoulders. Carefully putting his hands under her arms, he lifted her to her feet.

"Can you stand on your own?" he asked.

Again, she barely nodded.

"Good. I made some coffee and I'm going to make you drink about three cups of it." She may have smiled, but it was hard to tell through two fat lips.

While drying her, he took inventory of her injuries. She had a stubbed toe and numerous shallow cuts on her legs. A fresh, but healed, scar marred the inside of her right ankle. *Damn, she has nice legs.* He tried to stay focused as he continued drying her.

There was another fresh scar on her hip, this one more jagged. Carter knew he should be looking at her like a cop looks at an injured victim, not how a man looks at a naked woman. *An incredibly hot naked woman.*

He pulled his mind back from places it wanted to go and checked the cuts on her arms. She had a bad gash on her right tricep that needed a new bandage. Her face looked a little better now that the blood was washed off. She was going to have a hell of a black eye and there was an ugly purple bruise on her chin.

It could have been a lot worse. He knew it would have been if she hadn't managed to get away from Stewart and started running across the street. Where she was hit by a car. Carter looked at the bruises on her knees. Her legs plagued him again.

Damn it!

Kami winced, but that was the only emotion she showed. He helped her step out of the tub and asked where she kept bandages and antiseptic. She pointed to the cabinet under the sink. Wrapping her partly in a pink robe, he gently set her on the counter so she wouldn't have to hold herself up. After she was bandaged, he slipped her arm into the robe and tied the belt.

Taking a comb, he gently started to work the tangles from her hair. The whiteness of a thin scar just under her right ear drew his eyes. It was about two inches long and went diagonally down her throat. It didn't look like the other two scars on her ankle and hip. This scar was older.

Once her hair was combed, he helped her stand. Stepping behind her, he put his hands on her shoulders and led her to the living room. She sat down without a sound and he went to the kitchen to get the coffee.

Taking three or four deep breaths, he wondered how long it would be before he got the picture of her incredibly perfect body out of his mind. Naked. Don't forget naked.

It took two cups of coffee with lots of cream and sugar, but the color finally came back into Kami's face and her eyes lost the blankness. Wrapped in the robe, sitting with her legs under her on the couch, she was able to think more clearly than the hour before.

At first she'd been appalled with being so helpless. That and the fact a man she didn't know had seen her naked and crying. She had gotten over it and decided to find out who he was and why he was babysitting her. She wasn't sure what his angle was, but she would play the game until she found out.

"So, Ms. Johnson," Carter began, hoping she would volunteer some information. "How do you know Stewart Martin?"

Her eyes were the color of emeralds, but narrowed and cold. There was no emotion showing on her face and Carter wondered where the vulnerable woman of just twenty minutes earlier had gone.

"Agent Carter—"

"Please call me Michael or just Carter. That's how my friends talk to me." He smiled.

"Agent Carter," she said, her tone more clipped than before. "First of all, we are not friends, so I do not intend to call you anything other than Agent. Not Michael. Not Carter. Not Billy Joe Jim Bob. Secondly, I do not understand why you are even here. I gave my statement and now I want you to leave. Also, you may call me Mrs. Johnson."

Oookay, Mrs. Johnson the Ice Princess. Well, wasn't that interesting. Where's Mr. Johnson while you're getting beat up?

Carter glanced at her ring finger and saw nothing. Still, he had to fight the urge to smile. The saying about a redhead and her temper was right on the money.

Her voice held the trace of a southern accent, especially when she punctuated each word to show him how angry she was. Unless he played dumb FBI agent, this was going to be a very long night.

"Mrs. Johnson, I want to apologize for stepping on your toes. You see, when she was twelve, my sister was thrown from her horse. She received a mild concussion for her troubles. I remember she passed out a few times in those first twenty-four hours and my mom always said anyone with a head injury... well, anyway, I was worried about you." He plastered on his best Brad Pitt smile, showing his dimples.

His horse-riding sister had once told him his Brad Pitt smile could melt ice. It seemed to be melting the glacier known as Mrs. Johnson. Barely. That and the dumb routine.

"I'm fine. Thank you for your concern. Now leave."

She was serious, she didn't want to talk, dimples or no. Maybe he was losing his touch. Sister would get a good laugh.

"Okay, I'll leave after three questions." He paused to see if she would object and rushed on when she didn't. "Why was Stewart dragging you out of your car?"

Kami took a deep breath, suppressing a shudder. She set the coffee mug down on an end table. With her hands clasped in her lap, she said, "Stewart was looking for his girlfriend. I haven't seen her in two days. Karen and I have coffee almost every morning and Stewart knows that."

Although she thought she had given too much information, she figured he wouldn't leave until he got his three questions answered. "Question two, Mr. Carter?"

He smiled, again. She really wished he'd quit smiling.

"I was wondering if you knew where Ms. McKay was?"

"Ms. McKay?" she asked.

"Karen McKay. Stewart's girlfriend?"

"I didn't know her last name was McKay. I've only lived here for three weeks."

"So, do you know where Karen is?" Carter was getting tired of playing dumb.

"I don't know where she is. What day is it today?" For the life of her, Kami couldn't concentrate. That was strange.

"It's late, late Friday night. Almost Saturday."

"Karen was here Wednesday morning to have coffee and she told me she had a job deal in the works. I haven't seen her since." Kami rubbed her eyes.

"Thank you, that's very helpful. Now, I think it would be a good idea if you went to bed. I'm going to leave my card so you can call me if you think of anything else."

Carter stood and offered his hand. Being the stubborn person she was, Kami stood on her own. She got a head-rush, became dizzy, and had to sit back down.

"I don't feel very well. I think you should leave so I can go to sleep." Kami stood again, much slower this time. She looked up at Carter.

"Let me walk you since you're a little wobbly. I'll lock the door on my way out."

"I need to lock the deadbolts."

The thought of walking up and down those stairs wasn't pretty. But she'd do it because it meant the door would be locked and Michael Carter would be gone.

He moved toward the stairs. "Okay. But, please, promise me if you feel dizzy or nauseous in the morning, you'll go to the hospital and get checked out. I still think you have a concussion."

They reached the bottom of the stairs and were standing at the door. Kami thought things were good since she hadn't bounced or rolled down the steps and fallen into him. Maybe it wouldn't be a bad thing to fall into him.

Where did that come from? Maybe I do have a concussion. I don't have thoughts like that about men. At least, well, not since Thomas. Don't think about Thomas...

"Hellooo, Mrs. Johnson?" Carter said. "I lost you there for a second. You're not making me feel any better about leaving you alone."

Opening the door, she smiled. "I'm going to bed right now, I don't have a concussion, and I'm just fine. Have a good evening."

He picked up the baseball bat. "I'm assuming this is for protection. Why don't you use it as a cane to get back upstairs?"

She took the bat and leaned on it a little. Before she could shut the door, Carter pulled out his card.

"Here's how to get in touch with me. I travel, so the cell is the best bet."

She looked briefly at the card before putting it in the pocket of her robe. "You told me you'd leave after three questions. You only asked me two. What was the third?"

She was curious. Damn him.

"I guess I'll have to come back some other time and ask that third question. Have a good night, Kamielle. Call me if you need anything." He closed the door.

She locked the deadbolts and slowly climbed the stairs using the baseball bat. Once in her bedroom, she dropped the robe and bat on the floor. Climbing into the silk sheets and pulling the blankets up close to her chin, she wondered why she felt so good about the fact he would be coming back.

CARTER STARED at the house through his windshield. He wanted to see her again. Soon.

What am I doing? This woman has a lot of baggage and I don't need this. He thought about the bathtub incident now that he was alone. She had a body like Tyra Banks. Curved in all the right places.

Carter had a Marine buddy in Florida. The Marine had been invited to a Christmas party the year before last at the Senator's mansion. Tyra Banks had been there and Carter and his buddy had been introduced. As Carter drove, the pictures in his mind of his dream girl changed from Tyra Banks in designer wear to Kamielle in ripped up clothes or a pink bathrobe. Oh yeah, don't forget Kamielle naked crying in her bathtub.

He frowned at the thought of a woman who seemed so independent and strong falling apart the way she did. He decided he was going to fix whatever was plaguing her. That's what he did, he fixed things.

He pulled out his cell.

"Medina, it's me. I've got Stewart in local lockup, but nobody seems to know where Karen is. Drag your ass outta that hotel bed and be on the street in fifteen."

Twenty minutes later, Antonio Medina sat low in the plush Lexus seat drinking a cup of coffee he'd retrieved from the concierge desk of the hotel. Tony had wavy black hair he kept just long enough to curl at the ends, but short enough it didn't go 'finger in a light socket' on him.

He wore designer suits and Italian shoes and spent his days off with different women. He swore he'd never settle down because: "What's the point of marriage anyway? Every married guy I ever talked to complains his wife never gives him any. There's no way I'll settle down and lose the lovin'!"

Tony wasn't mean to the women he dated. In fact, he spent quite a bit of money on them. He'd buy roses, take them to a fancy restaurant, then they'd go dancing for a few hours at some of the clubs in whatever city he and Carter happened to be in that week.

Carter thought about how rough it would be on a relationship even if Tony wanted one. They were VCTF for the FBI. The Violent Crimes Task Force went wherever there may be a lead that would catch the latest psycho who was on the loose. Carter was Assistant Director of their Unit and Tony was the Profiler. He was the best Profiler Carter had ever worked with. Tony was ruthless enough to get in the heads of the psychos without losing his grip on reality. VCTF was one of the toughest jobs in the FBI because they saw all the horrible acts people were capable of.

"Whatcha thinking? I hate it when you get that look on your face." Tony raised an eyebrow.

"You can't see my face. And what look are you talking about? I have a poker face." Carter said, not taking his eyes from the road.

"I've been working with you for seven years, and we've been best friends for eight before that. We've shared the secrets of college life. I don't have to see your face to know what 'the look' is. You may have a poker face where everyone else is concerned, but I know you, buddy. Spill it."

"My first thought was about how sexy you look with your new haircut."

Tony smiled and fluffed his hair with a head shake. "I do look sexy, don't I?"

"The sexy hair made me think about your womanizing and how you wine, dine, and dance women right out of their clothes. I think it's time you grew up and got into a serious relationship."

"Serious relationship?" Tony said. "You're one to talk. How long has it been since *you've* had a serious relationship? Four years? Shit, man, how long's it been since you've been laid? A year? More?"

"It's been eleven months. Damn, it's kind of pathetic I know that, huh?" Carter shook his head.

"No, what's pathetic is that it's been that long, you loser!" Tony threw the cardboard sleeve from his coffee cup and it bounced off the side of Carter's head.

"I've had a date almost every weekend you had one. I just didn't take them back to their place to jump their bones like you did."

Carter threw the cardboard sleeve back and Tony caught it. *It's a good thing we can act like sixteen-year-olds when no one else is around*, Carter thought with a smile.

"Man, you have got to get over Crystal. It's not your fault she died," Tony said quietly. "She'd want you to move on with your life and be happy. You know that. It's the kind of woman she was."

Carter's jaw tightened. "The woman she was. *Was.* Because of me, we're not living on the Bay with our baby. That fuck killed her to get to me."

Carter was the best friend Tony had ever had and he'd only heard him utter the f-bomb four times in fifteen years. Four years earlier had been the other three times. They had been working a case on a doctor who had gone ballistic and killed his wife and three picture-perfect nine, eleven, and thirteen-year-old daughters by surgically removing their heads and mailing them to the VCTF.

Then the guy, nicknamed by the press as Dr. Blades, had gone on a killing spree. He seduced teenage hitchhikers, doing the same to them. The press had printed a picture of Tony and Michael at the crime scene in the L.A. Times. 'Dr. Blades' had latched onto Michael because the caption had "The Best of the Best" printed under it. The surgeon wanted to be the best and had to get rid of Michael Carter to do that.

Only Michael wasn't home when the psycho broke into the condo. Crystal, Michael's fiancé, was. Her head was delivered in a box to the VCTF the next day.

Jon, Michael's CIA older brother, had flown in from who knew where to help find the killing bastard. It took two days, but Michael, Tony, and Jon tracked the surgeon down with less than legal methods. A standoff ended with Michael shooting the doctor six times. Five in the chest and once between the eyes.

Michael had taken six months off and talked about quitting. He spent those months in Montana, where his brother and sister convinced him to come back to the job he loved.

Michael told Tony once, "Don't ask me about it and don't talk about Crystal. She's gone and there's nothing I can do to change it except bring down every psycho who destroys the lives of good people like her."

Tony knew they had both been thinking about the same thing in the minutes of silence.

"I know it hurts, buddy," Tony said. "And I know you told me never to talk about her. I care about you too much to see you waste away. And, if you ever tell anyone I said I care about you, I'll have to hurt you."

"Medina, the day you can hurt me will be a cold day in hell." Michael pulled his car into the parking garage at the Oakland Police Department. He turned to Tony. "By the way, I love you, too."

"Don't give me your Brad Pitt smile, you freak!" Tony laughed as he got out of the car. "I'm never going to live down that I told you I worry about you, am I?"

"You didn't say you worry about me, you said 'I care about you'. There's a difference. And no. I'm going to remind you every day," Michael said.

As they walked through the parking garage, Michael put his hand on Tony's shoulder. "I know I need to move on. I've actually been thinking about it for the last few weeks. I've had dates and sex and none of it filled the void. Crystal was my life. I lost her and thought I'd died, too.

"Jon called me last week and said almost the exact same thing you did. Coming from him, that's deep. It made me realize if Jon is worried, I need to change things. I'm working on it. Now leave me alone and let's go scare the shit out of Stewart."

Tony stood concreted in place as Michael walked to the officer on duty at the elevator. This was the most emotional conversation they'd had since Michael told Tony he was going to propose to Crystal. They'd also been really drunk at the time so Tony wasn't sure if that conversation counted.

"You coming, Medina?" Michael called.

"Yeah, I'm just getting over my shock," Tony said. He pulled back his jacket to flash his badge at the officer. When the elevator door shut, Tony turned. "Scare the shit out of Stewart, huh? What did he do this time?"

"Beat the hell out of his neighbor. A really nice lady who didn't deserve to be beaten up."

"Wait, you smiled. Was this 'really nice lady' hot?" When Carter didn't answer, Tony said, "She was hot, wasn't she? Why couldn't I have volunteered to look for Karen? Introduce me to the hot chick."

"You will not be introduced, she's too nice for you. And, I did have all the fun tonight. I kicked Stewart in the head for, well, for being an ass. I think I gave him a concussion." Carter smiled again. "And, I'm not going to introduce you to Kamielle, because I saw her first."

"Kamielle? First name basis already? I definitely have to meet the woman who put the spark back in your eyes."

Chapter 4

Hands tightened on Kamielle's throat as she struggled to breathe. Screaming made her flinch. Light glinted off something shiny and in the split second before it hit her in the face, she dodged the broken beer bottle. It sliced down her neck, right below her ear, and the blood flowed onto the pillow and stuffed animals on her bed.

The screaming made sense now. It was her mother.

Kami sat up, hands on her throat. *There's blood on me!* Her heart beat frantically as she pulled her hands away to look at them. They were damp with perspiration, not blood. She'd dreamed about the car accident and Thomas chasing her but she hadn't dreamed about the night her mother died in over five years.

Kami looked at the clock. 5:48 a.m. "Oh, yay, a little over five hours of sleep and here I am."

She swallowed a few times, touching her fingers to dry lips and wincing. Pain pounded in her temples. Blood had leaked through the bandage Mr. FBI had put on her arm but it looked like it was done bleeding for now.

Easing back on the pillows, her heart began to slow from the nightmare, and she tried to go back to sleep. Instead of the face of her father or the blood she thought she would see, she saw the smile of a man with beautiful blue eyes. Her eyes shot open. *Why am I seeing the face of a man I hardly know?*

She eased from the bed, taking her robe off the floor. When she reached the kitchen, Simon met her, meowing up a storm. Simon had adopted her the day after she moved in. She'd never had a pet so she loved the companionship. But since he was a tomcat, he didn't want to spend the night inside.

"Oh, kitty! I'm so sorry." He bounded down the steps as soon as she opened the back door.

The coffee pot was still over half full, so she warmed a cup in the microwave.

"Well, Mr. FBI, when are you coming back and what is the third question you have?" With the thought of the FBI agent came thoughts of Stewart. What was she going to do when he was released from jail? She didn't want to move because of Stewart. Maybe when Karen got back everything would be fine.

She started cleaning the house to get her mind off the day she would forever remember as 'the day life got worse than it already was'.

Friday morning, she had decided it was time to find a job. It wasn't like she was hurting for money, she just wanted a point to her day. Sketches in hand, she had gone to ten different boutiques to show her clothing designs. Almost every manager or owner she talked to wanted to know where she had gone to school and who she had worked for. Of course, there weren't any answers to the questions. She hadn't gone to school and there weren't any references because she had run her own business for two years.

Without addresses and proof of ownership, no one wanted to talk to her. They all said the same thing when she first walked in: "These are the best designs I've seen in a decade!

You're brilliant!" Then it changed to: "How do I know you didn't steal these from your previous employer and that's why you don't have references?"

Her heart and head ached. Then she had come home to the rain and Stewart. She shivered at the thought.

Kami stood in the living room looking around her spotless home. It wasn't dirty because there wasn't anything to get it dirty. No friends over for pizza, no feet tracking in dirt from outside. It was depressing to be alone.

"Well, at least I can take out the garbage. I have one skirt and shirt that will never see the light of day again."

She gathered up what little garbage there was and went outside. The lids were closed but there were two plastic milk crates stacked next to the dumpster. Kami carefully climbed on and threw back one of the lids. As she tossed the bag in, something red caught her eye. Actually, five things that were red caught her eye.

It was a hand with red fingernail polish!

Kami jumped off the milk crates and went running toward her back stairs. She tripped in the gravel, skinning her knees. Scrambling to get her footing, she ran up the steps and into the kitchen then slammed and locked her door. Stumbling to the far wall, she slid to the floor, struggling to catch her breath through tears.

"OhmyGod, OhmyGod, OhmyGod! Think, think. What are you going to do?" She was close to hysterical and knew she had to calm down. "Call the police. Cell phone."

Standing on shaking legs she went to get her purse from the downstairs office. At the front door, she stopped and leaned against the wall. She pulled the belt on her robe a little tighter, putting her hands in her pockets to try and warm up. Her fingers touched a thick piece of paper.

Special Agent Michael Carter
Asst. Director FBI, Violent Crimes Task Force
San Francisco, CA, Base Office

Violent Crimes Task Force? What had this man been doing at her house last night?

She used the wall to support herself as she went down the stairs. The clock said 6:26. She hadn't even been out of bed for an hour.

"Great. Now I have 'the day life got worse than it already was Friday' and 'the day life got worse than it already was Saturday'. I wanted excitement. This is what I get for being bored." She tried to smile and almost threw up.

She dialed the cell number on the card for Mr. FBI. It rang three times and she was afraid she was going to get his voice mail when the phone connected.

"Carter," a groggy voice said. When she didn't say anything he spoke again. "Hello?"

"Agent Carter," Kami's voice sounded strangled as she searched for what to say. She covered her mouth and choked back a sob.

Carter was immediately awake at the sound of a quiet voice he thought he may have recognized even after only two words. "Hello? This is Michael Carter. Talk to me."

"Agent Carter, I need your help."

"Kamielle? Are you okay?" Michael sat up. Her voice was strange, like she was struggling to breathe. "Stewart isn't back, is he? I left him in lockup just," he looked at the clock, "two hours ago."

Carter jumped out of bed, grabbing his slacks off the back of a chair where he'd tossed them an hour and a half earlier. Before she answered, he was getting a shirt.

"No. Stewart isn't here. There's, there's, there's..." she started to hyperventilate.

"Kamielle, listen to me," Michael said. "You have to calm down before you pass out or get sick. I'm going to help you and take care of whatever you need. I'll be there in fifteen minutes. Tell me what you need."

Kami felt her breathing slow as she concentrated on his voice. He had a way of calming her she wasn't sure she liked. She stopped pacing and sat down in her desk chair.

"I took my garbage out this morning and," she took a deep breath, "and I saw a hand. I think there's a body in the dumpster." She closed her eyes and leaned over with her head between her legs, fighting the urge to throw up again.

"I'm going to get my partner, Tony. Go to your front door and sit on the steps inside. Do not answer the door for anyone but me. Do you understand? Do not let anyone in but me." He pulled on his cowboy boots and shoulder holster. Then he grabbed his keys and jacket and was out the door on his way to Tony's room.

"Okay. I'll be right by the door. I'll be waiting for you. Agent Carter?" Her voice was small and scared again.

"What, Kamielle?" He was pounding on Tony's door.

"Please hurry."

"I'm going to be there before you know it."

KAMI SAT on the stairs by the front door rocking back and forth, trembling. She couldn't believe there was a body in the dumpster behind her house. She kept looking at her cell phone so she could see how many minutes it had been since she talked to Mr. FBI. Only twelve.

She touched her sore face. Going to the kitchen to get ice,

she looked in the mirror. She knew her lips had been split open and were fat, but she also had a bruise on her chin and a black eye. She had a flashback of hitting the pavement face first and being backhanded.

Ice in a baggie and wrapped in a towel, Kami went back to sit on the steps. She checked her phone again. Eighteen minutes. "Damn it! Where are you, Mr. FBI?"

She could almost relax when she had something to occupy her mind, but now that she was on the steps counting the seconds, panic was setting in. She hit redial and Mr. FBI answered on the first ring.

"Carter."

"Where are you?"

"Kamielle? Is everything okay?"

"No, everything is not okay!" she said. "There's a body in my dumpster and you said you would be right here. It's been eighteen minutes and you're not here!"

"Okay, okay. I understand you've had a really shitty two days. I also know if you don't calm down, you're going to pass out. You need to relax."

"Relax? You want me to relax?" Her voice went up an octave. "Have you listened to anything I've said? Were you really the one who was here last night? I don't think you should be telling me to relax! I think you need to get your ass over here to solve my problems!"

"What are you wearing?" Michael said.

"Excuse me?" Kami pulled the phone away, stared at it for a second, then put it back to her ear.

"What are you wearing?" he repeated.

"I don't think it's any of your business what I'm wearing! How does that help? I got beat up last night and there's a dead body in my dumpster!"

Michael knew he had successfully distracted her. He was

glad he was goading her over the phone and not in person. He thought of the baseball bat by her door and decided he'd let Tony walk in first.

"What the hell are you doing?" Tony asked, expertly weaving his truck through traffic.

"Are you wearing the pink robe? I bet you even have matching pink slippers." Michael ignored Tony and smiled in spite of the fact he was afraid she might attack him when they pulled up.

"Okay, Mr. FBI," she said, "it's been twenty-one minutes since I called you the first time. Where in the hell are you? Did you stop for coffee and donuts? Did you figure the *crazy* woman could take care of herself?"

"You have a hint of a southern accent," he said. "Are you from the south? By the way, you didn't tell me if you have matching slippers for your robe." Maybe she'd calm down.

"I'm from Texas and I have matching slippers. How did you know that? Why aren't you here?"

Then again, maybe not. "Kamielle?"

"What?" she snapped.

"Is that baseball bat still by your door?"

"What? No, it's upstairs. Why?"

"Open your door and don't hurt me." Michael ended the call. He and Tony were standing on the porch. Since she had been yelling, Kami hadn't heard the loud truck pull up.

She opened the door and Michael almost laughed. He may have if circumstances had been different. Her red hair was a rat's nest, both lips were swollen to twice their normal size, and she had a bruise on her chin.

To top it off, she had a blue towel balled up, he assumed with ice, over her left eye, covering half her face. It wasn't until she pulled the towel away that he quit smiling.

"Jesus. Can you see out of that eye?" He pushed by her

with Tony behind him. "It's practically swollen shut and has a gash above it. Why didn't the medics put anything on it last night? Why didn't I notice it?" *Maybe because you were too busy staring at her legs, you moron?*

She looked back and forth between the two men. The other man had come in silently behind Carter and shut and locked the front door. He seemed to be taking in everything. She could tell he was the quiet one and Mr. FBI was the obnoxious, go in first, guns blazing, ask questions later one.

"Kamielle?" Michael got her attention. "Let's go up to the bathroom so I can look at your eye."

"My eye? There's a body in the dumpster and you're worried about my eye? I can see almost perfectly fine. I could see well enough to tell there was a hand in my dumpster. Go get rid of her!" She was shaking as the words came out and Michael resisted the urge to put his arms around her.

"How do you know it's a 'her' if you only saw a hand?" Tony asked.

"Five long fingernails with red polish. There was also a gaudy fake ring on the middle finger."

"Okay. Why don't you show us where the dumpster is? The crime scene investigators will be here soon, along with the locals and the coroner," Tony said.

Kami looked at Michael then followed Tony up the stairs. Michael stood, frustrated, then finally raised both hands toward the ceiling as though admitting defeat and followed them into the kitchen. She pointed out the window to the dumpster and the men went out.

Halfway down the stairs, Michael turned to Kami. "Go back inside but don't lock the door." He stopped, staring at her legs between the folds of the robe. He marched up a couple stairs and pulled the robe back.

She slapped at his hands. "What do you think you're

doing? It wasn't enough you had to guess what I'm wearing? Now you want to know what I'm wearing under it? Nothing! Happy?"

"I swear. You need a keeper, lady. Why are the scabs on your knees torn open?"

"I tripped in the gravel when I was running back from the dumpster," she said.

"Go clean up. Tony or I will be back in to talk to you as soon as we check out the dumpster."

Tony was standing with his hands in his pockets. "You think we could do this some time today?"

"I'm coming. I have to keep our witness happy."

"I heard that!" she said, stomping into the house.

"Kamielle," Michael called. She poked her head out the door, glaring. "Put something on underneath whatever you change into and maybe later I'll guess what color it is."

Kami slammed the door.

"I don't think I've ever seen you act like this. What gives?" Tony stared at Carter for a moment then shook his head slowly. "You can't get involved with a witness."

"I'm not getting involved with anyone. Besides, I have a double date with you Monday night. And, Mrs. Johnson told me she's married." Carter pulled latex gloves from his inside jacket pocket and passed two to Tony.

Tony stepped on the milk crates and looked in the dumpster. "Your woman has a good memory. Long, red fingernails and a big diamond-looking ring on the middle finger. How did she notice the ring if she only looked in here for three or four seconds?"

"We'll ask her. And it's Mrs. Johnson, not my woman." Michael picked up a stick, handing it to Tony. "See if you can uncover the face."

"Why do you always make me do this shit? You should do

it." Tony took the stick and started to move garbage. Whoever had dumped her wasn't trying to hide her. "Oh, fuck." He shook his head as he jumped off the milk crates. "It's Karen McKay."

"Son of a bitch," Michael said. "From what I can piece together with Kamielle's statement and Stewart's rambling, Kamielle may have been the last person to see her alive."

"Well, we won't know for sure until we get back the autopsy results. There's blood on her face, but I can tell it's her. Go find out what Mrs. Johnson knows about this."

Once inside, Michael sat at the breakfast bar by the window, watching over the next ten minutes as the police, coroner, and crime scene investigators pulled up. He heard water running in the bathroom and when he heard the door open he yelled down the hallway, "Kamielle, can I make a pot of coffee?"

"Sure," she said coming into the kitchen.

Her hair was in a ponytail and her face glowed pink from being washed.

"I guess your eye didn't need any stitches. Sorry I overreacted." His voice was flat.

"What's wrong? Why did you go from joking and friendly, which kept me from becoming a basket case by the way, to emotionless?"

"That's what we have to do in the VCTF. We see nasty things every day and we have to be detached."

He turned away. Kami put her hand on his and he froze. She waited to speak until he looked at her.

"Last night, I didn't understand why you were acting dumb. Then I realized it was to make me feel superior so I'd answer your questions. That made me mad. Then, when you took control and got me to tell you what you needed, I was mad again. You were trying to be funny on the phone and trying to lighten the mood on the back porch. You are a man of many faces. Now I know you have to be because of the work you do. Don't let this job make you heartless. Stay relaxed and humorous so you stay sane." She squeezed his hand and started to pull away when he gripped her fingers.

"It's Karen in the dumpster."

"Oh!" Her eyes got big and rolled back as she fell.

Michael caught her before she bounced on the linoleum and added to her collection of bruises. He carried her to the living room and laid her on the couch.

Crouching down, he stroked her cheek with the back of his hand. "I was wondering when the stress was going to get to you. Rest, little one, I'll be here when you wake up."

"Carter!" Tony rushed through the back door. "You are not going to believe this." He ran his hand through his hair, which showed how distressed he was. He never risked messing up his hair. "Did you happen to notice two nights ago was a full moon?"

"You've got to be shitting me!" Michael said.

"Nope. She's missing her left ear and left ring finger. Our serial killer has moved into the city. There is one difference with her body and all the others, though."

From the look on Tony's face, Michael wasn't sure he wanted to know. In three years, they had thirty-three bodies with the same M.O. They had a serial killer who raped, murdered, and collected trophies from his victims. He also killed on a full moon every month, except for last month. Last month, they thought they'd been given a reprieve.

Tony frowned, "The missing ear and finger are the same. The difference is she has your name carved in her chest."

Chapter 5

Voices. Loud and soft. Male and female. Kami shot to a sitting position then fell back down on the couch, head swimming. The talking went on, so she opened one eye to get her bearings. There were at least four people in the living room with her and not one of them was Mr. FBI. She dropped her hand and slid a baseball bat from under the couch. There were two more hidden in the house along with the one by the door.

"Where's Agent Carter?"

At the sound of her voice, the talking stopped.

"Mrs. Johnson," a young woman said, "you remember me, don't you? From last night? Officer Petty?" Dana stared at Kami then turned. "Torres, go get Special Agent Carter. Tell him Mrs. Johnson is awake and needs to see him now."

"I remember you. Doesn't mean I trust you."

Michael came into the living room taking in the sight of Kamielle huddled at the corner of her couch with a baseball bat in her hands. "I think I'm going to get some stock in Louisville Slugger. How many of those damn things do you have around here?" He smiled.

"Michael," she said. The bat tumbled to the floor as she ran to the bathroom. She barely got the door closed as she began to vomit.

"Okay, show's over. I want everyone out of this house." Michael pointed to the backdoor. "Dana, will you get a glass of water and make sure she's alright?"

"She doesn't trust me. She wanted to talk to you. If I go in there, I think it will just make things worse."

"Fine. Go out and tell the techs I'll be in here for a while and don't let anyone else come in. They already have finger-prints for comparison."

Michael got a glass of water. He went to the bathroom, preparing himself for another verbal onslaught.

"Kamielle? It's Carter." He pushed open the door.

Her small frame was hunched over the toilet, sobs racking her body. He rubbed her back until she quieted then gave her the water.

As he pulled her up, he said, "I sure seem to be taking care of you an awful lot lately, don't I?"

"I'm sorry." Kami's eyes dropped and another wave of tears made her body shake.

Michael took her to her bed. She rolled to her side, pulling her knees up, and wrapping her arms protectively around herself. The look on her face made Michael's heart clinch with emotion he hadn't felt in a long time.

"Why is this happening to me?" she asked.

"I don't know, honey." He knelt down, wiping away a few tears. "I think it may be a classic case of wrong place, wrong time."

"I need to get out of here. I can't even drive my car and because of Stewart, I'm scared to walk anywhere."

"What do you say we go for coffee?"

"Could we really?" she asked. "You'd take me out?"

"Well, not a date, since you're married. I'll do my civic duty and take you out of the house."

"Married?" She stared at him.

"Yeah, married. You said you were a missus and made sure I knew it. Where is your husband?" Michael finally asked the question he'd been dying to know. He stood and looked around the bedroom. There wasn't a trace of masculinity. "If you were my wife, I wouldn't have let Stewart treat you the way he did." *If you were my wife... Where in the hell had that come from?*

Kami sat and straightened her shirt. She wouldn't meet his eyes. "Well, that's why you'd probably make a better husband to me than he did. I'm not married anymore."

"Why?"

"We're just not. Don't ask me about it, please." She stood and slipped on a pair sandals. "Can we still go for coffee? If not, will you at least drop me off somewhere?"

"I'm not going to drop you off," he said. "You're stuck with me for at least a couple days. Some really weird stuff is going on and I don't feel comfortable leaving you alone."

"Considering you just met me, that's a huge offer on your part." She couldn't hide the suspicion in her voice.

"I've seen you go through things in the last day and a half most people don't deal with in a lifetime. I'd like to see you come out of them smiling. I'm here out of obligation as an FBI agent." Michael turned to leave.

Obligation, my ass, I've never taken a witness out in my life. I think it might be illegal... if it's not, it should be. I'm going to go in and tell the boys to write up a law: No taking out women you've just met, who have been beaten up by their neighbors, have scars on their bodies from sharp objects, look incredibly hot naked, and seem to have a past that haunts their every move. Of course that would take all the fun out of getting to know Kamielle Johnson...

Kami stared as he left her room. She couldn't figure out if she was happy or not he was going to spend time with her because of his job.

Thomas Patrick stared out the floor to ceiling windows of his home office, gazing down on the pool in the back yard. Tiffany, his toy for the weekend, was sunbathing topless in the sunshine that had graced Chicago with its presence. She brought that damned poodle with her again. Thomas had told her not to bring it back after it shred a curtain in his master suite. Obviously Tiffany's IQ was the same as her dress size. Thomas didn't like being ignored.

He tilted back the two fingers of Scotch in his glass, taking a long swallow to savor the sweet burn of the expensive liquor. Setting the glass down, he took a draw from his Cuban cigar and turned his cold, hollow eyes to the oil painting hanging above his fireplace. Only one person had ever defied him and gotten away.

The bitch had heard things she wasn't meant to. Then she'd killed his unborn child and pretended to be hurt so she could plan her escape. He was going to enjoy cutting out her lying tongue when she finished begging for mercy.

Thomas had never been a violent man until Kamielle had forced him to become one. People would make their decisions and then face the consequences. He'd never had problems until he married a cute piece of ass. That's what he got for thinking with his dick instead of the brain he'd used to build an empire.

The phone on the huge mahogany desk rang. The voice over the intercom had a distinct New Jersey accent.

"Boss, I got a lead," Vinnie said. "She's not in Arizona anymore. I think she went to Vegas."

"You think? I'm not paying you to think! I'm paying you to find the bitch! If you can't handle the job, let me know and I'll put Marcos in charge. I'll also be a nice former boss and give you twenty-four hours to put your affairs in order and say goodbye to your sister."

"Sorry, boss. Marcos don't need to be in charge. I can handle this. I know she's in Vegas. She's dancing in a show under the name Camille Lovelace. I saw her picture on a reader board. Other than the fact she gots herself a boob job, she looks the same. Wild blonde hair, bedroom eyes, and a mouth that could suck a golf ball through a garden hose."

"You moron," Thomas said, "I know what she looks like! You have one week to secure her in our warehouse in Las Vegas then I'm flying in."

Thomas disconnected the call and hurled his glass at the painting above the fireplace. He pulled a .38 pistol from the hidden desk compartment and headed outside.

He strode to the pool toward Tiffany and her fucking yappy poodle. The same fucking yappy poodle that had just finished eating a hole in his new deck furniture. As Thomas raised the pistol to the dog, he spoke to Tiffany in a voice that was cold, clipped, and emotionless.

"I told you not to bring that damn dog back to my house. Pack your things and don't ever come back."

As the gunshot and screams finished echoing, the liquor puddled on the mantle just below the painting in Thomas's office of a blonde with bedroom eyes.

KAMIELLE AND MICHAEL walked into a small coffee shop and she immediately took in the surroundings. One bathroom, one entrance, and two people sitting at tables on the opposite side of the door. She figured she could check if there was a window in the bathroom right after she ordered her latte.

Michael asked what she wanted then went to the counter. She watched him walk away with a sexy swagger that would have caught her eye a few years back. She knew now sex appeal wasn't a reason to start a relationship. There were so many things she had learned about relationships and decided it was best not to have one at all. But if she was going to look, she'd look at Michael.

He came back with an iced latte for her and a plain, black coffee for himself. As his cell rang, Kami excused herself to the ladies' room.

"Carter," He answered with a smile as he watched her walk away. "Hey, Tony, what's up?"

"I just sent the body out with the coroner," Tony said. "I asked them to put a rush on it."

"Sounds good, buddy." Carter took a drink. "I'm at The Coffee House with Kamielle. I'm going to see what I can find out from her. Go back to the hotel and get some shut-eye. We'll go to the station later. I'm thinking we can hold Stewart a little longer on suspicion of murder. Maybe we'll finally be able to nail his ass to the wall."

"Buddy, you have my truck."

Michael laughed. "I guess I do. Ask one of the patrol cops to drive you."

"For shit's sake," Tony mumbled. "This is why I should never hand over my keys."

Kami came back to the table and sat down as Michael said, "I'll come get you later so we can question Stewart. Bye."

She sipped her latte. "Do you really think Stewart killed Karen?"

"To tell you the truth, I honestly don't know." Michael thought of the evidence that pointed toward the serial killer.

He didn't think Stewart was smart enough to be the murderer. There was no way this was a copy cat because certain details of the cases hadn't been given to the press.

He set down his coffee. "I know you don't want to think about last night, but what had you been doing for the last two days before I met you?"

She almost dropped her latte. "OhmyGod! You don't think I killed her do you?" She stood, mouth gaping, eyes wide.

"No, no. I was just wondering if you'd seen anything weird or if you can think of anything suspicious around your house the last few days." He stood. "Come on. We're attracting attention we don't need right now. Especially since you look like you've been beaten up."

As he ushered her out the door, she self-consciously touched her face and drooped her shoulders.

"I didn't mean to remind you," he said. "You look beautiful, black eye and all."

"Thanks. I didn't mean to freak out. I just figured that would be my luck. Getting arrested for murder would add to the horribleness that's been plaguing me for a few months."

"Want to talk about it?" he asked as he opened the passenger door of the big truck and helped her into the seat.

"No," she said and shut the door.

Michael walked around the truck and regrouped. He felt like they were connecting. *Connecting? Who am I kidding? I don't know anything about this woman.* He decided to try and get to know her on a more personal level even though she had just shot him down.

When he got in and started the truck, the first thing he did was turn on the stereo. "Do you like 90s music? I grew up with it, so it's my favorite."

"I don't mind Grunge. I pretty much like everything."

"Ah, Grunge. The good ole' days," he said. "I could wear

my ripped jeans and flannel shirts and no one cared. My cowboy boots weren't quite Doc Martens though."

She laughed. "I wouldn't be caught dead in flannel. That's like a total fashion no-no. Even when I couldn't afford to dress like all the other kids, I still knew the fashion faux pas." She blushed at the mention of not being able to afford clothes.

"You sound like my sister. She wouldn't be caught dead in flannel, either. Whenever I go to visit she complains about my clothes. I told her the horses and cows don't care."

"Your sister has horses?" Kami thought back to the few times the foster home had taken her and some of the other children riding at the local stables in Texas. She had loved the freedom and power of the beautiful animals.

"Yeah. We own a ranch in Montana and she runs it with her husband. I don't get to visit as often as I'd like. My job keeps me pretty damn busy."

"You own the ranch with her? How did that happen?" Kami looked years younger when she smiled. Her brows drew together and she crossed her hands in her lap. "I'm sorry. Am I asking too many questions? I'm being rude."

"No, you're not. I don't mind telling you about my family; I love them." Whenever Michael talked about Julie or Jon he always had a note of pride in his voice. "How about if we get together tomorrow and I'll tell you about them?"

Kami realized they had pulled into her driveway. The police vehicles were gone and so was her car.

"Tomorrow would be fine," she said distractedly. "Where's my car?"

"I told you I was going to have it taken care of. Tony drove it to a shop and he's going to deliver it back in a few hours. We have a little pull in getting cars fixed in a hurry." He smiled. "We've been known to destroy a car or two."

"Wow. It's been so long since someone has done something nice for me. Thank you."

They got out of the truck and went to the door. "I'm just going to check things out," he said.

They walked in and Kami turned to lock all the deadbolts when she shut the door behind them.

"It's a habit," she said when he raised an eyebrow.

So many people had been in and out of the house the carpet was dirty, the garbage was overflowing, and fingerprint dust covered almost every surface.

Michael frowned. "I'm sorry things are such a mess."

"You know what? It's okay. I haven't needed to clean since I moved in because one person doesn't get the place dirty enough. This will give me something to do tonight."

"I still think someone should have at least taken the garbage out." He walked over and pulled the bag.

"Really, I don't mind. I'll take it out." She took the bag from his hands and unlocked the back door. She pulled the door open and stopped.

Time away from the house with Michael had almost made her forget how the man had stumbled, or rather crashed, into her life. Karen was dead. Kami didn't think she could walk down the steps and throw the single bag of trash away.

Michael took the bag from her and went down the stairs. He was back at the foot of the steps when the door to Karen and Stewart's side of the duplex opened. He heard Kami's sharp intake of breath as a man who looked quite a bit like Stewart would have, if he hadn't been such a loser, started walking down the stairs. The man extended his right hand toward Michael when he was only halfway down.

"Hi, there. I'm Justin Martin, Stewart's brother. I've also been referred to as 'the better half'." He laughed and practically lunged toward Michael in order to shake hands. "I hear my brother went and got himself in a heap of trouble again. I'm his lawyer and he called me last night. You must be the neighbors. Anything I should know about the cops around here? Or about the mistakes my brother's been making lately?" The man didn't know when to stop talking.

Michael eyed him with suspicion and took a step back. It placed him on the first step up Kami's stairs and almost a foot taller than Mr. Martin, lawyer-boy.

"I'm actually the agent who arrested Stewart last night. What you need to know about the cops around here is they don't take kindly to men beating up women." He tilted his head toward Kami still standing at the top of the steps.

Justin Martin's mouth dropped open. "That bastard," he whispered. "My brother isn't a very smart or nice man. Our pa used to beat on our ma and Stewart seems to think it's okay. I'm sorry for his behavior, ma'am. Are you all right?"

Justin moved toward the stairs as though he was going to walk up to Kami. Michael blocked his way.

"No, she's not all right. That's why Stewart is in jail."

Kami moved down a few steps to get a better look. He was older than Stewart, although he looked younger in his facial features. Too many hard living years had aged Stewart. His brother, however, was perfectly manicured in a three-piece suit and shiny shoes. His hair was black with streaks of silver at his temples. The man exuded the aura of a lawyer; snake lawyer.

Michael felt Kami directly behind him. She said, "I hope... I hope Stewart stays away from here for a while. I don't want to see him."

"You can guarantee I'm going to let him sit in jail for a few days to think about what he did. I'm on my way down there right now to give him a lecture he won't forget." Justin went to leave. Then he turned back and gave Kami a piercing stare. "If there's anything I can do to make up for my brother's incompetence, please allow me to help. And I do mean anything."

He pulled a business card from an inside pocket and walked back. Michael took the card. The lawyer frowned and walked away.

"I imagine I'll be seeing you at the station later tonight," Michael said to his back.

"Yes. I imagine we'll be seeing a lot of each other, Mr. Carter," Justin said just before shutting the back door.

Michael turned to face Kami. She stood two steps above him and was looking directly into his eyes.

"I don't care much for that man," she whispered.

"Yeah, neither do I," he said. "Let's get inside. He might come back and try to put ice on your black eye."

Kami looked over her shoulder. "Thanks for not letting him come up the stairs. I didn't want him to touch me."

"I didn't figure you would. That's what I'm here for."

They entered the house and Michael shut and locked the back door. He looked around then placed a piercing blue gaze on her. "I don't think you should stay here tonight."

"And just where do you think I should stay? I don't have a car to drive, remember?" She put her hands on her hips then dropped her arms. "You know what? I don't want to stay here tonight."

"Tony and I are staying at the Holiday Inn. How about if we book you a room there for a few nights? I'll drive you down, then I know you'll be safe." He smiled. "Besides, this way we can have that lunch tomorrow while I tell you about my wonderful, overbearing family."

"I think that's a great idea. I'm going to look for a new place to live, too. I'm not sure I can live here anymore after what happened with Stewart and Karen." She frowned. "I still can't believe she's dead."

"I know. Death is hard to deal with when it's someone we're close to."

"It's not that we were close. It's just that I found her. That's the part that's so hard to deal with. I've already seen enough death to last me a lifetime," Kami said. "I'm going to pack my stuff. I'll be ready in about half an hour."

She walked to her bedroom and closed the door. Michael stared after her wondering again what secrets she kept hidden.

While packing her bags, Kami realized at some point in time, the man she had met last night had gone through a transformation in her mind. The odd, slow man who was Mr. FBI had morphed into cool, efficient Carter. Then he had somehow changed, yet again, to the more personal Michael. The name his friends called him.

Was he really her friend? Did she dare get attached to anyone?

Chapter 6

Michael checked Kami into the hotel under a false name. It was for her safety since she had found a murdered woman's body. He also didn't want Justin Martin to 'accidentally' find her and offer his services again. The man was a total snake and Michael didn't want him within one hundred feet of Kamielle. He wasn't sure when he had become so protective of the little redheaded spitfire. He figured it was some time between hitting her with his car and drying her off in the shower. Either way, it hadn't taken long for his possessive mode to kick in.

As they walked to the elevator to go to her room, Michael began to think about how to wrap this case up as quickly as possible. This was supposed to be his and Tony's last day in Oakland. Since Michael wanted to take Dana Petty to lunch and he was supposed to go on the double date with Tony, he was trying to decide which was more important. Definitely lunch with Dana.

He didn't feel like going on the date anymore. He knew Tony would be pissed when he canceled. Or, Tony would love the opportunity to go out with both women by himself. Wouldn't be the first time, wouldn't be the last.

"You're awfully quiet," Kami said once the doors shut. "I'm sorry you've gotten involved in all this. Truth be told, I'm sorry I'm involved." She lifted wide eyes to his.

"Believe me," he said, "this isn't your fault. I've been involved for more months than I'd care to count. I was on my way to talk to Karen when you ran in front of my car."

Kami winced. "I'd rather not think about that. You've already seen me at an all-time low. Let's not add to it with the need for a straight jacket." The elevator doors opened. "In the past I'd have an ice cream binge and cry session with my best friend, Shelby."

"Well, I could take you to this friend of yours and she could make all your troubles go away." Michael set the suitcase he had been carrying onto one of the queen beds. When he turned, Kami was crying. "Whoa. What did I say to trigger this?" He walked toward her.

"Nothing. I'm sorry." She backed away.

"Tell me what I said. It's your friend, isn't it? Does she live far away? Do you miss her?"

Kami wiped her nose on the sleeve of her sweatshirt and sniffled back a small sob. "Yeah, I miss her more than I thought I did."

"I'm sorry I mentioned it. I was just trying to help." Michael didn't know why he was apologizing. He never felt the need to defend himself to anyone.

"Don't worry about it. I didn't mean to fall apart on you again." She walked to the other bed and set down the laptop and duffel bags. "I think it would be a really good idea if I went to bed. I didn't sleep well last night." She wiped her eyes again.

Michael looked like he wanted to say something. She walked to the bathroom to get a drink of water then turned, too curious for her own good. She was dead tired, but didn't want to be alone.

"What is it?" She leaned against the door frame. "Are you trying to ask me something?"

"I was just thinking that if we were in a nicer place, we could order up room service and drown our sorrows in a pint or two of ice cream and some high quality bourbon." The smile he gave her was one that had been making the knees of young women weak for almost twenty years.

"Maybe we can do that some time when my life isn't out of control." She smiled back. "Thank you for being my friend, Michael, I needed one this weekend." She shut herself in the bathroom.

Michael stared after her for a moment trying to decide what to do. He enjoyed Kami's company more than he had enjoyed the company of any woman since Crystal had been killed. Except for Jon, Julie, and Tony, Michael didn't have a lot of normal conversations. Everyone he talked to any more had some connection to him from work.

What am I saying? Everything we've been talking about has to do with dead bodies and sleazy lawyers. Maybe... hell, maybe what? He wouldn't see her again when she was no longer needed for the case.

After she washed her face with cool water, Kami looked at her reflection. The dark circles under her eyes almost matched her bruises. She must have been a sight to behold at the coffee shop. She tried to maneuver her mop of red hair to make herself more presentable.

"What the hell am I doing? I've got split lips, a black eye, and I look like the walking dead. Fixing my hair isn't going to make me look any better." She slammed her hand down on the counter.

"Kamielle," Michael called. "Are you okay? I heard a noise." He paused then said, "You didn't fall, did you?"

Kami couldn't help it, she started to laugh. She opened the

door. "For the last year, no one has cared about me at all. Now I'm saddled with a six foot warrior who saves me every time I go into a bathroom."

"I am not a warrior and I do not rescue you from the bathroom. Okay, so the last few times I've been with you, I've rescued you in a bathroom, but that doesn't mean anything. I could have rescued you from other places." He ran a hand down his face.

She laughed harder. "You have made my evening much more fun, so, thank you."

"I tell you what, you try to stay happy like this for the next week and we'll forget you've been laughing at my expense. Don't tell Tony about this. He'll call me a Knight in Shining Armor for sure."

"You probably won't even see me again in a few days."

"I plan to keep an eye on you." He took her hand.

"Why?" she asked. "You don't live here. Why would you stay any longer? The local police will take care of the murder, won't they?"

"You sure ask a lot of questions. I can do whatever I want, I'm an FBI agent. And right now, this agent needs to go down to the station to question Stewart. Can I get you anything while I'm gone? I should be back in a few hours."

Kami looked at the clock between the two beds. It was already six in the evening. "A pint of Ben and Jerry's Cherry Garcia?" she asked with a devilish grin.

"I'll see what I can do." He stroked the skin between her thumb and first finger before dropping her hand. "See you later tonight. I'll call if I'm going to be too late."

After telling her goodbye, Michael stood in the hall for a moment. Was it a good or bad thing he was looking forward to bringing back ice cream and visiting with Kamielle?

His cell rang. "Carter here."

"Buddy, you have got to get down to the station," said Tony. "I just met Stewart's brother. You are not going to believe this, he's a lawyer."

"Oh, I met him at Kamielle's duplex, and the man is total pond scum."

"You're telling me. He's getting ready to post bail."

"You keep that son of a bitch where he's at until I can get down there!"

"I'm trying. Get your ass here and help me!"

Michael drove downtown as fast as he could.

The local police station was a hub of activity. There were beat cops pulling prostitutes and street pushers through the station. Michael weaved through people until he found the bail room. Tony was sitting next to the Chief of Police and Justin Martin.

"... hasn't done anything wrong." Justin was saying as Michael walked in. "This charge of resisting arrest is bogus. He was attacked by Agent Carter, not the other way around. Ah, Mr. Carter, speak of the devil."

"You've never met Carter, how do you know his name, Mr. Martin?" Tony stood.

Michael turned a questioning gaze toward Justin. Michael thought back over their conversation at the duplex. He'd never introduced himself and Justin had addressed him by name then, as well.

"We're not talking about introductions right now. We're talking about how my client, my brother, was manhandled and had his rights stepped on!" The lawyer turned back to the Chief. "I demand my brother be released and you think about what type of agents you align your department with."

Tony made a disgusted sound and walked out the door, Michael following.

"Can you believe this shit?" Tony asked. "I mean the guy

beats up his neighbor and his girlfriend is found dead in a dumpster behind their house. That's enough to hold him for questioning."

They watched Justin and the Chief argue through the glass walls of the room. Finally, the attorney threw his hands in the air and walked out. He marched toward Carter.

"I don't know who you think you are, but I am not going to let the abuse you put my brother through be forgotten." He stormed away.

"You've got twenty-four hours to link Stewart Martin to this murder. Resisting arrest is all I can keep him on," the Chief said. "If he had nothing to do with the murder we have to let him go."

"He beat the hell out of a woman," Michael began.

"And, she didn't press charges," the Chief finished. "Unless she does, there's nothing I can do."

"I'll work on it," Michael said. "Tony, keep seeing what you can come up with on our serial killer case."

"She's not going to do it, Carter, you already tried."

"Well, that was before she knew me and before she found Karen dead. Maybe now she'll be willing."

Michael left the station and went back to his car. He sat with his forehead on the steering wheel trying to figure out what to do. Finally, he pulled out of the parking lot and went to buy ice cream and a bottle of bourbon.

After a bath, Kami put on pajamas and wrapped herself in a robe. She set the laptop up on the small table in the corner of the room and picked an online jazz music channel. She slid the bag with the money under the bed.

It had been over a week since she'd been on The Chicago

Sun-Times website. As usual, Thomas Patrick's name was all over the Business and Social pages. The articles were about his booming restaurant and bar and his downtown buildings.

There was a picture of him on the arm of a beautiful, thin, blonde woman. The caption under the picture read "Millionaire Moves on with his Life". Kami sucked in a breath. The article confirmed her worst fears.

Successful business tycoon, Thomas Patrick, recently told the press his wife, Kamielle, had checked herself into drug rehab almost a year ago. It was after the devastating car accident that killed her best friend and turned her to a life of drugs and alcohol. Patrick, who cried during Tuesday's press conference, told the world his beloved wife died of a drug overdose over the weekend.

"My love just wasn't enough to keep her with me. I failed her and that means I failed in everything."

His heartfelt speech was concluded with a $500,000 donation to a Chicago drug rehab center.

"Maybe my money can help other families from having to go through the torment I have experienced over the last year. She left me for drugs and I haven't had a wife for eleven months; now she's physically gone. It's time to move on with my life."

Patrick appears to have moved on, taking model Steffie Magnolia to a business dinner after eleven months of attending all trips and dinners alone because wife, Kamielle, had been so ill due to her drug addiction and repeated hospital...

Kami stared at the computer screen. There was a picture of her with Thomas and Shelby. It showed a smiling couple, but looking at it now, Kami could tell she wasn't as happy as she had believed. Her hair was just below her ears and platinum blonde, her eyes held dark circles and her face was sunken from lack of food. She remembered the party and how easy life had been when she was oblivious to the horrible life Thomas lived.

She shut the top to the computer and threw herself on the bed face down. "That son of a bitch!" she yelled into the pillow.

Pounding her fists into the bed, she sobbed. If the rest of the world thought she was dead, no one would be able to help her if Thomas found out where she was. It wasn't *if* he found her, it was *when.*

Kami rolled over to stare at the ceiling. What would she explain to the police when she called 911 and they showed up? Thomas would be sitting on her couch in business suit sipping tea while his limo was parked on the street. *"We've just had a misunderstanding. The lady didn't need to call 911. Isn't your boss Mayor So-and-so? He and I go way back. We played Polo together in college. You let him know I said hi."*

It would be like always. Thomas would use his power and influence. The world would bow down to him.

Kami pictured Special Agent Michael Carter's smiling face. Was he one of the many men in Thomas's pocket? Kami didn't think Michael could be paid off. Of course, she'd only been around him a few days. She thought, again, of being able to confide in someone who might be able to keep her safe. She didn't think two days warranted enough of a connection to put her life in his hands.

She stared at the ceiling, lost in thought, for another twenty minutes before the hotel phone rang. She waited three rings before realizing no one had her number but Michael.

"Hello?"

"Kamielle, it's me. I'm on my way. I bought you ice cream. I just wanted you to know I'd be knocking on your door so you wouldn't be scared."

"Well, thank you. You know how to steal a girl's heart. Come bearing gifts of ice cream and they'll let you in every time."

It was after nine, but Kami wasn't tired anymore. She went in the bathroom and splashed cold water on her face. The redness from her crying was almost gone and she was getting used to the bruises.

There was a knock on the door and she opened it to Michael. He held her ice cream in one hand and a brown-bagged bottle in the other. His smile made her knees weak.

"Oh, my Knight in Shining Armor. Would you like me to eat this in the bathtub so we can stick with our bathroom fetish?" She giggled and tried to take the ice cream.

Michael held the container above his head and laughed with her. "You said you wouldn't mention anything about me being your Knight."

"You said I couldn't say anything to Tony. I'm going to rub it in your face every chance I get." She jumped again but he was too tall.

After some good-natured ribbing, Michael finally gave her the ice cream and a spoon. He pulled out the bottle of bourbon and set it on the wet bar.

"I'll get us some ice if you'll get the fine China plastic cups unwrapped."

He left with the ice bucket and Kami got the cups. When he came back, he put some ice in one.

"Do you want any?"

"No thank you," she said digging into the ice cream.

"Okay, but you're more than welcome to have some later.

Do you drink?" He poured half a cup of bourbon over the ice and lifted it to his lips.

Kami was frozen as she watched him. Her heartbeat sped up and her breath caught in her throat. She hadn't been attracted to a man since the first time she saw Thomas. This wasn't good.

"Kamielle?"

"Huh? Oh, yeah, I drink occasionally. I was a bartender for a little over three years, so I've tried just about every concoction known to man."

He walked to a chair at the table holding the laptop. She went to one of the queen beds and sat down, cross-legged.

"I like bourbon and beer. Beer on a tough day, bourbon on an extremely tough day." He took a healthy swallow.

"So I take it today was an extremely tough day?"

"This whole weekend has been tough. Of course, I think it's safe to say your weekend has been worse than mine." He saluted her with his cup.

She nodded. "You've made it tolerable."

"You used to be a bartender? You're not that old," he said. "How could you have been a bartender for three years?"

"I lied on a job application." She smiled and took another bite of ice cream. "I was only eighteen and I put I was twenty-one. The guy doing the hiring never checked out my age because he was too busy checking out my legs and boobs."

Michael feigned mock surprise, "You mean someone hired you based on your looks and not your qualifications?"

"Yeah, yeah, I know. Women get hired all the time based on their looks. But I was a damn good bartender." Kami hopped off the bed, putting her ice cream in the mini-fridge freezer.

Grabbing the bottle of bourbon and another plastic cup, she walked back to the bed. "I'm going to have one small glass of this. We'll call it pain reliever in a bottle."

"Oh, hell. I didn't even think about how sore you must be. How are you doing?" Michael stood and took the bottle and cup from her, looking her over from head to toe. "Your bruises are getting darker in color, but that means they're already starting to heal." He took her chin in his hand and turned her head from side to side.

"I'm fine, really," she said pulling away. "Pour me a drink, please." She sat on the bed cross-legged again.

"No problem. So, did you like being a bartender?" He handed her the bourbon and poured himself some more.

"It wasn't too bad. The customers were good because it was a pretty upscale place. Also, the owner didn't let anyone get away with treating his waitresses or bartenders poorly. He only hired women to work the floor. There was one guy behind the counter with me, but he was gay. Thomas didn't like his women being around other men."

"Thomas?"

"He was the owner of the bar." She looked away and took a sip.

"Sounds really interesting. Where was this?"

"Didn't you promise to tell me about your family?"

"C'mon, Kamielle. Haven't we moved beyond this? Why won't you answer any questions about yourself? Was the bar in Texas?"

"Texas? Why would you bring up Texas?" Her voice was shaky.

"You have a southern accent. You told me you were from Texas. I thought maybe that's where you worked."

"No, it wasn't in Texas. I really don't want to talk about it, please. It wasn't a happy time in my life." She finished the rest of the bourbon in one drink and held her hand out for a refill. She only shook slightly and was proud of herself.

"Okay. I'll tell you all about me and then you'll realize you can talk to me and trust me. You sure you want more?"

"Yes. Now tell me about this awesome family you have." She took the bottle and poured another half glass.

"I'll tell you everything you want to know about me after one more quick item." Michael set his cup down and put his hands on his thighs. "We need to talk about Stewart."

Chapter 7

Vinnie stood in a smoky room at the Brown Beaver strip club on the outskirts of Vegas. The name wasn't the only thing sleazy about the place. There were pay-per-view rooms right inside the front doors. He spent twenty dollars in one of the rooms before going to check out the women on stage.

Vinnie had been working for Thomas Patrick only four years. Patrick had inherited him and a few other guys when their former boss had gone to prison. Vinnie knew Patrick was too smart to get caught. Everyone in Chicago thought Patrick was a distinguished gentleman. Hell, everyone in the country thought he was God's gift to the world. Only a select few had ever seen his dark side.

In the time Vinnie had been doing clean-up for Patrick, he'd never seen the man as upset as the day they realized Kamielle was gone. Patrick had killed the two men posted outside his wife's door when they admitted the woman was missing. He'd shot them point blank. Most people preferred to be at a distance when they disposed of a problem. Patrick had just wiped the blood off his face with his silk handkerchief and made a drink.

A topless waitress rubbed against him and Vinnie smiled. Two things turned him on: sex and murder; usually in that order. In the forty years he'd been in the business, he hadn't been looking forward to an assignment like this in a long time. He'd been waiting for a piece of ass from Kamielle since the day he'd seen her bartending at Patrick's swank bar. The boss had quickly turned on the charm to the young girl and Vinnie hadn't even had a chance to cop a feel to initiate her to the world of working for the mob.

The men in the room began to chant "Lovelace" and the revving of a motorcycle engine and fake smoke filled the air to mix with tobacco smoke. As Vinnie squeezed his way between two sweaty men in business suits at the stools lining the edge of the bar, he got his first glimpse of Camille Lovelace, aka, Kamielle Patrick, pretending to be a stripper in Las Vegas.

Vinnie's pulse ratcheted as the blonde with huge tits rode onto the stage on a Yamaha motorcycle.

"I bet they can't afford a Harley!" The man next to him yelled over the sound of the motorcycle engine and chanting.

"Why the fuck do they need a Harley when that sweet piece of meat is sitting on stage?" his buddy yelled back.

Grunts of agreement moved down the line of men.

She didn't have much coordination on the bike. Luckily it was small because it almost fell on her when she came to a stop. Something about her didn't seem quite right. Was she too tall? A little too heavy? Must be the high heels and the angle Vinnie was sitting at below the stage.

He ordered a drink and sipped while the woman gyrated and stripped. Her eyes lit on Vinnie as he waved a hundred dollar bill. He figured it wasn't a waste when he'd be taking it back in a few hours. It got him her undivided attention for the remainder of her show. Stupid bitch didn't even recognize him.

At the end of the show, Camille, stripper by night and waitress by day, counted tips in her small dressing room. At a knock, she put the wad of cash behind her back.

"Who is it?"

The reply was the door being pushed open to reveal the seedy guy who had given her the hundred.

"Listen, buddy, I don't know how things work where you're from, but you don't get to come in here. Thanks for the kick-ass tip, but you don't get anything but the touches you already had. I ain't no hooker."

"Oh, I love you don't recognize me and your accent is different. I've come to take you back to Mr. Patrick. Of course, I get to have a little fun first."

"Who the fuck is Mr. Patrick?"

Vinnie went in, shutting and locking the door.

While Vinnie was in Las Vegas, a man in Oakland sat outside a Holiday Inn. He was in the front seat of a brown Chrysler smoking menthol light cigarettes.

There was a pile of cigarette butts outside the window on the pavement. It was after midnight and Agent Carter's car hadn't moved from the parking lot since he had pulled in a little after nine.

The man in the Chrysler pounded his fists on the steering wheel. She had to be there, she wasn't at her house! He had been so close to having her. Kamielle had to be with those FBI agents in the hotel. They were probably having sex. She would pay for this.

KAMIELLE GLARED AT MICHAEL. "I do not want to talk about Stewart! There is nothing to talk about!" She poked him in the chest. "The man is a total pig and that's it. I don't want to press charges. Why can't you get that through your head?" She tossed the cup in the trash and sat at the table.

"Damn it, I don't understand what's going on because you won't explain it to me."

"Isn't there a part of your life you'd rather not talk about? Something you'd forget, erase, or do over if you had that chance?" She stared at him with wide eyes full of tears.

"Yeah, there is," he said.

"Then please understand having to deal with the police and file official reports brings up painful memories." It wasn't just about Thomas being able to find her. It was also about dealing with the police when her mother had been murdered.

"Can I tell you something? Something I've only told two people in my entire life?" She wouldn't meet his eyes.

He took her hand and gave it a squeeze. "I didn't mean to push you this far. You don't even know me. I would really enjoy getting to know more about you and help you if I can. But don't feel like I'm forcing you."

She started talking before she lost her nerve. "My mother was killed when I was fifteen and I saw it all. In fact, I got hurt in the process."

She pulled her hair back from the right side of her face revealing the small scar under her ear. He traced it with the pad of his finger and she shivered.

"I saw this and wondered what it was from." He pulled his hand away. "What cut you, a knife?"

"No. It was a broken beer bottle. Mom's throat was slit. He tried to slit mine. I spent three hours covered in my mother's and my blood while giving my statement to the police. They wouldn't let me take a shower. They thought I was lying to them."

"I am so sorry. You don't like the police much, do you?" He tried to smile but couldn't.

"It's not really the police. It's the whole system."

"What happened to the man who attacked you and killed your mother?"

"I don't know. After he was arrested I was put into foster care and never kept tabs."

"Where was your father through all this mess? Why couldn't you live with him or another family member?" The thought of anyone seeing their mother killed, especially a fifteen year old girl, made him angry. He'd gone into law enforcement to protect people like Kamielle.

"I don't have any living family members. No aunts or uncles, my grandparents are all passed on."

"What about your father?"

"He's the one who killed her," she whispered.

"Are you kidding me?" Michael yelled. He stood, slamming his hands on the table.

Eyes wide, she watched as he paced the small room.

"I can't believe someone would kill their own wife! Try to kill their child. What is wrong with people? You think I'd be used to it with my job." He stopped and pushed his hands through his hair.

Kami stared, back rigid, eyes wide.

"I'm sorry. I'm *sorry*. You caught me off guard." He tried to contain his rage for her sake. He didn't want to scare her. "Kamielle, please, stop crying."

He took her hand and led her to a small couch in the corner of the room, pulling her next to him so their knees were touching. He decided to show her the same trust she had shown him.

"Four years ago, my parents were on a flight to Montana after visiting my fiancé and me. Their plane went down in a snowstorm when they were almost home. It was a small charter and everyone on board was killed instantly."

Besides the death of his parents, the fact he'd said fiancé registered in her throbbing head. She tried to stand. "You're married?"

Michael took her hand. "I'm not married. She died two months later."

Kami covered her mouth and fell back to the couch. "That must have been horrible for you to lose three important people so close together."

"It was a bad situation. Tony and I were chasing a serial killer, like we do on almost every job. This particular killer took a personal interest in me."

"He killed her, didn't he?" she whispered as she leaned in and touched his face.

The pain she saw answered her question. They were inches apart and she felt connected to him in a way she had never felt.

She'd only ever told Thomas and Shelby about her father. She knew now Thomas hadn't cared. Shelby had been sympathetic, but she had both her parents and had grown up with the wealthy of Chicago. She didn't really understand. Looking into Michael's eyes, Kami knew he did.

He wiped away the last of her tears and they sat for a moment, hands on each other's faces, lost in the memories. She finally closed her eyes. He put his arm around her and she rested her cheek on his shoulder.

"No one has ever understood my pain before now." She felt like she could relax for the first time in a year. She had been running and lying for so long.

As Kami drifted off to sleep, her last thought was maybe

things would turn out okay for once. Maybe she could figure out how to get her life back and how to trust people again. Trust Michael.

Michael felt her body relax and her breathing even out. He waited about twenty minutes before he stood, lifted her, and put her gently in bed.

"You're a mystery," he whispered as he brushed a kiss over her cheek.

He turned off the light and watched her in the shadows of the moon. He shook his head to clear his thoughts. Then he left.

KAMI WOKE SUDDENLY and looked at the clock. It was four a.m. She was still wrapped in the robe, but all the lights were off. There was a brief thought of having no idea where she was. The weekend rushed back and with a quick calculation she knew it was Sunday morning. She also remembered crying and telling Michael about her mother and father. She covered her eyes and moaned. Her black eye throbbed in time with her headache and heartbeat. She moved slowly off the bed and into the bathroom. Turning on the light made her head throb worse.

After a shower, she felt better. She took her time getting dressed and by the time she pulled her hair back in a loose, wet ponytail, it was almost five. Her mind was already working on where to move next and she tried not to think about Michael Carter.

Walking quietly out the door she whispered to herself, "Run before the feelings go away so you can take something good with you."

She went to the front desk and asked for a cab. It would be best to leave town because she had told Michael so much about herself. Some research about her mother's murder and then he would be able to figure out her real name and link her to Thomas.

She grabbed a newspaper and got in the cab. The ride was quiet and she counted street lamps for something to occupy her mind. If she timed everything right, she could have a new car and be packed before the evening rush hour traffic began.

Back at her duplex, she breathed a sigh of relief. Even if she didn't feel completely safe anymore, she knew Stewart was in jail and she would be gone before the day was through.

Spreading the paper out on the table she began looking at vehicles for sale. She'd have a cab take her to 'Auto Row'. There were at least twelve dealerships to choose from. It wouldn't take long to walk through and pick what she wanted.

She called and asked to be picked up at 7:45 a.m. An SUV was sounding good. Something with room and a DVD player in the back. That would be fun. She'd be able to sleep in it at some parks or something. The thoughts made her daydream about travels to come.

A horn honked and she peeked out the window to see a bright yellow cab at the curb. "You'd think he could come to the door," she said as she grabbed her purse. Keys in hand, she opened the door just in time to see the cab driving away.

"Wait! Come back!" Kami yelled as she ran out, waving her hands. The feel of something poking into her ribs stopped her next scream at the taxi.

A whispered voice in her ear made her blood run cold. "It's okay, you have me to take care of you now."

MICHAEL WAS ARGUING with the front desk clerk to find out which cab company had taken Kami. He still couldn't believe she hadn't been in her room when he had shown up with two cups of coffee and bagels. He'd kicked the door in to make sure she was okay.

His phone rang. Without looking at the screen he answered. "What?" There was a fuzzy sound like gurgling and hissing combined. "Hello? Is someone there?"

"Mich... Mi..." More gurgling.

"Who is this?"

"Help... me..."

"What kind of sick joke is this? Do you realize you're speaking with a Fed—"

"Kam... help... breathe... " The line went dead.

Michael looked at Tony who was still talking to the little geek on front desk duty.

"I've got the number for the cab company. I'll call and find out... what's wrong?" Tony asked.

"I think that was Kamielle. She doesn't sound good and I think she said she needs help."

"What do you mean you think she needs help?" Tony was asking the question to Michael's back because he was already running toward the parking lot.

"I don't know. I couldn't understand what she was saying. Call 911 while I drive. Get a police unit and paramedics sent to her home address."

"How do you know that's where she is?" Tony asked.

"I don't know where else she'd be."

Michael started his car, barely waiting for Tony to close the door before tearing out of the parking lot. He took off toward the duplex hoping Kamielle was there and not as hurt as she sounded.

Tony was speaking in hushed tones on his cell and kept glancing at Michael. When he hung up he said, "911 has already been dispatched. Someone walking their dog reported hearing gunshots from inside the house. They also saw a man running down the alley."

"Gunshots?" Michael yelled. "This woman gets into more trouble than anyone I've ever met."

It only took ten minutes for him to pull to a screeching halt behind an ambulance and police car. Two officers were trying to peek in windows, guns drawn.

Tony and Michael pulled their badges and drew their weapons as well.

"What's the situation?" Tony asked because Michael was already walking to the front door with keys in his hands.

"What the hell do you think you're doing?" the officer yelled. "What the hell does he think he's doing?" he asked Tony when Michael ignored him.

"Looks to me like he's going inside."

"How does he have keys to this house? Do you know the person who lives here?"

"Yes, we know the person who lives here." Tony jogged to Michael. "Where did you get keys?" he whispered.

"I took them off the key ring with the car keys. I thought these might come in handy if she locked me out. Ready?"

Tony nodded and Michael opened the front door. There weren't any lights on and the curtains were closed. A pair of heels lay inside the door. At the top of the stairs there was a small bloody hand print on the wall.

"Shit," Michael whispered.

He advanced up the stairs only to find more blood on the kitchen floor and splattered on the counters and walls. The chairs were knocked over. Yellow nylon rope was pooled next to one of the chairs and it looked like it was soaked in blood.

A knife lay on the kitchen floor. Not only was the blade bloody, but the handle had blood on it, too.

"Kamielle!" Michael called. If anyone else was in the house he'd kill them.

Tony had gone into the living room. The coffee table and couch were overturned. A baseball bat lay in the center of the mess. It looked like there were chunks of hair all over the floor, too, but Tony didn't have time to figure out what it was from.

"Get the paramedics in here!"

Michael looked under the kitchen table and found Kamielle huddled in a blanket. A cell phone was clutched in one pale hand.

"Kamielle, can you hear me?"

When she didn't respond, he went into FBI mode. He still couldn't tell where her head was so he went for the hand holding the phone. Her skin was so cold and she wasn't moving. Michael knew she was dead. He pulled the blanket away and saw she was naked and covered in blood. Her hair had been hacked off to her shoulders. He thought he heard a whimper.

He stood and ripped the table away from the wall, sending it clattering into the chairs. He grabbed Kamielle's wrist again, ignoring her clammy skin, but still couldn't find a pulse. Becoming frantic, he felt her neck. Her pulse fluttered lightly under his fingertips. Blood was now pooling under her body. There was an ugly looking hole just above her left breast. She'd been shot in the chest.

"Get in here now!" Michael yelled. "She's losing blood!"

Tony gripped his arm. "Come on, buddy, let's get out of their way. These guys are the best chance she's got of surviving. We'll follow them to the hospital and make sure everything is okay. We won't let anyone else hurt her."

Michael stood. "I don't know what's going on in her life, but you're right. I'm not going to let anyone hurt her ever again."

Chapter 8

Two days later, Tony and Michael sat at Kamielle's bedside in the Critical Care Unit of St. Francis Hospital. She hadn't moved, opened her eyes, or given any sign she might wake up any time soon. She was, however, breathing on her own which the doctors thought was a miracle in itself. Her heart rate was slow, but steady.

Besides the obvious gunshot wound that had punctured her lung, the knife wounds had caused her to lose a large amount of blood. The police and forensics concluded she had been tied up and sliced with the knife numerous times. Her hair had also been cut with the same knife.

Michael had been at her bedside since the night they brought her to the hospital. The only time he'd left was to get her clothes and some belongings from her duplex and pick up her cat. He had it locked in the hotel bathroom with food, water, and a litter box.

"Michael, buddy, go back to the hotel and get a few hours of sleep. I'll stay here. You look like shit. If she does wake up, you're going to scare her. Your clothes are dirty and you haven't shaved or showered in two days." Tony had just gotten back from the hotel.

"What if she wakes up while I'm gone? I want to be here when she opens her eyes."

"Why?" Tony asked. "You don't know this woman. She's trouble and you don't need this in your life."

"Why not?" Michael said. "She interests me like no one has. I don't want to go out on blind dates with you anymore because they bore me. I never have time to meet women and that whole 'move on with my life conversation' you gave me had a good point. I'm thirty-four, I've never been married, I don't have kids, and I haven't made any long term plans for the future. I'm not saying Kamielle is my future, but she doesn't seem to have anyone else and I've enjoyed her company."

Tony shook his head. "Fine, you want to spend more time with the woman, do it. Are you going to convince her to move to San Francisco so you can see her? In case you've forgotten, we're supposed to be back to work on Thursday. It's Tuesday."

"I know what goddamn day it is, Medina! I don't need you to remind me how to do my goddamn job."

"Carter, go get some coffee, food, a shave, and a shower. Come back when you're not going to be an asshole"

Michael stood and slumped his shoulders. "I'm sorry."

Before Tony could respond, Michael left the CCU.

Tony took a deep breath. He didn't think Michael was being an asshole; he thought he was being stupid. It didn't make sense this woman could intrigue him so much. Tony looked at Kamielle laying small and vulnerable in the bed. Maybe that's what had gotten into Michael. He wanted someone to take care of.

Sitting in the chair at her bedside, Tony said, "I don't know what's going on in your life, lady, but I hope you don't hurt my best friend."

"Shelby? Thomas?" she whispered.

"Kamielle, can you hear me?" He leaned closer and pressed

the call button for the nurse. Then he sent a text message to Michael.

"Where's my husband?" she whispered.

"What's his name and I'll find him for you."

"Thomas," she whispered. "He's on business. We have to get a hold of him so he can contact Shelby's parents. Is my car totaled?"

"Kamielle. My name is Tony Medina. I'm an FBI agent. Do you remember me?"

Her eyes drifted shut as she mumbled something else about Thomas.

Michael came running into the room and almost knocked down the nurse. "What's going on?"

"She opened her eyes and asked for Shelby."

"That's her best friend. She told me she missed Shelby." Michael stood on the other side of the bed and looked at Tony. "What else did she say?"

"She asked for her husband. I asked her if she remembered me and she didn't say anything."

"Kamielle, honey? Open your eyes for me. It's Michael. I need to know you're okay." He rubbed her cheek and held her hand.

Her lips moved. Her eyelids fluttered open and closed three times before she looked directly at Michael. "Who?" she said then recognition dawned. "Michael? Where am I? What's going on?" The words were stronger than before.

The nurse handed Michael a cup with water and a little stick with a pink, star shaped sponge on the end. It looked like a Blow-Pop.

"Run this over her lips and let her suck some of the water out of it," the nurse explained.

Michael did as she suggested and Kami closed her eyes at the sensation.

"I knew you'd save me," she whispered. "He told me he was going to kill me and I knew you'd save me." She squeezed his hand and tears slowly slid out of the corners of her eyes.

"I'll always save you, Kamielle. You just can't run out on me."

"I had to run. He might find me. I always run before he finds me." She closed her eyes again.

"The man who hurt you? Who, Kamielle? Who do you run from?"

But she had fallen back asleep.

"I'm going to do some research on this Thomas guy and her friend Shelby. I'll call the VCTF and get us a few more weeks," Tony said.

"Thanks for understanding, Tony."

"I didn't say I understand."

THOMAS STOOD in an airplane hangar in Las Vegas. He was screaming at Vinnie who was sweating profusely and trying not to look scared.

"You stupid son of a bitch! She doesn't even look like my wife. My wife is beautiful and pure. This woman is an ugly whore! Did you fuck her before you brought her here? I bet you did because you thought she was my Kamielle."

Thomas turned to the heap of woman cowering in the corner of the warehouse. Her makeup was smudged and her fake breasts were heaving as she tried to breathe through the gag in her mouth. There was a gash on her left cheek and it looked like she had a necklace of bruises. Her only clothing was a thong. It was what she had probably been dancing in.

"Only a whore would willingly go anywhere with you, you piece of shit! Did you think my Kamielle would be attracted to you?" Thomas turned to the woman in the corner. "Get rid of her body since she knows who we are!"

Vinnie watched Thomas storm from the airplane hangar which served many purposes to the Patrick Empire of Nevada. He almost threw up. He'd screwed up bad this time.

Thomas slid into the backseat of his limo, welcoming the cool air. He couldn't believe he'd lost control. While it had only been for brief moments, he felt as though his entire world was flipped on its axis. Kamielle was the last loose end and he had been so sure she was finally going to be his again. Of course, that goon had ruined everything.

Thomas took a few steadying breaths and dialed his phone. "Marcos, I want my wife found immediately. This has become unacceptable. I publicly announced she's dead. Vinnie's usefulness has expired. Dispose of him and his sister, Rosanna. I do not take kindly to mistakes."

Call ended, Thomas pushed a button that revealed a hidden compartment under his seat. He pulled out a syringe, pushed it slowly into his skin, and waited for his world to right itself.

One week to the day Kamielle had been attacked, her eyes fluttered open and she looked at Michael with a smile. She had been in and out of consciousness at least twice a day. Usually when the physical therapists were exercising her legs.

Michael spent his days reading magazine articles and telling her about his family. The stories had become her dreams about a ranch in Montana with beautiful children and a good looking cowboy.

She knew she was fighting a growing attraction to this wonderful man who had forced her to come back to life.

There was a part of her that didn't ever want to wake up. This was her second time hanging in the balance. She wanted to come back to life the first time because of her lost baby and a chance to make things right with her husband. There had been no reason to return to the world of the living this time.

Michael was a powerful force pulling her out of the darkness. As she lay in the hospital bed and stared into his eyes, she pulled his hand, which was gently clasped in hers, up to her dry lips.

Michael caught his breath as her lips touched his palm. "What was that for?" he asked as she put his hand on her still slightly bruised face.

"My way of thanking you," she whispered. "What kind of pain medication do they have me on? I'm feeling kinda strange."

"Well, they put you on a morphine drip and I've been pressing the button for you."

"I don't do well with pain meds. The last time I was in the hospital everything they gave me made me sick."

"Was that when your mom died?" he asked.

"My mom? Oh, I told you all that, didn't I? Alcohol and pain medication make me do things I wouldn't normally do."

"Before we get too far into any conversations that may be strange due to pain medication, you need to look in a mirror."

"A mirror? Is it that bad?" She frowned and slowly reached up to touch her face.

"How much do you remember?" His voice reminded her of the night she met him.

"More than I want to. My dreams have been a combination of a ranch in Montana and a psycho in a ski mask with a big knife."

She shuddered and Michael ran his thumb down the side

of her face. Since meeting the man, he was always touching her, and she didn't mind.

Or maybe it was the morphine.

"Montana?" he said. "Could you hear all the stories I was telling you?"

"Of course. You're the reason I'm still alive." Her smile was a ray of sunshine after sitting by her side for a week worrying.

"You're alive because you want to be alive. You're an incredibly strong woman."

"I decided to live because of you. I'm alone in the world, Michael. If you hadn't been here, there wouldn't have been a reason to live. You wove a story about a ranch and your beautiful nieces and nephews. It gave me something to dream about. Except, we're supposed to be speaking about the man who attacked me."

"Even stoned on pain medication, you're still eloquent and to the point," he said.

"He told me he was going to kill me and enjoy seeing the look on your face when you found my mutilated and raped body." Tears fell. "I kept thinking you were going to find me just like I'd found Karen. I wasn't ready to die yet, not like that." She shuddered.

"He took off my clothes and tied me to the kitchen chair. He kept slicing me with the knife and talking about how I didn't deserve to be so perfect. Then he saw the scars on my hip and ankle. He started screaming about letting someone touch me. Then he said my hair was wrong and he grabbed huge handfuls and cut it all off."

She used the remote control for the bed and moved to a sitting position.

Michael pulled a hand mirror from the drawer of the nightstand next to the bed. Short, Kamielle's hair had more wave in it. Her hair hung in layers from the tops of her ears down to her shoulders.

She started to laugh almost hysterically, running her fingers through her hair. "I wanted to cut it, but this wasn't really what I was thinking. Press that morphine button again, would ya? I think I need a few more drugs pumping through my veins."

He pressed the button and the machine made a noise as the cc's were injected into her IV. She closed her eyes and leaned her head back, letting the mirror drop to her lap.

"If you want to do this tomorrow, we can. You just woke up."

"At least the bruises from the Stewart attack are gone," she said. "Did I ever thank you for saving me that night?"

"I'm pretty sure you did. Of course I got to see you naked in the shower and that was thanks enough." He laughed.

"That's right, you're my Knight in Shining Armor who rescues me from dangerous bathrooms everywhere. You owe me, you know." Her voice was drifting out.

"I owe you what?" he asked.

"You owe me a chance to see you naked in the shower."

Michael lowered the bed back to a sleeping position for his little drug induced friend. Too bad she didn't know what she was saying so he could hold her to that promise.

MICHAEL WOKE the following morning in his hotel room feeling rested. While Kamielle had been in the hospital, there weren't many nights he hadn't spent at her bedside.

Tony had managed to get them two weeks of leave from the serial killer case. Their director hadn't been happy about the turn of events in which Michael's name had been carved into the chest of the latest victim. If Michael hadn't been so engrossed in the well-being of Kamielle, he might have been upset about the director wanting to pull him off the case.

Now, however, he felt he may have somehow put Kamielle in danger. Who had seen them together and wanted to hurt her because of him? Someone Stewart and Karen were connected to?

After showering and changing into a pair of jeans and cowboy boots, he pulled on a black t-shirt. A quick phone call to the hospital confirmed Kamielle was being moved to a regular room and no longer had to be monitored so closely.

She'd been lucky. The attacker had sliced deep enough to draw blood, but not cause nerve or muscle damage. He obviously knew how to wield a knife. That was the part that bothered Michael the most; Kamielle couldn't be his first victim. The attack was too organized. His only mistake had been attacking Kamielle, who chose to fight back.

At the hospital Michael was greeted with a surprising sight. Kamielle sat in a chair, visiting with a nurse. Her hair had been cut and styled.

"Michael!"

Her excitement made his stomach do funny little flips.

"I woke up in the middle of the night and decided after I was moved to my new room I was going to get my hair taken care of. It took a little convincing on my part. Everyone thought I may have been under the influence of too much morphine." She smiled again.

"I'm glad it was easy to fix," Michael said. He was having trouble thinking. Long, her hair had been beautiful. Short, it made her look down-right sexy.

She closed her eyes. Being moved to a new room and getting her hair cut had taken almost all her energy. She asked the nurse to help her back to bed.

"Hello, Mr. FBI." The nurse winked as she left.

"See what you started? Now they're going to call me Mr. FBI." He didn't sound all that upset about it, though. He was smiling as he pulled the chair she vacated up to the side of her bed. "How you feeling today, honey?"

"I feel good considering I'm in the hospital." She ran her fingers through her hair. "I couldn't stand the thought of my hair being so ugly because of that man so I sweet talked my doctor into letting someone from a salon come in."

"It looks beautiful," Michael said.

"Thank you. Even though I didn't have a choice, I actually kind of like it."

"Can we finish talking about the attack and then we can move on to talking about other things that hopefully won't be so upsetting? I don't want the nurse to kick me out."

Kamielle laughed. "Estelle won't kick you out. She'll let you be here as long as you want since she knows you're the one who stayed with me for a week straight in the CCU."

Michael ducked his head and Kamielle could have sworn he blushed. "Tony was there a few times. I left to shower and stuff. Who told you?"

"The CCU nurses told me this morning. They said they were going to miss seeing my cowboy. I told them hands off." She smiled, then took a deep breath.

"I don't remember much else about that night, Michael. I thought I was going to die and you were going to be the one to find me. I wasn't ready for that. He sliced me up and kept screaming at me to beg and cry for my life. The less I reacted, the more upset he got. I managed to wiggle enough to break the back of the kitchen chair.

"When he turned around and saw I had my hands free, he dropped the knife and lunged at me. We both fell to the floor and somehow I got the knife and cut him. I heard him scream, then he pointed the gun at me. That's the last thing I remember until I started having the dreams about you and Montana."

Michael reached out to hold her hand. "The doctors said you can go home in a few days. You'll have to keep your left arm in a sling until your gunshot is healed. You're lucky the lung wound wasn't severe."

"Go home. That's funny. Is Stewart out?"

"Yeah, we couldn't keep him since someone wouldn't press charges." He frowned.

"Well, it seems to me he's a minor problem in the realm of what has now become my world. I don't want to go back there." She grimaced and shut her eyes.

"I didn't think you would. So, Tony and I packed your stuff and he took it to a storage unit in San Francisco."

Her eyes flew open and she dropped his hand. "You took my stuff where? Where are my laptop and duffel bag? Why did you take my stuff to San Francisco?"

"Calm down before the nurse comes in and throws me out. I want to explain all this."

She crossed her arms. "This had better be good, Agent Carter."

He stood quickly and the chair slid back a foot. "Don't call me that, damn it! I thought I was doing something nice since you don't seem to have anyone."

She pointed at him. "You are not my babysitter or keeper. I want my stuff back here. I'm leaving this state before anything else bad happens."

"Will you please just listen to reason? Who is going to take care of you while you heal? Who will be there for you in the middle of the night when the nightmares start?"

"Don't do this to me!"

"What's going on in here?" Estelle came storming into the room. "I can hear you two screaming through the closed door. I don't know how they let you act in the CCU, Agent Carter, but on my floor, people do not yell."

"I'm just trying to explain to Kamielle that she needs someone to take care of her when she gets out of the hospital. She won't listen." Michael started pacing.

"You did not explain anything! You told me you moved my stuff to San Francisco!" Kamielle yelled. "Nobody bosses me around and nobody takes advantage of me!"

"I'm not taking advantage of you! I'm trying to help you!" When Michael realized he was starting to yell, too, he rubbed his hands down his face. "Jesus, nothing with you turns out the way I plan."

He walked to the door. "Your stuff is in the basement of my house in San Francisco, not a storage unit. Since you already hate me, I'll tell you the truth. I have a three bedroom house and thought you could stay with me until you decided where to go. My sister has some friends who sell clothes. I saw your designs when I packed your things. I thought I could hook you up.

"Tony will be by sometime before you get out of the hospital to take the rest of your statement and I'll make sure your things get back here to Oakland. Goodbye, Kamielle." He walked out.

"Michael! Wait! I didn't mean to get so upset. Come back, please!"

When he didn't respond to her plea, Kamielle put her face in her hands and dissolved into tears.

Chapter 9

"Please, Tony, you have to help me find him."

It had been two days since Kamielle had seen Michael. She knew she was wrong in getting so upset. Her natural instinct had always been to take care of herself. Michael made her want to give over control and it scared her.

"He's gone. He went home," Tony said. "What the hell did you do? You haven't even known him that long."

"He didn't tell you what happened?" she asked.

"No. He told me to get your stuff out of his basement. I'm not a moving service so I didn't do it."

"I yelled at him for taking advantage of me and he got mad and left."

"How exactly did he take advantage of you? The only thing he's done is be nice. Nicer than I ever would have been to someone involved in a case." He crossed his arms. "Stop the tears. You don't have me fooled, Kamielle Patrick."

At the mention of her married name, she inhaled a deep breath and began to cough. The coughing turned to dry heaves and more tears. She stood and staggered to the sink.

"What's the matter? Didn't you think anyone would find out your secret?"

"At least let me get dressed before you hand me over to him," she cried. "That bastard will not have the satisfaction of seeing me like this." She leaned against the wall. "I hope he's paying you well and you burn in hell with him." She wiped at her tears.

"What? You really don't want to see your husband? You must miss him," he said, playing along to find out what she really thought about Patrick.

"He stopped being my husband the day he tried to kill me and the day he killed my best friend! Of course, he doesn't care. If Thomas can't have something, no one can. You may as well tell him he's going to have to rape me for a child. I'm never going to give him a baby willingly again!" She reached for one of the flower vases.

She hadn't slipped. Drugged up and tired, she couldn't be that good an actress. She was telling the truth. Tony just wasn't sure if she was going to believe him now.

"I don't work for Patrick."

"Liar!" she screamed as she threw the vase. He sidestepped and it shattered against the wall behind him. "Oh, God, Michael works for him, too, doesn't he? I can't believe I trusted you two!"

She ran across the room and wrapped her hands around Tony's neck. The IV line ripped out and blood flowed down her wrist as she screamed. "Do you hear me? I'll disappear again! He won't find me! I will not live in that prison!"

The doctor and nurses came in, wrestling her to the bed, and injecting her with a sedative.

"Oh, everyone is in on it! You may as well quadruple the dose because I'd rather die than go back to him!" She thrashed and mumbled until the drugs took effect and her eyes closed.

Tony rubbed the back of his neck as the doctor stepped toward him.

"What's going on in here?" The doctor demanded.

"Ms. Johnson became agitated while we were discussing her attack."

"She's supposed to be released tomorrow. I'm keeping her for another day after this." The doctor left.

As Tony watched the nurses put in a new IV, he thought about what he had read on the internet and how Kamielle had acted at the mention of Thomas Patrick.

Even the best agents who were undercover had a difficult time staying in character when they had been in the hospital and on pain medication. He believed everything she said. Thomas was an evil man and Kamielle didn't want to be with him. It would explain a lot of things. The fake name, not wanting to file a police report. Was that who had attacked her at the duplex? Did Patrick want her dead or did he want her back like she seemed to think? Tony pulled out his cell.

"You WANT to repeat that one more time but slower? Why did they have to sedate her?"

Michael sat in his living room watching a baseball game. He had his phone in one hand and a bottle of Corona in the other. He put the footrest down and shut off the TV.

"She tried to strangle me and ripped out her IV."

"And she tried to strangle you because... ?"

"She thinks we work for her husband," Tony said.

"Why does she think we work for her husband? Who the hell is her husband? Why do I have to ask you so many questions?" Michael stood. "I need to come back to Oakland, don't I?"

"Okay, I'm going to give you the abbreviated version. When Kamielle got out of surgery and you left to clean up—"

"And you called me back to the room."

"Yeah, then. She started asking questions about her friend Shelby and her husband Thomas."

"Well," Michael said, "she was disoriented and had told me earlier in the week she missed her friend."

"Damn it!" Tony said. "Quit interrupting!"

"Okay, I'll try, but you don't talk fast enough."

"Shut. The. Hell. Up. Her husband is Thomas Patrick."

Michael stared at his dark TV. "Thomas Patrick? Chicago Mob Boss Thomas Patrick? The man we can't pin a crime on to save our collective asses, Thomas Patrick? She's married to *that* son of a bitch?"

"Uh, yes, to all the above. But, I don't think she likes him anymore. In fact, I think if we look closer, she hasn't seen him in a long time. She thinks he wants her back and she'd rather die than go back to him. That's why she tried to choke me. I might have, kind of, mentioned I knew her real last name. Now she thinks we work for Patrick."

"I leave for two damn days and you freak her out and now she thinks we want to kill her. Great. I'm glad you're so good at taking care of witnesses and damsels in distress."

"Back off, Carter, and can the sarcasm. I knew there was something fishy about her from the beginning. She's hot and you like her, but things aren't always as they appear. You know that. I'm going to do some more digging into her life with Patrick. I'll have her released to me day after tomorrow and then get her into a safe house near us in San Francisco." Tony was mentally going through all the things he needed to do to set up protective custody.

"You do the digging and I'll set up the safe house. I'll expect you Saturday afternoon. You might try to convince her we don't want to kill her or turn her over to her husband." Michael downed what was left of his beer.

"Easier said than done," Tony said. "You didn't see her try to strangle me."

THOMAS WAS SIPPING scotch when his private line rang.

"Sir," said a whispered voice. "The FBI has put in a request for a Kamielle, spelled with a K, Johnson to be moved into a San Francisco safe house."

"Very good." Thomas jumped out of the chair, but his words were calm. "It could be nothing. However, send me a photo of the woman on my secure e-mail. If it's her, I'll have two hundred fifty thousand put into your account and another two hundred fifty when I have her."

The man at the FBI felt guilty about passing along the information until the thought of five hundred thousand dollars sunk in. "Consider it done, sir. I won't let you down."

"Oh, I know," Thomas said and hung up.

If this was finally his Kamielle, he needed to be ready. Vinnie wouldn't be taking care of this particular job. Thomas smiled at the e-mail from Marcos.

Mr. Patrick,

The job you dispatched me to complete has been accomplished. While Vincent was upset to learn you no longer required his services, he was eager to leave town with my pay-off. He will be eternally enjoying the deserts of Las Vegas with his new dancing friend, Ms. Blonde Big-tits. His sister has also agreed to a long vacation. Please let

me know when you will require my services in the future.
It was a pleasure doing business with you.

Marcos was so professional about his jobs. Such a pity Vinnie hadn't learned to be as good.

Oh well. Thomas hit 'reply'. Maybe he'd let Marcos play with Kamielle a little before she came home for good.

As the black sedan crossed the San Francisco Bridge, Kamielle stared out the tinted windows. She hadn't said a word since the nurse wheeled her out to Tony's car. He had talked for almost twenty-five minutes straight about Michael setting up a safe house, how they didn't know her husband, wanted to find some kind of evidence to have him arrested, and were going to keep her safe.

Kamielle hadn't decided if she believed him. She'd been having nightmares for months about the day Thomas found her and this wasn't how it happened. The people who finally caught her weren't nice to her and they didn't offer to buy her lunch, coffee, magazines, or sunglasses.

Maybe Tony and Michael weren't working with her husband. Maybe she would finally be free. *Yeah, and maybe monkeys will fly out my ass.*

Tony kept looking at her. He wondered what the whole story was with her husband.

"Since you know who I am and that I'm alive, you'll find the Chicago Sun-Times website interesting," she finally said, glaring at him through her new sunglasses. "He announced me dead of a drug overdose almost to the day I met you and Agent Carter."

"I did past searches and saw the Social Section pictures of

the two of you at various functions together. You're not too bad as a blonde." He smiled.

"Thomas liked me as a blonde. Said it made me look sophisticated. He made me dye my hair while I was taking classes to lose my 'tacky southern accent'."

"Sorry. I think you look better as a redhead. Don't take it personally. I was just trying to make polite conversation."

She pulled her sunglasses down her nose. "Anything dealing with Thomas does not belong in the same sentence as the word polite." She pushed her glasses back up and turned to stare out the window again.

"I'm beginning to figure that out. Do you believe me that I don't want to kill you and Michael and I are good guys?" He sounded desperate, which made her more suspicious.

"It honestly doesn't matter what I think right now. If you take me to Thomas, I'll be dead in a year. If you don't take me to him, I'll have to disappear again."

"Why would you be dead in a year?"

She didn't answer.

"Come on, if I'm planning to turn you over to him, it won't matter if you tell me. If I'm telling you the truth, that I'm a good FBI agent and I'm taking you to a safe house, it'll be good for me to know why you're so scared." His voice had turned smooth and his Spanish accent added to the charm.

"Thomas wants a child. I'm the perfect person because the rest of the world thinks I'm dead. He won't adopt because then he won't have a blood heir. I have a baby then he kills me. He'll say he used my eggs and a surrogate mother to have our baby he has to raise without his 'poor dead wife'. I heard him plan the whole thing as I lay in a hospital bed."

Tony almost ran off the road. "You may not believe me, but I'm going to do everything in my power to put that bastard behind bars and see you get your real life back." He pulled the car into a rough neighborhood and parked next to his Dodge truck.

"Well, I'll know soon, won't I?"

She opened her door and stepped out as Michael opened the front door to what could have passed as a crack house. Two of the front windows were boarded over and the front cement steps were crumbling. She looked at him for a moment, drinking in the sight of the one person who had made her feel safe in almost her entire life.

He ignored her and looked at Tony. "Thanks, Medina. I'll take it from here. You know how to contact me if you need anything."

"Yeah, about that. I'm not sure this is such a good idea. Maybe we should talk first."

"I'm done talking." Michael turned to Kamielle. "Get your bags. We need to go over the safe house rules and regs before I leave."

"Leave? You're leaving? Why? Where am I going? He's here, isn't he?" She turned wide, scared eyes to Tony, rushing around the front of the car toward him.

Tony grabbed her and shook her slightly. "You're safe, damn it! He's just being a dick because of the way you treated him in the hospital. We're not going to let anything happen to you."

Michael registered Kamielle's real fear and instantly forgave her for the incident in the hospital.

"Kamielle," he came toward her and Tony. She hid behind Tony and Michael stopped. "Tony's right, I am being a dick. I'm not leaving you. I couldn't if I wanted to."

She poked her head from behind Tony. "Do you both swear Thomas is not in that house and you aren't going to turn me over to him?"

Michael's stomach did a free-fall. "I swear to you on the graves of my parents."

Tony gasped. "She knows about your parents? How?"

"The same way she knows I'd never do anything to hurt her," Michael said.

Kamielle nodded and slowly walked to the house.

"Carter, she's convinced Patrick won't rest until she's back with him."

Michael went to the trunk and pulled out her bags. "I found some interesting information on the Internet about Kamielle and her recent death of a drug overdose. Why does Patrick want the rest of the world to think she's dead? What does she know?"

"You should talk to her about that. She has a very good idea. I still don't know why he wanted her dead in the first place. I don't doubt her story about the car wreck. For some reason, he tried to kill her. Why?" Tony asked.

"Hopefully we can figure that out," Michael said.

They exchanged keys and shook hands.

"Good luck, buddy. Let me know if you need anything." Tony went to his truck.

Michael picked up the bags and went in the house.

Kamielle stood looking out a back window. "He'll kill me if you hand me over to him," she said.

"Damn it, Kamielle! I know he told the rest of the world you're dead. I read the newspaper website. That's what you were looking at that night in the motel, wasn't it? I saw your laptop out and you were in a strange mood. I don't turn innocent women over to killers and drug dealers."

She turned and dropped into a ratty chair. She briefly scanned the room and took in an even rattier hide-a-bed couch. When she met Michael's eyes, he was waiting patiently.

"Shelby and I found out about the drugs. Heroin. That's

why he had the brakes of my car cut. That's how Shelby died." She wiped away tears. "I've cried more around you and Tony than I've cried in my life."

"Maybe that's good. Maybe you need to let some of this go." He walked to the chair, put his hands on her forearms and pulled her up so she leaned into him. "I'll be your friend, I'll help you get your life back, and we'll go from there."

She pushed her face into his chest, closing her eyes. She breathed in his scent and wished her life could be different. Having someone to lean on, someone to trust, was so new. Shelby was gone and Kamielle had been living a lie of a marriage. What life was there to get back?

"I can't get my life back until Thomas is dead."

"Or he's in jail," Michael said.

Leave it to a cop to believe in the justice system.

"Jail doesn't keep people like Thomas. He's too rich and he knows too many people." She tried to scoot away from him, but he held her tight.

"Let's not talk about your... about Patrick any more tonight. Do you want dinner?" Michael brushed a kiss over her forehead.

"I'm really tired and would like to go to sleep. I don't have to sleep on that nasty hide-a-bed, do I?" She eyed the dusty couch and shivered at the thought of what might be living in it.

Michael chuckled. "The living room is just for show in case anyone sees in. The safe house has to keep up it's slum image so people in the neighborhood don't get suspicious. There's a fully functional house in the basement with everything we need."

"Oh good." The relief on her face made him smile. "I got prissy living in Thomas's rich world. There was a time that hide-a-bed would have been heaven. Now I love silk sheets and the scent of vanilla in the air."

"I'd give you silk sheets if I could," slipped out of Michael's mouth.

She stopped walking toward her bags and turned. "What?"

"We don't normally issue silk sheets to FBI safe houses."

"Oh. I thought you were, I mean, I wondered if you, never mind. Point me to the stairs so I can shower and go to bed, please." Color tinted her cheeks as she reached to pick up one of the bags.

"Just open the closet door and there's a panel that slides open to reveal the stairs to the basement." He pointed to the opposite wall.

"Closets with hidden stairwells? I didn't think the FBI threw money around like this. I feel like I'm in a bad spy movie."

"The FBI doesn't spend money like this. You're in a special safe house my brother, Jon, and I designed to prove we need more secure locations to hide witnesses. Not many people know about this place."

"Well, aren't you tricky?" She walked to the fake closet, opened the door, and disappeared inside.

Michael stared after her, wondering what he was really getting himself into with this woman. He'd made quite a few promises to her. He didn't make promises he couldn't keep so he hoped to God he knew what he was doing.

Marcos sat outside the safe house thinking about how stupid the FBI really was. They couldn't keep anything a secret; there was always someone who would leak information for the right price. Chivalry was dead in America, that was for sure. The mole had sold out Kamielle Patrick for a measly five hundred thousand. Marcos laughed. That was the wonderful thing about Americans: everything had a price. Greedy bastards.

His home in South America was a distant memory. His sisters had been beaten and raped by military in the area. Stupid girls deserved it, too. Always smiling and waving at the men. Then they had become pregnant and Marcos had to support a growing family. Since his father's death in a civil war years before, he was responsible for his mother and four sisters. Women were worthless. Marcos had decided it was best to dispose of his so-called responsibilities and go to America. He hadn't realized how well his talents would pay off. He had only been in the country for ten years and was rich beyond his wildest dreams. All because Americans put a price on life.

Marcos stepped from the truck and checked the canopy on the back. It didn't have windows and was double insulated so if Mr. Patrick's woman managed to remove the bonds and gag, she could scream until her voice was gone and no one would hear her. He fingered the taser in his pocket. Maybe he would wake her first so he could see the fear in her eyes, the question. This was so easy he would need some kind of excitement.

The back door lock was easy to pick. The rush Marcos always experienced flowed over his skin. He ran a hand down the front of his slacks to press his erection down. Mr. Patrick had only said to bring her back alive and not pregnant. The thought of making the *puta* submit to him was not helping his erection subdue. He ached with the thought of what he would do tonight. Hopefully more than once.

Walking silently down the hallway, he readied the taser. A peek in the first room showed the man who was supposed to be protecting her. His gun sat on a nightstand five feet away from the bed and he was sleeping in his underwear. Disgusting. Didn't he know it was impossible to guard someone when you had no pants, no gun, and you were asleep?

Marcos walked to the bed. He quietly lifted the second pillow and held it above the man's face. Quickly, he slammed the pillow down over the man's head and lifted his knee to smash down on his chest. The man struggled but could hardly move.

Minutes passed. The agent's distorted grunts could barely be heard and finally he stopped struggling. His body spasmed with a final movement.

Marcos's erection demanded release and he decided maybe he would have the woman here. He would leave some blood so they would know she was hurt.

Moving off the dead FBI agent, Marcos went to the next room. "Kamielle," he whispered, putting his hand over her mouth. "I've come to take you home."

Her eyes shot open and Marcos tasered her, reveling in the power. He removed his jacket and leaned down to breathe in her sweet scent. He frowned. Something was wrong. Turning on the bedside lamp, Marcos glared at the unconscious woman in the bed. This was not Kamielle!

He cursed, closing his eyes. When his breathing calmed, he smiled. Well, he could leave or he could have some fun.

At least the night would not be a total loss.

He undressed her limp body. Pulling a condom out of his pocket, he surveyed her nakedness. She was plump in all the right places. He laid the condom on her bare stomach and began to undress.

Chapter 10

"Leave me alone! Get off me!"

Kamielle's screams echoed through the basement. Michael jumped up from the computer. He knew the nightmares would start at some point.

"Kamielle, wake up. You're dreaming." He sat on the bed and pushed the hair off her forehead. She thrashed, eyes closed, sweat glistening on her face.

"Help me, Michael!" She became frantic. He pulled the covers back and picked her halfway out of the bed.

"Wake up, honey." He shook her gently.

She took in her surroundings. "Where are we?"

"We're at the safe house in San Francisco, remember? No one knows where we are but Tony, and he won't tell a soul." Michael lowered her back to the bed, but she shot up and wrapped her arms around him.

"It was horrible. I was back in the house, tied to the chair, and he was slicing me with that knife. I wanted you to be there, to show up and save me." She shuddered.

"I'm sorry I couldn't be there sooner, baby, I would have saved you from him." He kissed the top of her head and pulled her into his lap.

"You did save me."

"No, you saved yourself. I showed up too late."

"Or just in time. I didn't die that night like he planned." She pulled back to look at him. The lights were so dim she could barely make out his features. "You always seem to come just in time." She laid her head back against his chest.

She shifted her bottom against his lap and he almost groaned. He should not be trying to seduce her while she was in his protective custody. Of course, she wasn't at a real safe house and Tony was the only one who knew where they were. His iron-clad resolve was crumbling. His arms flexed around her, pulling her closer to him.

"Kamielle," he began, only to be cut off by her fingers on his lips.

They sat in silence for a few minutes as she ran her hands up and down his biceps and he massaged her neck.

"I want you. I want you to help me forget everything that's going on," she said. Then she pressed her lips to his.

The touch made Michael's body harden. She shifted again on his lap, and this time he did groan. "You make me feel things, Kamielle. Things I don't want to feel." He took her head in his hands and kissed her. "I was so pissed when you accused me of taking advantage of you. I've never in my life taken advantage of anyone during a job or otherwise. I didn't have any reason to be that mad. I never lose my temper with witnesses."

"A job," she said as she pulled away.

"You're more than a job to me now. When you fell asleep next to me at the motel, I realized I'd been talking to you like a friend. I laid you on that bed and wanted to lie down next to you. When you went into the bathroom to change tonight and walked out in a pair of boxer shorts and an AC/DC shirt, I nearly attacked you. Instead I told you good night and shut off the lights."

Michael pushed her down and covered her body with his. He put his nose next to her ear and breathed in the smell of her hair and skin. Her breath caught and her heart beat faster. He put his mouth on her throat and she closed her eyes on a sigh. He pushed his fingers into the hair on both sides of her head, moving his lips over hers.

Heat ran from the top of her head to the tips of her toes and warmed everything in between. Everything. She thought she'd been in love with Thomas, but he hadn't made her body feel like it was on a roller coaster ride. This was lips brushing and she was moving while laying down.

She'd known Michael for only a few days before she'd gone into the hospital. She shouldn't be having this reaction to him. Yet, she felt like she'd known him for months. He knew more about her than Thomas ever had.

Against his neck, she mumbled, "I've only ever had sex with one man. I haven't even been turned on in over a year."

She pulled one of her legs free and wrapped it around his calf. Her foot moved slowly along the denim causing a delicious friction. He groaned and pushed against her. She groaned and pushed back.

Michael slid his hand down her rib cage, past her waist, cupping her butt. The movement caused her to push against the erection straining the fly of his jeans. He pulled, she pushed, and a rhythm began. Their lips feverishly melded together as tongues danced and clashed in first her mouth then his.

She pulled her head back to gasp in some much needed air as he slid his hand from under her butt up to the front hem of her shirt.

"I always liked AC/DC," he panted as he began to slide the shirt slowly up her stomach, "but they might just be my favorite band now."

His careful ministrations revealed smooth skin and a flat stomach with a small belly-button ring. Unable to resist, Michael slid down Kamielle's body. When his tongue flicked out to lick the small hoop, and her belly-button in the process, her moan of protest turned to desire.

"Shake me all night long," she said in a wobbly voice as his hands continued to slide her shirt up.

"That's the plan," he said as he revealed her breasts to the cool air of the basement. "You're beautiful."

"I've got scars," she said. "That's not beautiful."

He slid back up her body to look in her eyes. His hand palmed her full breast as he bent his head to kiss her. "You're beautiful inside and out. A few scars don't matter. I have some, too. I'll show you later if you're really, really good." His smile relaxed her once again.

He rocked into the V of her thighs and all thoughts disappeared from both their minds. She wrapped her legs around his hips and thighs, pulling him closer and rubbing shamelessly against him.

Michael couldn't stand it anymore. He lifted the upper part of her body and ripped the t-shirt over her head. It revealed the bandages on her healing gunshot wound and reality came crashing around him.

"Kamielle, stop. I don't want to hurt you."

"The only hurting that's going to happen is me hurting you if you don't make me come. Right. Now."

She pulled against his hips with her heels and bowed her back. Unable to deny the lady, Michael latched his mouth over her nipple and she screamed in release as tremors washed over her body. She quit pulling him with her legs, but he kept rubbing against her to get every last wave.

"Oh, my." She pulled him down for another bone melting kiss just as a phone rang.

Michael pulled back from the kiss and rested his forehead to hers. "Shit! This cannot be happening."

"You better answer it." She looked at the clock. "You wouldn't be getting a call this late unless it was important." She groped around the bed for her shirt with one arm thrown over her breasts.

"Look at me." The soft command in his voice made her still and look into his eyes. "I don't do this, Kamielle, ever. You're special to me." He slowly moved off her and his body protested.

Before she could respond, he went to the desk and picked up his cell. The fact he was still fully clothed hit her like a ton of bricks. She found her shirt tangled in the sheet and pulled it over her head. Her shoulder was throbbing, she just hadn't noticed before.

"Carter," he barked into the phone, "someone better be dead for you to call me at two in the morning, Medina!"

After about a solid minute of listening, Michael dropped into the chair. "I told you we have a leak! Contact the director right away and let him know I switched the reports on purpose. Find out who accessed the report in the last three days. Has anyone examined the body yet?"

At the word body, Kamielle sat up.

Michael went to the stairs and mouthed, "Stay here, I'll be back."

Once upstairs he continued. "Have they found the woman's body? Do they think she could still be alive? Shit. I cannot believe this. I thought there would be a break-in and the son of a bitch chasing Kamielle would realize she wasn't there and leave. Dammit!"

Tony continued talking. Michael could only think about the dead agent and missing woman. He should have set up a sting, not changed paperwork. Shit!

"I'm going to need to meet with the director myself to explain what happened," Michael said. "The only good thing is now I can prove someone is leaking information. Come to the safe house and take Kamielle back to my house. Yes, my real house. I'm already in trouble so I don't care right now." Michael ended the call and turned.

She stood at the door. "I never could follow directions worth a damn." She smiled. "I need some Vicodin out of my small bag. I forgot to take it downstairs."

"How much did you hear?"

"I'm going to your real house and you're in trouble. That's all. Why are you in trouble? Is it something I did?"

"Nothing you did and everything I did."

"It's about me, though, isn't it?"

"Let's go talk while we wait for Tony to get here." Michael grabbed her bag. "This thing weighs a ton and you take it everywhere. What do you keep in here, weights? I know your baseball bats wouldn't fit."

She reached to take the bag from him, but he wouldn't let her. "Your arm hurts. I'm not going to make you carry your own bag."

She eyed the bag, shrugged one shoulder, and went downstairs. "I have some things I need to tell you about my life with Thomas before you get yourself into more trouble."

"You don't have to tell me anything you don't want to." He set the bag on the bed.

"That's the thing, I want to tell you. I can't believe I want to share these things with you." She shook her head. "Thomas doesn't just want me back for a baby. He wants me back because I took this." She pulled out a stack of money.

He stared at her, the money, then back to her. "You stole money from him? Are you insane? It's probably dirty!"

"Wait, it's not his, it's mine. Shelby taught me to invest. I didn't keep a separate account because I didn't think I needed to. I only took half before I left. It was my shopping account. It's all legitimate, I swear."

"How much money are we talking here? A couple hundred grand?"

"It was a little more than that. I took three million. I knew I was going to need cash so he couldn't follow me."

"Three. Million. Dollars." Michael sat down on the bed. "How do you know he wants the money back? Doesn't he realize it's yours?"

"This is Thomas Patrick we're talking about. Everything in the world is *his* according to *him*. I'm property, so anything I have is his property."

"You swear to me this isn't drug money."

"I swear. You know how you said you never do this?" She waived her hand in the air toward the bed. "I don't do this either. I'm running for my life and I didn't stop so I could get it on with you, or anyone else, for that matter."

"I believe you." He took her hands. "The money changes a few things. Patrick gave a press conference stating you're dead. You know about the drugs and you 'stole' three million dollars from him. This just keeps getting better and better."

Michael began pacing the room. "I'm betting the attack was one of his men sent to retrieve you," he said. "But then why was he toying with you at the house? Shouldn't his job have been to deliver you?"

"Just forget about me and I'll leave." She tried not to show any emotion. "You have so many problems because I'm in your life. Forget about it all and move on."

"Forget about it? Forget about you? Not happening. My

sister says things happen for a reason whether you believe in fate or not. You're stuck with me, lady. When Tony gets here you're going to my house while I explain things to my boss. I'm going to request leave because of my rash actions and tell him you left me a note saying you're going to... to somewhere. I'll have to file an official report and it will put whoever's on your tail on a wild goose chase. Where's somewhere you haven't been?"

"You can't lie to your boss for me." She looked outraged, but she also looked so vulnerable. Michael knew she wanted to depend on him yet wanted to save and try to protect him. Too bad.

"It's too late to tell me what to do. If I hadn't known I was going to help you before now, those moments on that bed with you made up my mind for me. Not because of sex," he said when she opened her mouth. "But because we feel something for each other. If we had met at the coffee shop, we'd have already had more than six dates and I'd have you at my house every night I could get from you."

She smiled with the first hint of acceptance. "Does that mean you think I'm easy? Six dates and every night possible already spent together? Too bad I had a brief hospital stay. It all sounds so *normal*. And very, very wonderful." She put her arms around his neck to pull him down for a kiss.

After a few moments, he pulled away, breathing hard. "Tony's here. Grab your stuff and change while I go fill him in. No one gets to see you in that AC/DC shirt but me." He smiled and leaned down to brush a kiss over her lips.

"How do you know Tony's here? Don't we have a few more minutes?"

"The security system light is flashing to tell me someone pulled in the driveway. We'll be alone soon and then we'll see where this is headed."

As he went upstairs, she looked at the bed again. "Oh, I think we know where this is headed."

***

THE MEETING with the FBI Director could have been worse. Michael didn't get in as much trouble as he expected because there was paperwork documenting both safe house occupants. The only difference was his name and Kamielle's name were on the paperwork of the safe house that had been broken into.

The missing woman had been found two blocks over in a mall parking lot with no attempt to hide her body. The killer could have left her alive, yet her neck had been broken.

The coroner told Michael what he already knew. It's much harder to break a neck than people think. You have to know how much pressure to apply in order to have a clean break. Michael and Tony had once seen marks all over the neck of a victim. Muscles torn, but not a severed spine. The killer ended up strangling the guy.

This break was clean, efficient, and perfect. If there was such a thing in a murder. Michael figured the guy for ex-military. Who knew, though? The only thing Michael was completely sure of was Kamielle was in more danger than he originally thought. Thomas wanted her back alive and he had sent someone to get her.

The dead woman had been raped before her neck had been broken. That meant whoever was after Kamielle got to use her before she was delivered.

***

KAMIELLE STOOD in the living room of a beautiful two story home. Michael had a talent for decorating. It was kind of a surprise. She hadn't expected leather furniture and art prints on his walls.

"Don't think he did this himself," Tony said as she looked around. "His sister has a degree in design and her first project was this house."

"You just ruined it for me," she laughed.

"Friends?" Tony asked quietly.

"What?" She turned.

"Do you forgive me for what happened at the hospital?"

"It's almost like a different lifetime," she said. "I realize you thought I was using you guys and you were protecting Michael. Friends. Now tell me what's going on."

"Well, Michael told me I could tell you everything. I don't agree with what he's doing, but I haven't seen him care about a woman since Crystal died."

"Crystal was his fiancé, right?"

"When did he have time to tell you about her?"

"Before I was attacked. The night he got me the hotel room we told each other lots of things. Also, while I was recovering in the hospital, I remember bits and pieces of the stories about his family and his plans with Crystal. She sounded like a wonderful woman," Kamielle said.

"She was. He doesn't live in the past, though. He cares about you enough to tell you things he never tells anyone. And, he's putting his career on the line for you."

"He told me he's going to lie to his boss. I don't want him to get in trouble. I don't want him to get hurt."

"We changed the names on the safe house documents so we could see if someone was leaking information to your husband. The agent and woman at the safe house that was supposed to hold you and Michael? They're dead."

"Dead?" Her face paled. "Thomas had them killed, didn't he?"

"From what we can tell, the agent was killed and the woman was kidnapped. We think the guy who took her realized it wasn't you then killed her and dumped her body. There isn't any evidence on her we can find."

"Was she raped?"

Tony waited a beat then nodded.

"If there was semen and she was shot or stabbed, I'd say it was Vinnie." She sat on the couch with her arms wrapped around her middle. "If there's no semen and her neck was broken, then Marcos killed her. He never leaves a trace and he's evil."

"Okay, whoa, you know way too much about this. You just described the dead woman's body. I have to make some calls. Do you know Marcos or Vinnie's last names?" He pulled out a small notepad and his cell phone.

"Vinnie had an east coast accent, Jersey maybe, greasy and fat. Gave me the heebie jeebies. Marcos is Latino, shaved head. He seems normal and good looking, almost, until you look at his eyes or he talks. The only reason I know anything is because Vinnie had too much to drink one night and was asking how to break a neck. I heard part of the conversation and then Marcos heard me in the hall. I went to bed."

"Okay, you go get Michael's luggage from his room while I make some calls." Tony went to the table.

Kamielle walked down a hallway past two rooms before coming to a large bedroom. It held a king bed covered by a black comforter. She knew it was Michael's room by the smell of his cologne. Her skin warmed as she ran her hand over the blankets.

There were photos of people on his dresser. One showed a couple in their mid-thirties with three kids standing around them, two boys and a girl. The kids looked between the ages of six and twelve. All five had matching smiles. The boys looked alike, but Kamielle could tell which one was Michael by his eyes. The other boy's eyes were different, darker. The girl was holding the hands of both. Blue sky, green grass, and snow-capped mountains were in the background.

A family. Kamielle's heart ached at all she had missed out on in her life. She thought when she married Thomas they would make the family she never had. That didn't quite turn out as planned.

Another picture was of Michael and a man—his brother—standing with their arms over each other's shoulders. Michael was wearing a graduation cap and gown. Kamielle shivered. Michael's brother wasn't smiling. She was glad Michael looked like he cared about things. His brother looked like he'd kick ass first and take names later. He looked like the men Thomas kept company with. She didn't know if she wanted to meet Jon.

Luggage. She needed to find luggage, not be mooning over pictures of the Carter family. She glanced around the room then went down on one knee to look under the bed. There were three matching suitcases.

"Well, I can make myself useful and pack some clothes or I can go sit in the living room like a lump."

She went to the closet and slid open the door. She grabbed two shirts and a tie that would match both. She walked to his dresser and pulled open the top drawer. It contained socks and underwear.

"Boxers or Briefs?" she asked herself.

"Both."

Kami spun and dropped a pair of socks. "Oh, you scared me."

Michael was leaning on the door frame. "Find anything interesting?"

"I wasn't snooping, I was just—"

"Looking at my underwear, I know. I'll show them to you if you ask nicely." His hand moved to the snaps of his jeans and he smiled.

She reached behind her for a handful of underwear and threw them at him. "I thought you were mad at me."

"Why would I be mad? I sent you guys here to pack."

"You sent Tony to pack."

"So, what are you doing in my underwear then? Are you packing or snooping?"

"Packing. I couldn't handle just sitting. Too many things are going through my mind."

"Well then, no big deal. My jeans and t-shirts are in the next two drawers. We can do laundry at the ranch."

Kami stopped grabbing clothes. "Ranch?"

"Yep, we're going to Montana. I'm sending Julie and the kids to Disneyland for two weeks. My brother, Jon, will be meeting up with us in a week. He's going to do some looking into Thomas Patrick and the people he hangs around with."

"You don't want your family involved with Thomas. He's evil." Kami put the last of the clothes in the suitcase. Michael walked over to zip it.

"No, Thomas doesn't want to be involved with my brother. He's Black Ops CIA. Anything you think you know about Thomas? Multiply that by one hundred and you have the type of things my brother knows about and deals with. Jon could eat Thomas for lunch and not even break a sweat."

She pointed to the pictures. "Is that him?"

"Yeah. That was my college graduation. I didn't think he was going to make it, but he showed up the night before. He was covered in mud and who knows what else, and had a stab wound on his thigh. My mom took one look at him and almost fainted. Then she almost hit him. I told Jon he better not have blown any missions for me and he said family always came before National Security."

"He looks scary."

Michael shrugged. "He is. But he'll lay down his life for you if he thinks you deserve it."

"He doesn't know me, why is he going to help?" She wrinkled her forehead in confusion.

"Because I asked him to and because I know you."

"You don't really know me." She ducked her head as he came closer.

Michael put his hand to her cheek. "I know you're brave, I know you're beautiful, and I know you don't deserve everything that's happened to you."

She looked at him with tears in her eyes. "Thank you for believing in me."

Michael pulled her close. "Thank you for letting me."

They stood silently, wrapped in each other's arms for a few moments. They forgot someone was trying to kidnap her and they pretended life was normal.

He broke the silence. "Do you want to drive or fly?"

"Could we really drive?" Her eyes lit up at the possibility of spending time like a normal couple on a site-seeing trip.

"I was hoping you'd want to. It'll give us time to get to know each other even better and I'll have your undivided attention. It will also give Jon more time to do some digging into Patrick's background. We can drive straight through until we get tired and then switch or we can stop and get motel rooms. Or we can do both."

"How about if we start out driving straight through and we'll stop and get a room when we need it." Her voice was low and he didn't miss the reference to getting a room, not rooms.

"Okay," he said. "We'll stop and get a room when you tell me we can."

"We might be gone a long time. Think Tony will watch my cat?" She smiled and ran her finger down the side of Michael's face.

It was going to be a long drive.

Chapter 11

They rented an SUV so they would have plenty of room. Kamielle almost talked him into a Camaro or a convertible Mustang until he remembered their luggage and his long legs. Damn woman made him forget the strangest things. Like he was too tall to drive a sports car from California to Montana.

She'd picked a cherry red Tahoe, paid for a two month rental, and away they'd gone. It was just over two hundred miles from San Francisco to Reno. They made great time traveling in the middle of the day and were on the outskirts of town in about four hours.

"You've really never been gambling before?" Michael looked at Kamielle who was staring avidly out the window.

"Until a year ago, I hadn't been anywhere but Texas and then Illinois. Sometimes I'd pretend I was just on an extravagant road trip while driving across the country. It made it easier to deal with. Ohh!" She squealed as they crested a small hill and Reno came into view. "I bet it's beautiful in the dark!"

Michael had to smile. It was like having his nieces and nephews around. She made everything a small miracle and didn't seem to let anything get her down. Considering she had almost died a few weeks before, she was entitled to enjoy the world right now.

She turned wide, pleading eyes to him. "Can we stay here for a few days, please? No one knows where we're going except Tony."

"Stay the night? Nights?"

She waved her arm toward the window. "It's so pretty and it looks fun here. All the people, the lights. I really want to see it in the dark and I want you to teach me to gamble."

He couldn't tell her no. She had pulled her legs under her and was sitting sideways in the seat, practically bouncing up and down. She looked radiant and it was the look of a woman with no cares in the world. The look Michael wanted to give her.

He shrugged. "Okay."

She squealed again and leaned across the center console to grab his head and kiss his cheek. Twice.

They decided on Harrah's. When valet parking drove away with the Tahoe, Michael turned around and she was gone. He panicked until he heard her laugh coming from the doors. She was arm in arm with the young man who had loaded their luggage onto a trolley.

"Sir?" The voice next to him drew his attention from Kamielle's butt.

Michael pulled out his badge. "I need to see your head of security."

"Uh, yes sir, right this way, sir." The bellboy was tripping over his feet when he caught sight of the shoulder holster and pistol.

"Kami," Michael called. "Wait up." When he reached her, he took her hand and pulled it away from the other bellboy. "You need to stay with me, sweetheart. I know this is like a vacation, but we have to be careful." He lightly ran his hand over her eye and touched her shoulder.

"Oh. I know, I just got excited and forgot for a minute." She squeezed his hand and brought it up to the side of her face. "I figured we'd get a suite with two rooms and two bathrooms. That way we can be together but separate. You don't mind sharing a room, do you?" She kissed his palm.

"Uh, no. Ask if we can get a room near the stairwell."

About that time, the first bellboy came back with a man in a light colored suit. The head of security. Michael turned to both bellboys. He pulled out fifty dollar bills and handed one to each man.

"Keep her with you while she books the room." To Kami he said, "We should be ready about the same time." He leaned down and kissed her cheek.

Michael and the head of security talked for ten minutes. Without giving too many details, he let the man know if anyone was snooping around asking questions, he wanted to be alerted. They went over the layout of the building and security protocol. When Michael was satisfied, he shook hands with the guard and went to find Kamielle.

She was sipping a drink, listening to the bellboys talk about the piano bar. When she spotted Michael, she gave both young men a quick kiss on the cheek and slipped them another tip.

Michael didn't want to acknowledge the feeling of jealousy rolling in his gut. He'd never been with a woman who attracted this much attention. Everyone stopped to stare at her. Employees, customers, males, and females alike. He put his arm protectively around her shoulders and asked one of the bellboys to deliver their bags in about fifteen minutes.

"You have to quit kissing people you don't know," Michael said as they boarded an elevator.

When a couple tried to get on with them, he pulled his badge and asked them to wait for the next one.

"What did you do that for?" she asked.

"What floor?"

"Twenty-two. What did you do that for?" She waited while he pushed the button then crowded him into a corner.

"You're drawing too much attention to yourself. I don't want anyone remembering we were here," he grumbled.

"You're being paranoid." She poked him in the chest. "People are less likely to remember one unimportant woman than one larger-than-life FBI agent who doesn't let others ride on elevators." She poked him again. "And, about kissing people I don't know, those young men were very helpful."

"Yeah, and they'll remember what you look like down to the color of toenail polish you're wearing because you gave them so much attention!"

The look on her face told him she didn't understand.

He looked up, sighed, then met her gaze. "Okay, I apologize for sounding like such a jerk. I don't like being in situations I can't control. I'm worried about you and I'm worried about the people looking for you."

The doors opened and she took him down the hallway.

"Stairs." She pointed. "That way if we have to get out quickly, we only have to go about twenty feet. And, I've decided I'm safer with you than I've been my entire life. You know why I've been in such a good mood? Because I have you, Michael Carter, FBI, Knight-In-Shining-Armor, Agent Extraordinaire." She used the key card to open the room.

Before he could come up with a reply, he was stunned speechless by the suite. It looked bigger than his house. There were huge picture windows taking up almost one side of the room. The gauzy curtains let in the last light of the afternoon sun. There was even a mini kitchen with a wet bar. He walked to the master bedroom. The attached bathroom was bigger than his bedroom at home.

There was a raised dais in the center of the room that held a bathtub large enough for four people. On one side of the bathroom was a double stand-up shower.

Kamielle looked under his arm. "Excellent. I told them I wanted a room with a huge bathroom since I couldn't use the pool." She wedged herself next to him. "Why don't you want me kissing people?"

"Because while I'm around, I'm the only one I want you kissing." He turned and took her in his arms.

"That's a good answer, Mr. FBI." She wrapped her arms around his neck and pulled his mouth down to hers. Just like when they'd kissed before, it was fireworks.

He sucked her tongue into his mouth and worked his fingers through her hair. His thumbs rubbed her cheeks and he tilted her head to the side for better access. For two full minutes, they dueled with their tongues. Her moans made him even more desperate.

He lifted her and spun her against the wall. His hand dug into her butt as she wrapped her legs around his waist.

She broke the kiss, panting. "I was hating you were so tall, but it's okay now. You're forgiven."

"That's good." He nuzzled her neck, bit down on the muscle there, then licked it.

"Oh," Kamielle's head thumped against the wall. She tightened her legs and moved her hips up and down.

"Shit, I forgot you don't play fair."

"Last time, I had all the fun. I think I owe you one. Or two." She smiled, then bit his lip.

"I had fun last time. But that doesn't mean you don't owe me." He braced his hand under her again and walked them to the bed.

They hit the mattress and sank into it. Michael pulled his head up. "What are you paying a night for this room? Everything in it is nicer than my house. I don't think I've ever slept on a bed this comfortable."

"You don't want to know what I'm paying for the room. Who cares about that right now? Don't you have some scars you promised to show me?" She pulled at his jacket until he took it off.

He sat up and took off his shoulder holster, setting it on the night stand by the bed. She grabbed his forearms to stop him from taking his shirt off.

"Uh-uh, I've been waiting to do this." She pulled the shirt out of his jeans and ripped it over his head.

"Slow down, Princess."

"No. I've wanted you since the day we went out for coffee. I kept thinking about how gorgeous you were and how you were taking care of me. Me."

"I've wanted you since right after I hit you with my car." He laughed and unbuttoned her shirt.

A ring sounded. Michael stiffened. "What the hell?"

She looked toward the door. "It's a doorbell. Most large suite's have them because you wouldn't hear someone knocking. It's probably our bags."

"Of course it's our bags. My shirt is off, yours is almost off. There has to be some kind of a distraction." He groaned as he rolled to his back.

"Just think of how great it will be when we finally get to be alone. I'm going to fix my clothes and hair while you get our bags." She went to the bathroom and shut the door.

Michael picked his shirt off the floor and glanced at his pistol. He left it there and walked to the door of the suite.

"Who is it?"

"It's your bags, Mr. Johnson. I also have a fruit basket and Presidential Suite basket."

He opened the door and let in the two bellboys from the lobby. They set the complimentary baskets on the table.

"Your wife explained you were celebrating a late honeymoon so we combined the Presidential and Honeymoon baskets. You've got condoms, strawberries, chocolate, whipped cream, bananas." The bellboy blushed.

Michael held up his hands. "Okay, that's enough details. Which restaurant do you recommend?"

After getting the name of the hotel's more romantic restaurant and tipping the guys, again, Michael waved them out the door and went back to the bedroom. Kamielle was spraying hairspray.

He met her eyes in the mirror as she fluffed her hair. "It seems to me the people who can afford this room can afford their own hairspray."

"It's not about affording, it's about convenience. When you have money, you get things." She turned to him.

"Honeymoon?" He arched a brow.

She winced. "I hope you don't mind. We're Michael and Kamielle Johnson for two or three days."

"Why didn't you get us the Honeymoon Suite?" He walked toward her and she backed up until her lower back bumped the counter.

She put her hands on his chest as he moved into her personal space. "I, uh, didn't want to embarrass or pressure you."

He lifted her until she sat on the edge of the counter, staying between her legs. "Shouldn't that be my line?" He kissed her neck.

She sighed. "We're two adults with an obvious attraction. I

figured getting a room we shared would put the ball in your court, so to speak."

"We've established we want each other." He kissed the other side of her neck. "You're stuck with me until I can prove your husband's trying to kill you." He held the sides of her head and looked in her eyes. "Tell me now if you want me to step back and be professional instead of leading with my emotions."

"Can I have both? You make me feel safe and special. I want you to help me get my life back but I also want to have you as a man for as long as I can keep you." She wrapped her legs around him and pulled. "Did you notice we're in a bathroom? Again?" Her smile was just this side of wicked.

"I did notice that, yes." He rocked his hips.

In the silence of the room, her stomach growled and it sounded doubly loud. She giggled.

Michael gave her a gentle kiss on the lips, stepped back so they were no longer plastered to each other, and took her hands in his. "Okay. Because I don't think I can be around you and keep my hands to myself, I'm going to protect you and I'm going to do that twenty-four-seven. With you every day. With you every night. But first I'm going to feed you and let you gamble for a few hours so I can have you to myself for the rest of the night. No interruptions."

His gaze was so intense she looked away. He pulled her head back. "I don't take sex lightly, Kamielle. Do you want to be with me? If you don't, I'll respect that."

"Yes, I want to be with you. I think I've made that pretty clear over the last few days. Quit second-guessing me, okay?" She kissed him hard and pushed him away so she could hop off the counter. "I like your plan of a few hours downstairs. Let's go."

Jon Carter had no patience for someone who betrayed their country. He had even less patience for people who dicked with his family.

"You're going to make another phone call. This time you're going to tell the son of a bitch what I want you to say."

Jon's voice was like ice running through the man's veins. He sounded scarier than Thomas Patrick ever would. Being tied to a chair didn't help.

The FBI agent who had been given half of his payment to inform Thomas about Kamielle had left his office Friday night, but never made it to the parking garage. The footage from the security camera didn't show anything and never would. Jon had asked one of the few people he trusted at Langley to help him with the computer end of this fact-finding mission. AJ Jensen would work without emotion and he wouldn't interfere. That's what Jon needed right now.

Nathan Jorgensen was a little weasel of a man who worked a desk for the FBI office in Chicago. His application to become a field agent had been turned down three times in the last four years. He couldn't pass the fitness physical or the shooting test, and his psych evaluation showed he would 'most likely cave during a physical interrogation'. One of Jon's many specialties was interrogation.

It hadn't taken a genius to find the leak. Jon knew whoever it was probably lived in Chicago. It would be easier for Patrick to keep his thumb on a flunky who was nearby. Nathan also didn't know how to hide the fact he'd come into a considerable sum of money.

He'd bought himself a Porsche Cayenne and promptly shown it to anyone who would look. Too bad it would never see the light of day again. Jon would have it sold and scrapped by the end of next week with the money donated to charity.

"You're kind of like Robin Hood," AJ said to Jon's scowl.

Jon walked behind the chair Nathan was secured to. Fifteen feet away, at a table, AJ had a Satellite phone and a laptop waiting for the call to Patrick to be placed.

"Do you know what happened to the FBI agent and woman in the safe house? Do you?" Jon grabbed a handful of Nathan's hair, ripping his head back. Nathan squinted against the pain.

"No! Nothing! I don't know!" He started to snivel and tears pooled in his eyes.

Jon pulled harder. "The agent was suffocated; smothered to death with his own pillow. He had broken ribs from where the bastard sat on his chest to keep him from moving. How about if I hold you down, break your ribs, then let you come up for air when you can't stand it any longer? I'll keep doing it until your brain can't get enough oxygen. Maybe I'll leave you hooked to machines like a vegetable for the rest of your life.

"The woman's dead too." He leaned down. "Did you even think about what would happen to my brother and the woman he's protecting when you ratted them out?" Jon pulled a knife from a scabbard strapped to his thigh.

"I didn't know it was your brother! I didn't even know you were real! You're like a myth, a legend, a CIA Black Ops ghost. Someone who's made up to blame the worst jobs on."

Nathan was very close to pissing his pants. He wasn't sure if that would be the final insult or not. He'd piss his pants if it meant he could live. Someone from the CIA couldn't kill an FBI agent, could they?

"Stop, you'll make him blush." AJ looked up from his laptop to stare at Jon. "He hates when we bring up his stellar reputation."

Jon glared at AJ. This was one of the problems of working with someone.

He waved the knife in front of the traitor agent's face.

"Shut up, Nathan. I'm obviously real. You fucked with the wrong people this time around. The woman? She was raped, beaten, and her neck was broken. I'm a big believer in 'an eye for an eye'. I know some people who would enjoy raping and beating you. You wouldn't like that, would you?"

Nathan shook his head violently and held back the urge to throw up. Jon Carter would probably kill him for puking on his boots.

"I could fly you over to Russia and leave you in one of the many whore houses there. They'd drug you up and sell you to the highest bidders. Leave you there for a few months. You'd be begging someone to kill you. Begging someone to put a bullet in your fucking brain. I don't like people like you. People who hide in the shadows and sell the souls and lives of others. You signed your death warrant when you sold out my brother."

Jon took the knife and rested it against Nathan's neck. It was so sharp the shallow movement of breathing caused the knife to break the skin. A small stream of blood trickled down his throat to be soaked up in the collar of his white dress shirt.

Jon leaned down to meet Nathan's scared gaze. "So here's the deal. I'm going to pay you in minutes of your life instead of money. You're going to call Patrick and tell him his hit man screwed up. Tell him Michael Carter was too smart for you guys. Then you're going to tell him Carter and Kamielle have disappeared and no one knows where they've gone.

"But because you're so smart, you searched for next of kin and figure he's on his way to Montana to the family ranch. You do or say anything to mess up this phone call and I'll gut you where you sit. I'll send the pieces of your body to your mother in a box with a letter explaining you died because you're a pussy who sold out his country. Ready to make a phone call?"

Nathan gulped and stuttered, trying to keep calm. "Yes, yes. I'll do anything you want. Anything."

"I know you will. That's why you're here. Just remember whatever you thought Patrick could do to you, I can do worse." Jon untied one of Nathan's hands and gave him the sat phone. "Call Patrick on his cell instead of his secure line."

Jon walked to AJ and the computer.

"You're one scary son of a bitch, you know that, Carter?" AJ said.

"I've been told."

"Remind me never to piss you off." AJ shook his head and looked back at the laptop.

"It'll be too late if I'm reminding you."

Jon checked the computer and walked back to Nathan. He ripped open Nathan's shirt and set the tip of his knife just below his belly button.

"Remember. I'll gut you and not even bat an eye."

The phone call went well, even if Nathan's voice was shaky. He was over-acting a bit, too. Said he was scared about what was going to happen when the Director of his office found out he'd been searching files on California cases. Patrick kept telling him to calm down and not worry about it. Marcos's name was finally mentioned when Patrick said he'd be flying into Montana if, and only if, the information Nathan was telling him turned out to be true.

One thing Jon had learned was to stick to the truth as often as possible. He always used his own first name when under cover. That way he'd answer when someone talked to him and if he ever ran into different contacts in the same place, everyone knew him as Jon. Last names were different; no one was ever surprised about that.

Another thing about the truth was it kept stories straight. Patrick would find out the wrong agent and woman were dead and Michael and Kamielle were missing. He'd even find evidence of a family ranch in Montana, but only because Jon would let that part slip through. He'd buried the deed so deep under other names, no one would be able to find it if they weren't supposed to. Family was always kept safe.

However, when Patrick, and whoever Marcos was, showed up in Montana, they'd get a surprise. It wouldn't just be Kamielle they found. It would be Jon and Michael Carter. It wasn't going to be a fair fight.

When the call was over, Nathan breathed a sigh of relief. "Did I do good?" His voice was still shaky.

Jon grabbed the hand he had untied earlier and re-secured Nathan to the chair.

"Do you realize that Patrick is going to have you killed? He didn't get mad at you for your mistakes. He told you not to worry about it. Do you think he'd let a slime-ball like you live? He knows you'd rat him out at the first threat of pain."

Nathan stared into Jon's eyes and knew he was going to die. This time, he did piss his pants. Then he started to cry.

"Jesus!" AJ stood. "That right there is why you were never meant to be a field agent. No one's even hurt you and you're wetting yourself and crying! I'm out of here, Carter, I can't handle being around this pussy." AJ started to pack his gear.

"That's okay. I was going to have you leave anyway. Thanks for your help." Jon walked to him.

"That's what friends do, Carter, help each other. Even if you don't think you have friends, there are enough of us who respect you."

Jon shook his hand. "I'm building a cover for an op in Russia. Find out what you can about my new partner. That dick, Kimball, knows I hate working with anyone. He's planning to send me in with some woman. Elana Miller."

AJ stopped. "Elana? She's hot. Worked in records and just started in the field. What's Kimball doing sending someone like you on a mission with someone like her?"

Jon shook his head. "Fuck if I know. She must have pissed him off. Either that or he thinks sending me out with a newbie will make me screw up. Man's had a hard-on for me since he became Deputy Director of our unit."

"Listen, watch your back." AJ raised his chin at Nathan who was crying silently in his chair. "That little prick isn't worth shit."

"I brought you here because of your ability to work without emotion. Don't go getting worried about me now. I've been doing this job for fifteen years. I won't screw up when it's the most important thing I've ever done. No one fucks with my family."

AJ walked out of the dilapidated building in the old factory district of Chicago. In the SUV he uploaded all the information Jon would need to track Patrick's movements. He also started searching for Marcos in the database of Patrick's associates. Since the Feds had been trying to build a case against him, there was a lot of information on the man.

Until yesterday, AJ had known Jon Carter as Jon Matthews. Carter was a ghost. When Jon had approached him about doing an unsanctioned op, AJ had been intrigued. Surprised the hell out of him to find Jon was even more ruthless when someone he knew was being threatened. AJ didn't think Jon could get anymore coldhearted than he already was. It surprised him he had a family to protect. It figured he'd have a brother in the FBI. Bet those family get-togethers were interesting.

Back in the warehouse, Jon circled Nathan like a shark would its prey. "You're not worth my time. I don't like loose ends and you've just become one. Patrick would have had you tortured."

Jon moved behind Nathan and leaned down to whisper in

his ear. "Do you believe in God? Because if you do, that means you're going to Hell."

Nathan scrounged his last bit of courage and turned his head to look into the dead eyes of Jon Carter. "If I'm going to Hell, then you're definitely going to Hell."

"Of course I am. The Devil and I have a deal. I'm in charge when I arrive. I'll see you there."

The bones of Nathan's neck snapping barely made a sound.

Chapter 12

Kamielle gambled, drank, and had the most fun she'd ever had. They looked at nightly shows and decided on one to watch the next evening. Finally, they held hands and walked the balmy streets of Reno, people watching and talking.

"My brother is kind of scary when you meet him for the first time. I know I already told you he's CIA, but that's kind of a secret. You can't tell anyone. Since he's black ops, our government won't claim him if he gets caught."

"Why would you tell me such a big secret?"

"You've trusted me with most of yours. I wanted to share one of mine. Jon and I help each other when we can. We both love Julie, but she doesn't understand our lives. She's always harping on us about getting married and having kids."

Kami squeezed his hand. "You had Crystal. Does Jon have anyone?"

Michael shook his head. "No. And he never will. He thinks having attachments are weaknesses. He doesn't realize he can protect and love someone the way he does Julie and me. If he'd let himself love, he'd be just as strong as he is now."

Kamielle stopped walking. "Why can't more men be in

touch with their feelings like you?"

He shrugged. "I have a minor in psychology. I've seen things that would make people never love because they'd only see the evil and loss. After working for the VCTF for a few years, I decided life was too short to not take chances. That's when I asked Crystal to marry me. We lived life to the fullest until I lost her.

"When she was killed, Jon was on my doorstep in less than forty-eight hours. We hadn't released her name to the press so I don't know how he knew. He finds out everything."

"He loves you very much." She'd never felt love that fierce from anyone. The fact it was his brother made it that much sweeter.

"He told me because I'd loved her so much, that would help me heal. Then he told me if I'd never fallen in love, I wouldn't be hurting. Tony, Jon, and I went out to find that doctor. I killed him."

She pressed her hand to his cheek. "I know. And you stopped him from ever making anyone else feel the pain you had to feel." She pulled his head down to hers and kissed him.

He wrapped his arms around her, pulling her close. He could feel her breath and tears through his shirt.

"I understand why Jon has never fallen in love," he whispered. "I felt like my heart had been ripped out when she died. He's seen more horrible things than I ever will. He's been in almost every country in the world and helped remove the scum of the earth. But he also misses out on this." He squeezed her tighter. "The feeling of rightness when you're with someone you care about."

Wide eyes met his and her lips moved but no sound came. He laughed at the look on her face.

"I'm not professing my love. I've slept with a few women since Crystal died, but not one of them has made me feel the way you do. I just want you to know I'm not emotionally shut off and you'll always know where you stand with me." He kissed the tip of her nose and wiped away her tears.

She took a deep breath. "I'm not as good at this feelings thing as you are. I've always been a little like your brother; if you trust people they hurt you. Maybe you can teach me?"

He raised an eyebrow. "Are you still drunk?"

"I wasn't drunk." She stepped away and put her heels together. Touching her finger to her nose, she said, "See, officer, completely sober."

"Good, I don't want you passing out too early." He took her hand again.

They walked back toward the hotel. This time they didn't talk about anything emotional. Michael told her about the pranks he and Jon used to play. She told him about the foster family that had taught her about computers. They talked about her fashion designs and how she wanted to open her own shop when her life was in order.

Riding up the elevator, she wouldn't make eye contact.

"You don't owe me anything," he said.

She finally looked at him. "I know. You're not like that. Should we leave tomorrow?"

"No. You are going to have three days of total relaxation. I don't want you to think about him once. We'll talk about everything when we start driving again, okay? I'm the only person you are to be thinking about."

He pulled her out of the elevator and walked her to the door of the suite. "I was thinking you could invite me in for a drink." He winked. "Then you could take a bath and relax."

The lines around her eyes smoothed as she smiled.

"Well, you were such a good date. Dinner, gambling, drinks, an emotional walk in the moonlight. You're every woman's fantasy date. I suppose I could offer you *one* drink."

He picked her up in a fireman's carry and unlocked the door. Her scream of surprise was laced with humor and need.

"One drink? Oh, I get more than that, Princess."

"SON OF A BITCH!" Tony stared around the office he was sharing with Michael at the police precinct.

The desk drawers had been pulled out and flipped over, the tops wiped clean. All contents of the filing cabinet were spread on the floor.

He called the captain. "Who has access to the offices after regular hours?"

"Shit, Medina, any civil service agent, the cleaning service, lawyers, judges, you name it."

"Are there security cameras on this floor?"

Tony looked for the file on Kamielle. He had a sneaking suspicion her being missing and her file going missing were not just coincidence.

"In the hallway, yes, the offices, no," the captain said.

"Can you get me the name of who I need to talk to so I can review the tape?"

"Meet me in thirty minutes."

Tony hung up and tried to call Michael. Kamielle's file was missing along with the files on the murdered prostitutes. The cell rang four times before going to voice mail. Tony cursed and left a message.

IT WAS midnight and Kamielle had been in the bathroom for almost an hour. Michael finished his drink and walked to the bedroom.

He knocked lightly on the bathroom door. "You okay in there?"

"Yes. I'm just getting out of the bath. I took your advice of relaxing a little. Why don't you order up a bottle of champagne from room service while I take a quick shower?"

Michael tried to open the bathroom door, but it was locked. "Kamielle, we can go to sleep. In separate beds. I told you I wasn't going to pressure you."

"Don't be silly. I'll be out in less than half an hour."

She closed her eyes. The stitches in her shoulder could be removed later in the week. Michael told her they would go to a doctor in Kalispell. The skin was pink and new and no longer hurt when she touched it. The black eye was gone, but she could still see the ugliness of it in her mind.

She surveyed her naked body in the full-length mirror. Too thin after months on the run and being in the hospital. What did men notice when they had sex on their minds? She laughed. They didn't notice anything except insert Tab A into Slot B. That was her experience.

She went to the double shower, turning on the faucets at both sides. The spray quickly filled the enclosed space with steam. The water felt wonderful beating down on her shoulders and she sighed. She could call for Michael. They could learn each other's bodies and she could completely let herself go. Except she was scared to death. When they were partially dressed and in the darkness of a bedroom she was fine. The thought of baring herself completely, body and heart, was too much.

She took a moment, closing her eyes and enjoying the water spraying at her from all directions. She ducked her head under the water and jumped when a hand touched her hip.

"You are the most beautiful woman I have ever seen in my

life." Michael stood in front of her in all his naked glory. And what glory.

Sputtering and wiping water from her face, she opened and closed her mouth a few times until she finally said, "What? What are you doing? I locked the door."

She tried to cover the upper and lower parts of her body with her arms. She was doing a very poor job. His eyes traveled to her breasts, then lower.

"I'm good with locks. You've been in here for an hour. I decided if I took the decision of when to invite me out of your hands, things would move much faster."

He gave her a devilish grin and stepped closer. The hand on her hip tightened as his erection brushed her stomach. They both drew in their breath.

He leaned to her ear, and in barely a whisper said, "I haven't thought of much else than you since the safe house. You brought your AC/DC shirt, didn't you?"

She was having trouble thinking. "Yes."

"Good." He kissed her ear and reached up to tilt the shower head so it sprayed on the wall and pushed her back. The water cascaded behind her, warming the cold tiles. The heat radiating from his body warmed her front.

"You'll tell me if I hurt you?" His eyes searched hers.

She licked her lips. "You'd never hurt me."

Michael reached up and ran the palm of his hand over her nipple. It pebbled beneath his touch and he let out a breath he hadn't been aware he was holding.

She pushed her body forward and filled his hand with her breast. He instinctively reached up with his other hand.

"You feel so good," he said.

Leaning forward, he kissed her forehead, her right eye, her left eye, her nose, then her mouth.

The kiss exploded between them and went from sweet to

hot. She put her hands over his and squeezed. His body rocked forward and he rubbed against her stomach. Their hands kneaded her breasts and their mouths fought for the best angle to swallow each other whole.

He moved his lips a fraction of an inch from hers. "I have to be inside you. Later, I'll take you in the bed with more control. We'll make love later. Right now, I have to fuck you."

Kamielle had never thought she was one for dark sex talk, but as soon as the words left his mouth, her stomach tightened and she grew even more wet between her legs. "Yes! Now, please!"

Her head rolled against the shower wall. She watched through slitted eyes as Michael reached behind him. There was a condom sitting on top of the shower railing. He held it in one hand and ripped it open with his teeth. He looked as out of control as she felt. It gave her a new sense of urgency.

She peeled her body from the wall and took the condom from his hands. Dropping to her knees she gripped his penis. The breath hissed out of him and he shouted when she pressed her lips to the tip. Breathing out through her nose, she took him into her mouth and sucked.

"Oh, hell! Jesus, Princess, you're gonna kill me."

She gave a few more hard swallows before he gently tugged her hair so she'd release him from the wet heat of her mouth. Still on her knees, she rolled the condom down his length.

Strong hands gripped under her arms and lifted her until her feet didn't touch the ground. He held her above him so her breasts were level with his mouth. He licked and sucked first one nipple then the other. Her legs shot out and wrapped around his lower back. She pulled with all her strength until she felt his body at the entrance to hers.

"Look at me," he said.

Her eyes opened and locked with his as he pushed her

against the tile and dropped his hands to her waist. He pushed down with his hands and up with his hips, sliding all the way home in one thrust.

Her sharp cry made him still.

"I'm okay." Her words were rough. "It's just been so long and you feel so good."

He rested his forehead on hers, breathing harsh, eyes closed. She could feel him pulsing inside her, like a heartbeat, like they were one.

She turned her head and lightly bit his ear. "Fuck me, Michael, you promised."

The whispered invitation was all he needed. His hips pistoned up and down, slamming her body against the shower wall. He moved one arm under her ass and the other behind her shoulders to cushion the movements.

Whispered words told her how beautiful she was, how much he wanted her, how he would always keep her safe. It could have lasted for five minutes or thirty, they lost all track of time. His thrusts slowed and he moved the arm from behind her shoulders to the spot where their bodies were joined. He rubbed and pinched while he kissed and bit her neck.

"Come for me. I need you to come." He rocked in and out of her steadily. The rubbing inside her body mixed with the rubbing outside pushed her over the edge.

She screamed his name and her body convulsed in his arms. He shoved into her one last time and stilled. Through the haze in her brain she felt him pulsing inside her again. It was stronger than last time.

They slowly came out of the moment, noticing the water had cooled. Michael lowered her feet to the floor and kissed her. "That was..."

"Amazing," she finished.

He pulled out and she mourned the lost connection.

Rolling off the condom, he leaned out the shower and tossed it in the trash.

"Good thing you're so strong," she teased. "You could have dropped me and injured us both."

"Not a chance." He slid the door closed and turned up the hot water for both shower heads. "What do you say we finish this shower and move our party to that huge, soft bed?"

"Don't you need some time to, uh, recuperate?"

They both looked down at his semi-hard erection.

"Apparently not."

They laughed as she reached for the body wash.

<hr>

KAMIELLE WOKE to the feel of a hand running lightly up and down her back. Goose bumps pimpled her flesh, but it wasn't from cold. Her half-opened eyes focused.

Two empty champagne bottles lay inside the bathroom door, the glasses sat on the edge of the tub. Condom wrappers littered the floor near a plate of half-eaten strawberries and chocolate sauce. Room service had been very, very good to them last night.

The hand on her back wandered lower and brushed over the sensitive flesh of her bottom. She giggled and moved the lower half of her body.

"You keep wiggling like that and I won't be responsible for my actions," Michael said, voice gravely.

"No, please, I can't take anymore." She rolled to her side and trapped his hand between hers.

"That's what you said," he looked at the clock, "three hours ago. Then you poured half a bottle of champagne all over your chest."

She giggled again. "I'll have you know I was just making sure we didn't have to drink warm champagne."

"I still drank it. It tasted wonderful." He leaned down and licked the spot between her breasts.

"Yes, well, that may have been part of my plan, too." Another giggle escaped. Sounding exasperated she said, "I don't giggle! You keep making me giggle."

"What's wrong with that? Women who are sexually satisfied and do not have a care in the world giggle. How about I make you giggle some more?"

She shrieked as he rolled on top of her and pinned both hands above her head. He quickly lowered her shoulders a little so the stitches wouldn't pull. Then he raised an eyebrow and flipped her to her stomach in a flash of movement she barely had time to register.

"Michael."

The feel of his warm, hard body pushing her into the mattress weakened her resolve to take a break from the outstanding sex.

"Are you sore? You told me about an hour ago to get my hands off you because you were sore."

She wiggled beneath him. "I lied. Please."

"Please what?" The humor in his voice told her he knew exactly what she wanted. "How many condoms were in that gift basket, Princess?"

"Six. I had them double the regular amount. I thought it would be enough."

She arched her back against his body. The groan that escaped him was almost payback enough.

"Six? We used six condoms in six hours?" he said.

"Is it really only six in the morning? Jeez, get off me and let me get some sleep. Wake me up at noon when you come back with more condoms." She reached behind her and wrapped her fingers around his penis every time he moved up her body enough for her to reach him.

"We're out of condoms. You better stop." He moved his body against her a little faster.

She started to lift herself to her knees as his body moved back down. It caused his morning erection to slip inside. She was tender and swollen from so much sex, but so turned on it almost counteracted the tightness. The warm head of his penis was lodged in her body. With one thrust back, she could have him all the way.

"Kamielle, baby, what are you doing?"

"My doctor said I probably won't be able to get pregnant. I need to feel you inside me."

All the blood rushed from his brain. The heat of her was drawing him in and keeping him from thinking straight. She rose higher on her knees, forcing him further inside.

"It feels different touching you skin to skin. Stronger." He pushed forward and pulled her on her knees in front of him. He slid all the way in. His voice was tight. "I'll pull out, just to be safe."

"I don't care. I want you moving."

Throughout the night, they had been frenzied, as though it was their only night or last night together. They had explored each other like new lovers do. Now, it was different. Dawn light filtered through the heavy curtains and the room was silent except for their labored breathing.

He took her slowly, feeling every thrust. She moved with him, pushing back when he pushed forward. Whenever she tried to rush it, he held her still. Finally, she couldn't take it anymore and fell forward. He followed her down, pulled out part way, and rolled her to her side. He kissed away the tears on her eyelashes.

"It's too much. You're too much." She buried her head in

the crook of his neck and surrendered to his body.

He worked her to the brink of orgasm over and over until she finally exploded. She wrapped her leg around his hip and held him to her when he tried to pull out.

"No," she said.

They both felt him empty into her. She kissed his neck, cuddled into his body, and fell asleep.

Kamielle woke for the second time that morning. She was alone and the bedroom door was closed. She suffered a brief panic he was gone, afraid her emotion of the morning may have scared him away. Then she heard a hushed, violent voice coming from the main room.

She pulled the satin sheet the rest of the way off the bed and wrapped it around her. Although her inner and outer muscles protested, she walked to the door and cracked it open. Michael was pacing in front of the mini-bar wearing only his gray boxer-briefs. His features were hard and he was whisper-yelling into his cell.

"Tony, you're not making any sense. What do you mean the files are missing? They were in a freaking police station for God's sake!" He listened intently for a moment. "The security cameras show nothing? Did you have any handwritten notes in the file?" Pause. "No, I don't think you're a rookie idiot. I just need to be sure no one knows where we are."

Kamielle felt like she was eavesdropping so she opened the door. Michael held out his hand.

"Yeah. I'll call Jon and see what he knows. You feel like coming to Kalispell? I'll see you in a few days." Michael pulled Kamielle into his arms and kissed the top of her head as he ended the call.

"What's wrong?" She wrapped her arm around him, holding the sheet to herself with the other.

"Tony went to work last night and our office in the precinct had been ransacked. Your file and the prostitute serial killer files are missing. We can't decide if they were after your whereabouts and took the other files or wanted to know about the serial killer case and got your file by mistake. We have everything on a flash drive, but the files are still important."

She shivered. "Do you think it's Thomas?"

"Well, I'll have to call Jon and see if his message has been delivered."

"Message? What message?" She pulled back and looked at him. "What did you guys do?"

"I want you to have your life back."

"What did you do?" She stepped away.

"Jon found the leak in the Chicago FBI office; the guy who's been keeping tabs on you for Patrick. Finding leaks is one of the things Jon does. He was going to use the agent to contact Patrick so we can draw him out and arrest him."

"When were you going to tell me this?" Part of her wanted to be outraged. Her heart, on the other hand, wanted to trust Michael.

"Remember when I told you I wanted you to relax and enjoy these few days and we'd discuss everything on the rest of the trip? I was going to tell you on the drive. I'm not keeping secrets from you. I will never keep secrets from you." He stepped toward her, but she held up her hand. "Kamielle, I didn't have anything to tell you. I don't know if Jon met with the agent."

She shook her head, swatting at his hand. "You have to keep me informed. What if I walk around a corner and, bam, there stands Thomas? The man makes my blood run cold. I have got to be prepared if I'm going to see him! Dammit, this is my life!"

He pulled her into his arms despite her protests. "I'm sorry. I didn't think about what seeing him would do to you."

She sighed. "I want to trust you. I know you're trying to protect me and do what you think is right. But remember we're messing with my life. I have got to know what's going on. Please."

He rubbed his cheek on the softness of her hair. "You're right. Let me contact Jon so we know what's going on. I'm sorry."

"You really don't have anything to apologize for. I just don't like not knowing."

"Okay, from here on out, you'll know everything as I do it. How about if you go shower and get ready for breakfast?"

She kissed his cheek and went back to the bedroom, letting the sheet drop just as she got inside the door.

"Damn it, Princess! You don't tell a guy you're showering alone then flash that fabulous ass."

She blew him a kiss and closed the door.

"I am so screwed," he said as he started punching in the number to Jon's message service.

The automated system was routed through who knew how many satellites before it linked to South America, Asia, and then Europe. Sometimes it took Jon weeks to return a call. It always depended on whether he was in a position to call back. He should have been contacting Michael soon anyway.

It took eight minutes.

"Hey, little bro. I was going to give you a call in about an hour. Wasn't sure if you'd be up and ready to go being as how you're shacked up in Reno with a hot chick," Jon said.

"It's nine o'clock in the morning. I don't know what time it is in the country you happen to be in. But, yeah, I am shacked up with a hot chick. How the hell do you know I'm in Reno?"

"I know where you and Julie are at all times, Mikey. I'm back in the good ole' U.S. of A. Chicago to be precise."

"That didn't take you long."

"The leak cracked like an egg. Patrick knows you're on your way to the ranch. I have his place under surveillance to see if he moves or sends someone else. If he thinks it's just going to be his wife and one FBI agent he'll show up with his hired hit man to take the two of you out. Too bad for him he doesn't know you're not a regular Fed."

"Also too bad for him he doesn't know the infamous Jon Carter will be with me," Michael said. "You do realize you scare the shit out of most normal people."

"I've been told. It's helpful in many situations."

"I bet. We have a problem. Tony called. Someone stole Kamielle's file from our temporary office in Cali. It might be nothing. Our serial killer case files are missing, too."

"Considering what's been going on with Kami, I'd bet it's her file they were after. I'll put out some feelers but I doubt I'll get anything," Jon said. "I'm gonna stay here until I find out who's going to Montana to try and wipe you two out. Will Tony be coming?"

"He's headed out in a few days."

"Okay, you know I always want an accurate head count. I'll let you know when I've got movement from this end. Does our girl know what's going on?"

"Yeah. She's wanting to be a part of everything. She knows this guy and I think it's important we use that."

"I agree, Mikey, but I already know everything I need. He's a sick son of a bitch. Patrick brings home a prostitute almost every night and he's not nice to them. I thought I was going to have to take him out last night. Luckily for him, he blew his wad early and didn't finish beating on his fuck-toy. I did, however, take the opportunity of being in the house to check out his computer. Have Tony stop by Vegas on his way to Montana. This Marcos guy sent an e-mail about a man named Vinnie taking a vacation. He's buried in the desert."

"I don't know how you do it every day, Jon. Put up with these people and not take them into custody. I deal with it, but I get to arrest the scum."

"I get to kill the scum, so it evens out in the end," Jon said. "Marcos is going to be a handful. He'll be the one Patrick brings with him, I'm sure of it. I don't want you or Kamielle anywhere near him."

"Don't worry, I'm going to keep her as far away from both of them as possible. I'm hoping for a quick and easy bust. Patrick made the press announcement about Kamielle being dead. When Tony and I arrest him, we'll be able to prove he knew she was alive."

"It's easier to just make people disappear, Mikey."

"I still have faith in the system, Jon."

"One of us should," Jon said. "I gotta go, baby bro. My target is on the move. Kisses to the girl."

"You wish."

"You don't know how much. Adios." Jon hung up.

Michael went to the bedroom.

"Well?" she said.

"Jon set the bait. He's keeping an eye on your husband and his hired man, Marcos. We're ready. We can leave today, tomorrow, or the day after."

"First of all," she walked to him, "don't call Thomas my husband. Second, we're leaving tomorrow. I want one more night and day with you before this nightmare begins."

"Whatever you want, Princess. We have show tickets tonight anyway. That, and I need one more round in the shower to store in my memory."

Chapter 13

Thomas was connected. Not only did he have dirt on almost every important person in the eastern U.S., he also kept a steady heroin supply to those who needed it discreetly. He hadn't developed his own addiction to the drug until the year before Kamielle had run off. It started with recreational use during sex. The first time he'd picked up a man and a woman together, he'd needed the drug to take off the edge. It had turned out to be the best sex of his life.

Unfortunately for the couple, the big-mouthed woman had recognized him and wanted money to keep quiet. Marcos had enjoyed quieting her while Thomas and the husband watched. Then the bodies had needed to be disposed of.

The reasonable part of his brain knew he couldn't kill everyone he had sex with. After that incident, he made it a habit to pick up prostitutes who wouldn't have a leg to stand on if the police ever had to be involved. He always sent them on their way with enough money to go to the hospital if they needed to. He liked rough sex. It wasn't his fault people bled so easily.

Marcos cautioned him about making good decisions. They were considering involvement in the sex-slave trade market out of South America. This would let Thomas have an uninterrupted supply of teenage boys and girls who wouldn't know they could go to the cops. It was the best plan he'd ever had.

Well, maybe not the best plan. Of course, the plan involving Kamielle was the best. An heir without a mother who could steal him. The world thought Kamielle was dead. She would bear him a child and then die. She would have made a good mother until she decided to betray him.

Snooping bitch had started asking about the extra money coming in. Why couldn't she have been a typical woman and happy with more money? She started talking to their accountant and wanted to know about money market accounts and how Thomas was investing. That damn Shelby hadn't helped any either. She taught Kamielle how to play the stock market. Kamielle wasn't dependent on him if she could make her own money.

Then she had figured out money coming in was being routed through a dummy company. It hadn't taken her long to find the paper trails on the computer. The woman was too smart for her own good. When he realized she had put everything together about the drug deals, he'd decided to cut his losses and have her erased. No one would miss her since she didn't have any family. He had mourned the loss of his wife while planning the accident. Things would have been perfect if she had kept to her place in his world.

It was her fault he now liked breaking in virgins. He needed to find them younger and younger to satisfy his new tastes. Thinking back, he wondered how she had even gotten pregnant at all. Sex with her had become boring and he hadn't touched her much in that last year.

Then she'd gotten pregnant and killed his heir.

Thomas picked up his private line and pressed a button for his secretary. "Delores, start getting things ready for Marcos and me to fly to Montana. Book some site-seeing events for the clients I'll be meeting in Kalispell."

Delores didn't know there weren't any clients. The names were bogus.

"Yes, sir. I'm sorry, sir, but there aren't any first class tickets available. Also, the only tickets I could arrange won't allow you to leave until Thursday. I'm so sorry, sir."

Three more days. Thomas grimaced. He'd sent his private jet to South America with a few associates in order to get a feeling for business down there. It was easier to fly in and out of another country when you had your own jet.

"I guess that will be fine. It will give me time to finish business here. Change my meetings for the rest of the week. We should only be gone a few days."

He hung up and called Marcos to outline the plan for once they landed.

It didn't take a genius to figure out why Jon was being paired with Elana Miller for the Russia op. She was young, inexperienced, and hot. Kimball wanted Jon to screw up and thought this was going to do it.

Jon watched her leave her condo and walk to the bus stop. Her hair was black and hung to the middle of her back. Her lean, lithe body screamed at him. The reaction wasn't lost on Jon. He never let his dick do his thinking anymore and Elana Miller was causing his little head to think too much.

He followed the bus and parked when it got to her stop. She'd never seen him before and would never know he was watching her.

Elana walked for half a block then went into a building. She took stock of her surroundings without letting others know she was watching them. Jon hung back, noting maybe she wasn't as inexperienced as he thought.

The door to the building had "Parson's Ballet Studio" stenciled in gold letters on the glass. Great. He was going to have to watch that body bend, fold, stretch, and dance. Shit. Maybe it was time to head to Montana and meet Mikey and his new woman at the ranch. Anything would be better than this torture.

Jon's mind didn't have any control over his body. His legs carried him to a bench in front of the plate glass windows. He sat, pulling a folded newspaper from under his arm. His mirrored sunglasses blocked his eyes, and to anyone walking by, it looked like he was reading.

Elana stepped from the changing rooms five minutes after she walked in. Her hair was secured with a braid and sweatband. Oh, sweet Jesus, she was wearing a one piece leotard suit leaving nothing to Jon's imagination. It was a tank style: hugging her breasts, flaring at her hips, following a truly spectacular ass down, ending at her calves. Her feet were encased in pink slippers laced with ribbon.

She stretched and dipped and Jon snapped his mouth closed. This was *so* not good. For jobs, he'd been in strip joints with completely naked women shaking their various body parts in his face. He'd gotten lap dances that didn't turn him on. Now, here he sat on the streets of Langley, Virginia, pretending to read a newspaper and he had a hard-on for a woman he'd never met. Who was wearing a giant, one-piece spandex suit. Oh yeah, she was also his partner for the mission to Russia.

Fuck.

Elana stood, raising her arms over her head. Her eyes connected with Jon's. There was no way in hell she could see him looking at her. She continued to stare as she slowly dropped her arms. Feeling trapped, and more than a little turned-on, Jon stood and folded his newspaper. Before he did something stupid, like introduce himself, he walked away.

It was time to go hunting for a couple of mob boys. Jon would deal with his weird reaction to Elana Miller when Mikey's woman was safe.

THE TICKETS KAMIELLE and Michael got were for a variety show. There were dancers, singers, comedians, and small acrobatic-like stunts.

One of the singers came off the stage and sat on Michael's lap, singing solely to him. The slit of her sequined dress showed more skin than necessary. The spurt of jealousy going though Kamielle surprised her. She didn't have anything to get jealous about, did she?

The sex was fabulous, he was in touch with his feelings, and she wanted to keep him. Oh, hell. She wasn't using her real name, she was on the run for her life, and she didn't have anywhere to live. Why would Michael want to spend any time with her after Thomas was in jail? What if one of Thomas's goons hurt Michael? She'd never be able to live with herself if something happened to him because of her.

The singer moved to the next table and Michael took Kamielle's hand. Pulling it to his lips, he kissed the tops of her knuckles. "Looks like you're thinking too much and not enjoying yourself enough." He kissed her palm.

Her stomach flipped. "You're right, I was thinking a little too much."

"Well stop it. The only thing you should be thinking about is me." He kissed her palm again and let his lips linger.

"I *was* thinking about you."

"No, now you're thinking about me. Before you were

thinking about something stressful. Now you're thinking about sex."

"Shhh! Someone might hear you." She glanced around. "People shouldn't talk about sex in public."

"Sex in public? Do you have a fetish I should know about?"

She swatted at him. "That isn't what I meant and you know it."

"No one heard me, I promise."

He took a drink of his beer and pulled her hand to the side of his face. The slight stubble tickled her palm and made her blush as she thought of what had happened when they were getting ready for the show.

"I didn't give you whisker burns earlier, did I?" Michael's eyes held a mischievous twinkle as he rubbed his cheek back and forth against her palm. "I'd be willing to kiss it and make it better if I did."

She thought back to standing in her high heels, bra, and nothing else as he had knelt in front of her. He'd pushed her to the bed and given her whisker burns, all right.

She ran her finger over his lips and leaned close. "I may have some I'll need you to inspect and kiss better."

His nostrils flared and he bit the pad of her finger. He was tempted to walk out right now with her thrown over his shoulder. She brought out a playful and barbaric side of him. Oh yeah, and a sex maniac side. He'd never had so much sex in such a short period of time in his life. Made love. It wasn't just sex. It hadn't been from the beginning.

Losing Crystal and his parents had taught him life was too short to sit around waiting for things to happen. If you wanted something, grab it with both hands and take it. He was going to grab onto Kamielle and never let go until she made him.

Losing her mom and living with the violence of her father hadn't given her much of a sense of security. Being married to

Patrick couldn't have been a picnic, either. Since her 'relationship' with Michael had started so strangely, would she give him a chance to take her on dates when this was over? Now *he* was thinking too much.

He grinned and pulled her over for a quick kiss. "Quit distracting me and enjoy the show."

An hour later, the house lights came on. She looked around the room.

"It's midnight," Michael said from behind her. "No clocks so you won't worry about how late it's getting. They don't want people to stop spending money."

She laughed. "I suppose it's time for me to get a watch. I left mine during my last move."

"Will you tell me more about your life? You know almost everything about me." He took her hands, pulling her close.

"Yes. I'll tell you anything." Her voice was breathless and she felt slightly annoyed he had such an effect on her.

"Let's go." He led her to the elevators.

Back in the room, Kamielle changed from her dress into shorts and a tank top. Michael put on boxers and a shirt. He pulled the cushions off the couch and put them in front of the fireplace. Stripping the sheets and blankets from the spare bed, he created a bed on the floor.

Lighting the propane fireplace, he pulled her down.

"I wanted to look at you in the firelight. I've seen you in the setting sun, the moonlight, and the light of dawn." He brushed a lock of hair behind her ear.

"God, you're good."

"It's not a line." He frowned.

"I know. That's what makes it so good."

He tackled her and they rolled across the cushions to the floor. She was laughing and having trouble catching her breath.

"Don't make fun of me," he said. "I'm bigger and will win any wrestling match we have."

She laughed harder. "How are we supposed to have a serious conversation when you do this? I have whisker burns you're supposed to check on."

Kamielle was on her back, Michael pinning her from above. He growled and bent to kiss her. She turned her head and bit him on the shoulder.

"I swear you're going to kill me. No making love for a while, I need a break." He glanced up and saw the new gift basket on the table by the door.

Room service was still being good to them. New basket meant six new condoms. It had possibilities. She licked the spot she had bitten and he rolled away.

"You are not going to distract me with sex. You promised to tell me about your life. In fact, you promised to tell me anything I wanted to hear." He moved back to the cushions, pulling her next to him.

"You know most of it. My mom died, I went into foster care, and I lived with some okay people. One of them taught me a lot about computers. I moved to Chicago, started working in a bar, and met Thomas Patrick."

"He owned the bar you worked in, didn't he?"

Michael couldn't stop touching her. He ran his fingers up and down her arms and played with her hair.

"Yeah. How did you know?"

"Just a guess from when you mentioned your job that night in the hotel. I put it together when I found out who you married. Was he good to you? Did he ever hurt you?"

Kamielle thought for a moment. "Thomas and I were together for six years. He never raised his voice to me and he never lifted a finger. I saw him get angry at others and always wondered if I'd do anything to provoke his temper. I watched him change over the years. He became more withdrawn and his anger got worse."

"Did he know about your dad?"

"Yes. He and Shelby were the only ones. I'm sure the families I lived with in foster care knew, too, but I never told anyone voluntarily. When people asked me about my family I said they had passed on."

"Do you ever wonder if your dad is still alive?" Michael rolled her so he spooned her back, hoping by not having to meet his gaze, she'd open up some more.

She snuggled into his arms and bent her knees in front of his. "At first, I did. I wanted him to die. I hated him so much. Then I realized my hatred was keeping me from living. I decided to just not care about him at all. As far as I'm concerned I don't have a dad."

He wrapped his arms around her, pulling her closer.

"It was the last year of our marriage when I realized Thomas was different. He wasn't the man I'd fallen in love with." Michael's muscles tensed. "We had more money than usual. He was throwing parties for people I didn't know and he didn't want me to spend as much time with Shelby. He was also gone more on business.

"Before, he'd take me with him on trips and we'd go shopping and out to dinner. All of a sudden he didn't want me with him but he also didn't want me doing anything else. I even think he might have been having an affair." She rolled so she could look at Michael.

She shuddered in his arms. "He never hurt me physically, it was all emotional. I think I loved the thought of being someone's wife, of having money, having someone to take care of me. He made me take classes to get rid of my southern accent, he liked my hair blonde, so I colored it. I don't know who I am anymore." Tears pooled in her eyes.

Michael tucked a strand of hair behind her ear. "I know who you are."

"No, you don't. Do you know my last name? When my birthday is? How old I'll be?"

He shook his head. "That doesn't matter to me. I know you're strong inside and out. I know you go through life with a fierceness that has made you survive. I know I care about you. A lot." He wiped the tears and hugged her tightly.

"My name is Kamielle Lynn O'Shea. I'm twenty-six and my birthday is next week on June fourteenth. I don't feel strong, except when I'm with you. I know I care about you, too. A lot."

"Well then, sounds like we're going to be just fine."

"I want to tell you about the car accident that killed Shelby." Her lip quivered. "I couldn't go to the funeral because I was in the hospital."

"I want you to tell me everything. But if it's too much, it can wait."

"After months of Thomas coming up with every excuse why I couldn't do anything with Shelby, he told me she and I should go shopping for my birthday. We had been fighting about his work because I suspected he was using a dummy company to ship drugs and launder money. I was stupid and ignored what was right in front of my face."

"You couldn't have known your husband was such a bad guy," Michael said.

"I should have. Hell, even Shelby didn't really like him and she liked everybody. Anyway, I went to call Shelby and tell her I was free to go out, and on my birthday even. There were car keys I didn't recognize by the phone and Thomas told me my present was in the driveway.

"I'd always wanted a Mustang. Thomas was into Mercedes and BMW and wouldn't let me have one. Yet, for my twenty-sixth birthday he got me a cherry red, Mustang GT convertible. I was so excited. I thought it meant we were going to get back to the way things were." She swallowed and shifted slightly in Michael's arms.

"Shelby and I spent the entire day shopping. We were heading down a hill when Shelby said she wanted me to smell the new perfume she'd bought. She undid her seat belt and turned to dig in our bags. The stereo was up and we were both singing along.

"A stoplight turned yellow and I tried to slow down, but nothing... nothing happened." Tears ran down her face. "I screamed at Shelby to turn around and put on her seat belt. But she didn't move fast enough. I tried to avoid the other traffic at the light, but I couldn't. We were hit on Shelby's side. She was... thrown... and that's all I remember. Her screams and watching her tumble like a doll."

"Shh. It's okay. You don't have to tell me anymore." He rubbed her shoulders and arms.

Kamielle forged on, knowing she had to finish the story. "I woke up in the hospital and the doctor told me Shelby was dead and I'd had a miscarriage." She swallowed. "Thomas was furious. He wanted to know how long I'd been pregnant. I hadn't known. We'd barely been having sex and I was on the pill. I found out what would unleash the wrath of Thomas Patrick. Vinnie and Marcos had to pull him out of my room.

"I overheard him later that night saying whoever had 'done the brake job' had done it wrong." Kamielle pushed her head into Michael's chest and breathed in the smell of him. It calmed her nerves. "I couldn't believe he'd tried to have me killed. Then he said I was a liability and I needed to disappear."

She mumbled into his chest, "I've been running from him since. I spent months in physical therapy, dragging it out so I could plan. I took the money, worked my way west. Then I met you." She opened her mouth on his chest and kissed him there.

He rubbed circles on her back. "I'll help you get a life back. We'll work on everything after that together."

She lifted her head. "Together?"

"You're not going to get rid of me easily, Princess." He gripped her face. "So, your birthday is next week, huh? Have you ever heard of the concept of celebrating a Birthday Week so you get seven days instead of just one?"

She shook her head and smiled, drying the last of her tears with her fingers.

"Well, let me introduce you to the Birthday Week."

Then he kissed her and they both forgot about car accidents, killer husbands, and how sore they were from so much sex.

"OFFICER PETTY? My name is Antonio Medina."

Tony reached across a messy desk to shake hands with the officer. She had a no nonsense look about her, which Tony appreciated. Carter had said she was pretty, but Tony was used to women in tight clothes who wore makeup and fixed their hair. Dana had her plain black hair back in a ponytail. She didn't have any bangs, wore no make-up that Tony could see, and her mouth looked a little too big for her face.

She stood to shake hands and Tony was temporarily taken off guard by the fact she was almost as tall as him. Her body was fit and did good things for her ugly brown uniform.

"I know who you are, Agent Medina." She frowned.

"I'm sorry, have we met?"

Dana sighed and shook her head. "I was on scene when Karen McKay's body was pulled from that dumpster. Special

Agent Carter was going to set me up as his contact partner. He no-showed me for lunch."

"I'm sorry I don't remember you." He shrugged.

"Right. That happens to me more often than not. Are you here to try and make up for Carter ditching me?"

"No ma'am. Carter said you two clicked and he thought maybe you and I would as well. May I sit?" He waved his hand toward the plastic chair in front of her desk.

"Yeah, sorry. Listen, we need to start over. I'm in a bad mood. It's been a rough couple days and you caught me off guard."

"I know what you mean about bad days. I've had about three tough weeks in a row." He laughed.

She leaned across the desk and offered her hand again. "Officer Dana Petty. How can I help you and Carter?"

"Well, we have a witness in protective custody. We'd like your help."

She frowned. "What is it you think I can do to help?"

"I'm a Profiler. Michael and I work so well together because we work differently. He said you seem competent and I thought I'd check you out."

"Is this some kind of interview, Agent Medina?"

"No. Don't get defensive. Carter no-showed you because he was hiding our witness, not because of something you did."

"I'm assuming the woman is Kamielle Johnson."

Tony nodded. "Sure is. Michael and I want your insight into the prostitute serial killer case we've been working. We also need any information you might have about Thomas Patrick."

"Wow, those are two totally different subjects. First of all, how do you think I can help with your case?" She grabbed a notepad and pen from the clutter on her desk.

"Since the latest victim was here, we thought we could

have you help us, well, help me, review old case files. We think our guy has been here all along; at least in California. He carved Carter's name in the last victim."

"I read that in the report. Crazy. What about Patrick? Is he tied to the serial killer case? Seems odd a businessman from Chicago would have anything to do with this."

Dana knew who Thomas Patrick was and where he lived. It was like knowing Bill Gates was in the Seattle area.

"Patrick doesn't have anything to do with the case. We just need to know about his businesses here and any assets he may have in the area. We also want to find out about recent business transactions in California. If you can help us out, I'll fill you in on all the details."

"Of course I want to help. But we're shorthanded here. Captain isn't just going to let me drop everything I've been doing and run away with you," she said.

"The Bureau will cover all expenses and pay the department for your time for at least three weeks. Don't worry about your captain, he'll want to work with the FBI." Tony stood and handed over his card. "You okay with leaving town for a few weeks?"

"Hell yeah. The days I've had, it's time to get away."

"Don't you want to know where we're going?"

"As long as I don't have to wear this uniform, I don't care."

"Okay," he said. "We'll spend tomorrow going over old case files and unsolved cases with a similar M.O. of our serial killer. Depending on how long that takes, we'll spend some time researching Patrick."

Tony wouldn't have to spend as much time researching Patrick because Jon was taking care of most of that on his end. They knew Patrick hadn't been in town when Kamielle had been attacked, but had he sent someone?

"Cool. I'm here for another hour. I'll get all my paperwork caught up. You're sure Cappy will go for this?"

"You get your stuff taken care of and I'll go do my part. In an hour I'll come back here to get you. We'll grab a drink and get to work."

Chapter 14

ana was wearing jeans and a t-shirt when Tony came back to get her. Her captain had jumped at a chance to put one of his officers with the FBI. He'd tried to talk Tony into one of the male officers, but Tony made it clear he and Michael wanted to work with Officer Petty. While most cops had good training, Dana had gone to college and received a degree in Criminal Psychology. Her insight would be valuable.

"We're good to go," Tony said. "You're officially working with Michael and me on the serial killer case for the next three weeks."

"Wow! I'm so excited to be working with the FBI. Are we going to start tonight?" Dana vibrated with energy.

"I figure we'll go over the files Michael and I have compiled over the last two years. It'll be good for me to have another set of eyes look at the evidence. Since our original case files are missing, I need you to print these." He handed her a flash drive. "If you can print the photos, too, that would be great."

She plugged the drive into the USB port and started printing the files and pictures.

"You don't mind working in close quarters, do you?"

She looked at him. "Not in the least."

"Good, because we're driving to Montana tomorrow."

"What's in Montana?"

"Well, as soon as we're on the road, I'll tell you. I'm not sure I trust everyone in this precinct anymore. Those case files had to have been taken by someone who works here."

"It might not have been a cop, though." Dana hated the possibility of someone she may have trusted her life with being responsible for stealing FBI files.

"Just to be safe, as of right now, you are working with me. No phone calls to anyone unless I know about it and absolutely no discussing what you're doing."

"You got it, Agent Medina."

"Let's get that straightened out, too. I'm Tony and you're Dana. None of this 'Agent Medina' or 'Officer Petty' shit, okay?"

Dana smiled. "I can handle that."

After the last photo printed, Dana put them in file folders. When everything was gathered, Tony motioned toward the door with his hand.

"Do I pack three weeks worth of clothes?" she asked when they were outside.

"We'll do laundry when we need to. I don't need you lugging six suitcases around with us."

"Hey, that's not fair. I know I'm a woman, but I'm not as girlie as most. If I can wear jeans and t-shirts the whole time we're gone, I'll only need one bag."

"Sure, I'll believe that when I see it. Casual wear will be fine. Pack one nice dress in case we need to go out."

"My apartment isn't too far from here and I have a spare room. Do you want to get checked out, come to my place, and we'll go over the files? Wouldn't that be more comfortable than a hotel room? I know this great Thai place that delivers and I have beer in my fridge."

Tony was tired of staying in the hotel. "Sounds good."

They spent fifteen minutes at the hotel. He packed quickly as she stood at the door watching. Tony pondered the fact he hadn't actually worked with a female partner before. He wasn't so sexist he didn't think they could do the job, he just hadn't had an opportunity to work with many female agents. He was always afraid his hormones would get in the way.

Dana was simple, straight-forward, and seemed easy to work with. There wouldn't be any hormone problems with her. She was pretty in a wholesome way, but Tony hadn't dated anyone wholesome in a long, long time.

Hotel checkout taken care of, they drove to Dana's apartment. It was a quiet neighborhood and there were only ten units. She showed him where to park.

Her apartment was simple, like the woman, with family pictures hanging on the walls. There were a few movie posters tacked in the living room and a decent entertainment center.

Dana pulled a few takeout menus from a drawer. "You like Thai food? We could get something else."

"Thai is fine. I like all spicy food. My mom and dad were both born and raised in Mexico so everything I've eaten since I was young was seasoned with jalapenos or habaneros."

Once dinner was ordered, Dana pulled two beers out of her fridge. "I've only got MGD, that okay?"

"I'm not too picky when it comes to beer." Tony took it and had a long drink.

He spread the pictures on Dana's coffee table by date and there was nothing pretty about any of them. He pulled out the most important ones. There were three shots of each woman. One showed the placement of her body, one showed the left side of her face, and one showed her left hand.

"Does the missing ring finger represent something about marriage or maybe lack of marriage?" She picked up one of the pictures.

He was impressed by her psychological take on the symbolism. "I think so, yeah. All the women are prostitutes. I figure our unsub, unknown subject, sees them as dirty and worthless. He takes the ring finger because they're having sex with people they're not married to."

"What about the left ear?" She studied one of the pictures more closely.

"That, I'm not sure. He obviously takes the trophies for a reason. I'm a little worried about what he's done with them. I'll see when we catch him." Tony grimaced as though trying to picture and *not* picture what someone would do with thirty or more ears and fingers.

"*When* you catch him. I admire your confidence. You know it's a man?"

"All the women are raped and have their ear and finger cut off before he slits their throats. The fact they're overpowered and the wedding ring idea both point to a male attacker."

The doorbell rang forty-five minutes later. Dana pulled out plates, chop sticks, and two more beers. They ate in comfortable silence and made a plan to go over each case from the beginning.

It was midnight when they looked over the final pictures. The ones of Karen McKay.

"So this has become personal for the unsub." Dana traced her finger over the letters carved in Karen's chest.

"It happens sometimes. The press can be our best friend or our worst enemy. When a case goes on this long, word spreads about who is working it and how well, or not well, they're doing. The killer wants to taunt Carter."

"Why just Carter? Why not you, too?" she asked.

"Who knows? There are some things I try not to over-analyze."

She yawned and covered her mouth. "Sorry. I was on patrol all morning."

"It's okay. It's been a long day and we've got at least two days of driving ahead of us. Let's call it a night."

Tony stood and started gathering the pictures and printed reports. Dana loaded the dishwasher and turned it on.

"I've only got the one bathroom and towels are under the sink. I'll be up for a little bit." She grinned at him shyly. "My first year I learned to read a book before I went to bed. I'm less likely to dream about serial killer photos if something else was the last image in my head."

"Smart." He turned to walk to the room he'd be sleeping in. "I'd like to leave at seven. That okay with you?"

"I'll be ready to go." She went to her room.

Three weeks of working with the FBI. Tony was easy to work with and she remembered Michael being the same way. Maybe she'd prove herself and move up at work. This was going to be great.

AT NINE TUESDAY MORNING, Tony and Dana had already been on the road for two hours. Michael and Kami, however, were cuddled in bed.

"Jon should be checking in with me sometime soon. He'll have more information on Thomas and Marcos."

She shivered. "I want this to be over."

"I know, baby, I know." He pulled her closer and kissed the top of her head. "We'll head out in a few hours and get to Idaho tonight. We can stay there or drive through to Kalispell."

"I'd just like to get to your ranch. If we take turns, we can drive the rest of the way, can't we?"

"Yeah, we can do that. I think you'd better go put some clothes on, Princess, so I can do some work." He kissed her long and hard then rolled out of bed.

Michael logged into the FBI secure mainframe using Kami's laptop. She sat silently next to him as he checked his e-mail and clicked on a message from Jon.

Thomas and Marcos had plane tickets for the day after tomorrow. Michael cursed under his breath. They weren't going to beat them to Kalispell by much. Jon also told Michael to watch his back and that he'd be at the ranch before Thomas and Marcos got there. The last reminder was for Michael to send Tony to Las Vegas to check on the death of stripper Camille Lovelace along with the missing Vinnie and his sister.

After reading the e-mail from Jon, Michael went through the information compiled on Thomas. There were photos with reports. The first picture showed Thomas making the press release about Kamielle being dead. The next picture was of Thomas and model Steffie Magnolia. The last picture was of Thomas, Kamielle, Shelby, and Tyra Banks.

Kami traced her finger over her face then Shelby's. "I didn't even want to go to this party. Shelby convinced me to. She said if I could get Tyra to model my designs, I'd be a hit."

Michael looked closely at the photo. "Holy shit, that's the Senator of Florida's Christmas party, isn't it?"

"How do you know that?"

"I was there. My buddy in the Marines got invited and brought me along. I was checking into Thomas's background, trying to figure out who he was working with. I met Ms. Banks that night. I practically drooled all over myself."

"She has that effect on men. Some women, too." Kami smiled. "She was so nice to me, though. She liked my designs and told me to get in contact with her during the summer because her winter and spring were booked. I had the accident before I could get her my ideas."

Michael scrolled through more information. There were pictures of Thomas having lunch with known mob connections, but lunch wasn't a crime. The FBI hadn't been able to set up audio surveillance because they didn't have enough proof to get a warrant. Michael figured Thomas had a few judges in his pocket who were holding up the warrants for audio surveillance and phone taps.

"That's Marcos and that's Vinnie." Kami pointed to a picture of the two men escorting her into the back of a limousine.

"Jon's pretty sure Vinnie is dead. He thinks Marcos killed him."

Kami laughed without humor. "Figures. Vinnie wasn't smart enough for Thomas. He didn't know when to keep his mouth shut. He wasn't a good man. He was always nice and polite to me, but I got the feeling it was only because Thomas had threatened him. I'm not sorry he's dead. Does that make me a bad person?"

"No. Jon also thinks Vinnie is dead because he was supposed to get you and found the wrong woman."

"Someone's dead because Vinnie thought it was me?"

"We don't know for sure, that's why I'm having Tony go to Las Vegas."

"Someone else *is* dead because of me." She stood, wiping away tears.

Michael stood and took her hands. "Quit making this your fault. You didn't kill anyone. Patrick is to blame for all the deaths following you around."

"I would have expected him to send Vinnie or Marcos to get me. Obviously Vinnie found the wrong person. Who found me in Oakland? Why did he try to kill me if he knew I had to be brought back to Thomas alive?"

Michael thought for a moment. "I don't think he was trying to kill you. I think he wanted to play with you and scare you. He didn't expect you to fight back and he panicked."

"Thomas doesn't hire men who panic. The attack still doesn't make any sense."

"We know it was Thomas's doing because Marcos was sent to the safe house for you."

She shivered at the thought of Marcos getting his hands on her.

He squeezed her hands. "They won't touch you. I'll kill them first." The steel of his voice reassured her.

"What about the law, Michael?" she whispered.

"My job is to uphold the law. I'm planning on arresting Marcos and Thomas and sending them to jail for the rest of their lives. But if either of them tries to hurt you, I'll kill them."

She shook her head. "Don't break the law for me."

"I'll do whatever it takes for you."

In that moment, Kamielle realized she had fallen in love with Michael. She couldn't pinpoint the exact instant it had happened. He'd been her rock for so many weeks. The feeling in her chest was different than anything she'd ever felt. Different than the day she'd married Thomas and the day she'd lost her unborn baby.

Now what did she do with this information? She didn't want to scare him away, so she'd have to wait for a good time to tell him. Maybe when she wasn't being chased by her lunatic husband and Michael wasn't on the trail of a sadistic serial killer? That sounded like a plan.

Michael watched the different emotions play across Kami's face. He wasn't sure what was going through her head. She smiled and pulled him in for a hug. Whatever conclusion she had come to was good, though.

He wrapped his arms around her. "As much as I've enjoyed the last two days of being in our own little world, we have to get going. This will all be over by the end of the week, I promise."

It was Tuesday morning. If they could be in Kalispell by Wednesday morning and Thomas got there Thursday, Jon and Michael could have him confessing by Thursday night.

She snuggled into his arms. "Can we have one more shower together before we leave this incredible hotel room?" She couldn't believe after two days of nonstop sex she still wanted him.

"You make me forget some of the important things going on. I never did tell Tony to go to Vegas. Shit. You start the shower and I'll call Tony. He's going to be pissed at me."

"Tell him you'll make it up to him somehow. He gets to spend a few extra days with Officer Petty."

"She's not really his type. Tony goes for flashier women." Michael pulled out his cell.

"Sometimes when you spend a lot of time with someone you realize what you thought was your type really isn't. Sometimes the person you least expect is."

"Speaking from experience?" he asked.

"Maybe." She shrugged.

Michael didn't have a chance to ask anything more. Tony answered after two rings.

"Hey, Medina, I forgot to tell you something yesterday." He paused. "Jon found an interesting e-mail on Patrick's computer. He's pretty sure Vinnie is dead and his body is in Las Vegas with two others." He paused again. "I know Las Vegas is east and you're headed north. Jon's meeting me in Kalispell, I won't be alone." Pause. "I have Montana under control. Take Dana to

Vegas and find out what's going on. I'll e-mail you Jon's thoughts."

Tony argued briefly. He didn't like that he wasn't going to be Michael's backup. Grudgingly, he agreed Jon was the best backup a person could have.

"Since you're driving and cell service is iffy through some of those mountains, I'll get the Las Vegas FBI branch checking any recent homicides. I'll also find out if anyone has reported the stripper missing. I want you to actually be there and I'm sorry I didn't ask you about this sooner." Pause. "Yeah, I've been just a little distracted. Tell Dana I said hi. Keep me updated. Bye, buddy."

Michael heard the shower start and felt his heartbeat speed up. He turned his back to the sound knowing he had to get business taken care of first.

His next call was to the director of the VCTF. He let his boss know he'd gotten a tip and Tony was on his way to Las Vegas to check it out. The director wasn't happy about Michael dealing with tips while on leave. After a brief discussion, the director gave him a contact name and number for the Vegas Field office.

Michael called Agent Steve Lange and outlined what he could: an informant was sure there was a triple homicide involving a mob enforcer, his sister, and a stripper. Wanting to keep things running smoothly for Tony, Michael gave Agent Lange Tony's name and cell number. He let him know they were following this lead because of a witness in protective custody from the mob. Lange promised to review the information.

It was ten minutes before Michael was off the phone. He couldn't hear the shower running anymore and sighed at his missed chance. He went to the master bedroom. Kamielle sat on the bed watching TV and her hair was dry.

"I started the shower and poked my head out to see if you were ready to join me, but you were on the phone. I decided to wait for you." She stood and untied the sash of the robe, pushing it off her shoulders to the floor.

"I still can't believe the effect you have on me." Michael walked to her.

"You keep saying that like it's a bad thing."

"Oh, it's not a bad thing at all. I just want to keep reminding you I'm not getting tired of you."

The shower lasted over a half an hour and was almost as intense as their first night together. By the time they had dressed and packed it was almost noon. She put the bag with the money and laptop on the hotel luggage cart and Michael loaded up the two suitcases. With one last look around the suite, she sighed.

"Don't worry, Princess, I'll take you wherever you want to go when all this is over. We'll be able to spend as long as you want living on room service."

"Promise?" she asked.

"I promise."

By 12:30 p.m. they were on I-80 heading north.

"Will you use my phone and send a text to Tony?" Michael handed over his cell. "Ask him to call me when he gets to Vegas."

Kamielle sent the text. "Do you think he'll find their bodies?"

"I don't know. It's hot and there are scavengers that add to the decomposition of bodies. Unless we get lucky, we might never find them."

"Because of the e-mail Jon found, will you be able to tie Thomas to the murders?" She fidgeted.

"Don't worry, honey, Thomas is going down for every horrible thing he's done. If we can't tie him to those three murders, we should be able to link Marcos. While his e-mail was vague and didn't say 'I killed three people', it might be enough if we find the bodies."

"Are you still in trouble with your boss about the stuff that happened at the safe house?"

"He's not thrilled with me, but I am assistant director. I have the authority to do what I did. I hate that two innocent people died and it's something I'll have to live with. It could have been us and I won't ever forget that. It helped me prove we need more secure places. I made my point, but not the way I wanted to."

She reached across the center console and took his hand. "That wouldn't have been us. You wouldn't have let anything happen to me."

He squeezed her fingers. "I'd like to think so, too, but everyone has to sleep and even the best agents run out of luck. I won't let anything happen to you."

"I know. If I didn't trust you completely I wouldn't be here and I never would have slept with you."

He glanced at her and squeezed her hand again.

They drove the rest of the afternoon with the radio playing in the background and various discussions about life in general. They took the time to get to know one another even more. They discussed current events, popular music, and the latest movies. It surprised her how much of the same things they liked.

About halfway through Idaho, they stopped for gas and dinner. When they were done eating, the sun was setting.

"We should keep driving. Are you doing okay?" He rubbed her shoulders as they walked across the parking lot.

"I should be asking you that. You've done all the driving. How about if I take over for a while? You can relax or take a nap."

"I think I'll take you up on that." He walked to the

passenger side and tossed her the keys. "I might sleep, I might not. I enjoy visiting with you."

"Same here." She got in. "This is beautiful country."

"If you like the Middle of Nowhere, Idaho, then you're really going to like Kalispell, Montana. The area is littered with trees, farmer's fields, and wide open land. We own quite a few acres and the neighbors are pretty far from the ranch."

"I can't wait to see it."

Michael's cell rang. "It's Tony. He must be in Vegas. Hey, buddy, how was the drive? That's good. Thanks, again. Were you able to talk to agent Lange yet?"

Kamielle listened in as she drove.

"Great. I hope you're able to find something. I'll send you a text when we hit the ranch."

After a few more comments, Michael ended the call. "Tony and Dana made it without any problems. It seems Agent Lange's been a busy guy since I talked to him. He found out the stripper's real name, Vinnie's sister's name, and may have a lead on where to find the bodies."

"Wow. Does the FBI always work so fast?"

"No. Tony didn't have all the details but it sounds like a hiker may have found some bodies in a shallow grave."

"Well, that would make things easier."

"You're telling me. I'm going to find out how close Jon is to the ranch. We'll switch driving again when we get into Montana."

"Okay, but I'll drive for as long as you want me to."

Her head crowded with thoughts, Kamielle changed the radio station while Michael called Jon. By early Wednesday morning, she'd be at the ranch and close to coming face to face with Thomas. She wasn't sure if she was ready.

Chapter 15

Lucky. That's what Michael, Tony, and Dana were. There were thousands of unsolved murders in the country; hell, hundreds of thousands. They'd gotten lucky when a hiker and his dog stumbled across a shallow grave in the mountains outside Las Vegas.

While it rarely rained in the city, the mountains often got downpours that were on the verge of miniature flash floods. Apparently Marcos hadn't wanted to dig too deep a hole for three bodies. A couple rainstorms had washed away a few inches of top soil and the dog had smelled a scent he couldn't resist.

Tony and Dana pulled up to the crime scene, stepping out to flood lights attracting all kinds of desert bugs. A man in a wrinkled suit marched toward them.

"I don't give a flying hell which paper you work for, get out of here!"

Tony pulled back his jacket to show the badge clipped to his shoulder holster. "Agent Lange, I presume?"

The man stopped. "Please, please tell me you're Medina."

Tony looked at Dana. "I've never had a man so happy to see me before."

"Oh, I just bet." She rolled her eyes.

Tony held out his hand. "Call me Tony."

"I've been up for almost twenty hours straight. I don't know if it was good, bad, or dumb luck that had your partner calling me and then three bodies are found. The longer I'm stuck here, the more I'm thinking it's bad luck."

Lange was in his mid-thirties and everything about him seemed average. Average height, brown hair and eyes, plain face. Dana figured he might be okay to look at when his hair wasn't finger-combed to one side and his suit didn't look like he'd rolled around on the ground.

"Why don't you point us to the locals in charge and take a break." Tony would have loved to pick the guy's brain some more, but he looked ready to drop.

"No way. This is my effing case. Even if your partner hadn't called, I'd have still been brought in on a triple homicide. Besides, I just sent some guys out for Red Bull and donuts."

Dana grimaced. "What about coffee?"

"I gave up on coffee around five o'clock this evening. All it made me do was have to piss."

Dana laughed. "I so love working with the FBI."

"Oh yeah, sorry. I forgot introductions." Tony waved his hand between Dana and Lange. "Oakland PD Officer Dana Petty. Las Vegas FBI Agent Steve Lange."

Tony watched Agent Lange transform. He ran fingers through his hair, stood up a little straighter, and held out his hand to Dana. The effect was something similar to a sci-fi movie. Lange's hair magically settled in a tousled, sexy look. The wrinkles on his suit seemed to flatten out, and he now appeared inches taller. He oozed charm.

"Ma'am, I do apologize for not being more professional. Oakland PD? Very brave and honorable."

Agent Lange didn't need his Red Bull and donuts after all. Dana Petty had woken him right up.

"I think being FBI is even more brave and honorable. But thank you so much, Agent Lange, for the compliment." She smiled.

"Please, call me Steve. May I call you Dana?"

"Of course. As I've told Tony, I want to be comfortable while we're working on this case."

"Tony?" Steve seemed confused.

"Yeah, Tony, remember me? The other FBI agent?" Tony's voice sounded surly, even to his own ears.

"Agent Medina, of course. Sorry. As I may have mentioned, I've been up for—"

"Almost twenty hours, yes." Dana finished. "Can you tell us what you know about the bodies?" She lifted her chin toward the group of people.

"Yes, my dear, I sure can."

She touched his arm. "Just a minute, Steve. Tony and I need to get some items out of his truck. We'll meet you right over there by the flood lights."

Dana walked Tony back to the truck.

"Did you see that guy? It was like "Invasion of the Body Snatchers". One minute he seems like he doesn't want us here and the next he's," Tony paused, "well, different."

"Undressing me with his eyes?" Dana said with a snort.

"Yeah, something like that."

"You haven't worked with many women, have you?"

"No."

"Well, it goes like this. Forty-nine percent of other 'cops' treat me like a piece of meat. Forty-nine percent pat me on the head and try to keep me from being hurt."

"What about the other two percent?" Tony asked.

"The other two percent treat me like you and Michael. Capable and like it doesn't matter I have boobs."

He laughed. "You're not what I expected. Every time I think I have you figured out, you do stuff like this."

"A woman is a mystery, Tony, don't go putting me in a box." She patted his cheek. "So, as much as I hate to do it, I'm going to put these boobs to use and get Steve to tell us things faster than I think he would have." She looked over at the agent in question for a moment. "I haven't decided if I think he's a creep or not."

"I think he's a creep."

"You only think that because he ignored you."

"No, I think that because of how he's acting."

"Don't get chivalrous on me. Next time you're out with a woman, pay attention. I bet you treat her differently than someone on the job."

"Of course I do. If we're out on a date, I'm treating her like a woman. Hand holding, brief touches, whispered jokes. She should be treated special." Dana was staring at him with her mouth open. "What?" he demanded.

"I, uh, nothing."

Dana pictured what Tony described. She'd never been on a date where the man gave every bit of his attention to her. Of course, she'd been dating cops, and they never really saw her as a woman.

"Let's go find out what Agent Steve knows," she said.

"Please, by all means. You and your boobs lead the way. I'll just be behind you if you need anything." He had a mixture of humor and annoyance in his voice.

"Now you're getting it, Medina." Dana grabbed her notepad from the truck and tromped up the hill to Lange.

"I've got an initial report from our field medical examiner, but the official autopsy won't be performed until the bodies are taken to the morgue. The M.E. there is remarkable. He really knows his stuff. Not that our field M.E. isn't as great." Agent Lange raised his voice just enough to try and flatter the M.E. who was knelt next to the hole containing the bodies.

"Cut the crap, Steve." The woman lifted her head and Dana met blue eyes outlined in thick black eye-liner. Her blonde and black hair was up in a haphazard ponytail. She was wearing a blue jumpsuit with the words 'Las Vegas M.E.' embroidered on the chest pocket.

She stood, pulled off one of her gloves and reached a hand over to Dana and then Tony. "I'm Clarissa Hunter, M.E. I should be at a kick ass Rave right now." She indicated her over-done make up and wild hair. "I happened to be out," she glared at Steve, "when I got the call to come to this little party."

"Clarice, tell them what you told me." Steve put his hands in his pockets, rocking back on his heels.

"Clarice? I thought your name was Clarissa?" Dana said.

"The boys think it's fun to call me Clarice like Clarice Starling from "Silence of the Lambs". I told them I'd sick my psycho boyfriend on them and they thought that was super funny." She stage whispered, "They won't think it's funny when I tell them his name is Hannibal."

Dana instantly liked her.

"Tony, how about if Clarissa and I talk about the bodies and you and Steve talk about the case?" Dana winked at Tony and turned her back on the men.

"Seriously, you'll get more out of 'Steve-my-jockstrap-is-too-tight-Lange' than your partner will."

"I know. I'd rather talk to you, though. Dana Petty, Oakland PD." She held out her hand again.

"Oakland? What the hell are you doing in Vegas?"

"I got super lucky and was asked to work with the FBI," Dana said.

"If I had to work with boys like Lange, I wouldn't count myself lucky." Clarissa rolled her eyes and put on a new pair of exam gloves.

"Well, apparently I've gotten extremely lucky or met two men unlike any other FBI agents."

"Two? Where's the other one?"

"He's not with us right now."

"What's that one's name?" Clarissa lifted her chin toward Tony. "He's gorgeous. Looks like the guys that were at the club I had to leave."

"Tony Medina. I'll let you talk to him when we're done. I might have a few more tidbits to get out of Steve." Dana rolled her eyes this time.

Clarissa's laugh was low and husky. "Oh, honey, didn't take you long to figure him out. Too bad you're not wearing a button-up shirt. You'd be able to undo a few and he'd give you anything you wanted. Including his first-born child, if anyone was dumb enough to reproduce with him."

They both laughed.

"Okay, I love talking to you, but I have a club to get back to. We'll begin with the unknown male since he's on top of the pile." Clarissa pulled out a hand-held recorder and pressed a button. "White male, approximately mid-fifties. Maybe five foot seven, five foot eight and around two hundred fifty pounds. Black, thinning hair, balding at the crown. Single gunshot wound to the back of the head, appears to be small caliber. Hands bound at the wrists, behind the back. Feet bound at the ankles." She looked at Dana and handed over a pair of gloves from her jumpsuit pocket. "Help me roll him over, please."

Dana pulled on the gloves and knelt. She grabbed a shoulder and pulled while Clarissa pushed. The body rolled and Dana's breath left her in a whoosh as she plunked back into the sand on her butt. "Oh, my God."

Tony jogged to her. "Dana, what's—" he stopped when Clarissa started talking.

"Holy shit. Duane, get over here with the camera!" Clarissa yelled for her assistant then she addressed Dana and Tony. "The bullet that entered the back of his head wouldn't have done this."

This was that the face of the victim was gone. His chin, mouth, nose, eyes, and part of his forehead. His skull was empty and it appeared everything inside of it had run into the hole.

Dana covered her mouth with her hand, realized she still had on the gloves, and ripped them off. "What? What happened to him?"

"Not just him. Them." Tony peered into the hole, pulling out his flashlight. Beneath the man's body were the bodies of two women.

"Can I get you anything, Dana?" Steve put his arm around Dana and his head was very close to hers.

"Unless you want me to puke on you, I suggest you move away."

Steve repelled himself back.

Clarissa got Dana's attention. "I want you to take a few deep breaths with your head down and then I want you to shoot back one of those Red Bulls."

"Shoot it?" Dana asked.

"You need to go out more often, girlfriend. Shoot back? Chug? Drink really damn fast?" Clarissa said.

"Why?"

"Because I said so. Now do it." Clarissa had also taken off her gloves and she popped the top on the can.

Dana took it and smelled the contents.

"Don't smell it!" Tony and Clarissa said at almost the same time.

Dana plugged her nose and chugged the Red Bull. When she was done, she grimaced and held the can away from her. "That was disgusting!"

"Yeah, but you're not nauseous anymore, are you?" Clarissa was smiling.

"No."

"Got your mind off the bodies?"

"Yeah."

Tony looked at Dana. "You going to be able to talk in full sentences anytime soon?"

"Maybe." She grimaced again.

"Let's switch. Steve wasn't telling me anything anyway." Tony shrugged.

"I can handle this now. I just wasn't expecting *that*." Dana pointed at the hole.

"I believe you. You looked at a table full of serial killer victim pictures with me. Just go talk to Steve and when he's told you what we need, come back over. Okay?"

"Okay." Dana took a deep breath and walked to where Steve was hiding after her warning of puking on him.

Tony looked at Clarissa. "Tony Medina. Steve didn't introduce us."

"Dana told me. I really want to get a look at these other two bodies. Let me get the CSIs over here."

It took over an hour for the three bodies to be removed from the hole. Each one was photographed and placed on its own tarp. Tony followed behind Clarissa and listened as she recorded her notes.

"Victim two is female in her mid to late thirties. Dyed blonde hair. Wrists and ankles bound like victim one. Clothing missing and there appears to be pre-mortem bruising on her pelvis and thighs. Possible rape."

She walked to the last tarp.

"Victim three is bound like victims one and two. Mid to late forties, female with black hair. Missing clothing along with similar pelvic and thigh bruises like other female victim.

"All three have gunshot wounds to the back of the head and all three are missing their, uh, the front and jaw portions of the skull. Weapon will need to be determined by official autopsy." Clarissa paused.

"The only other major differences in the bodies are the female victims are both missing all ten fingers at the first knuckle. They appear to be cut off with shears or a knife of some kind."

Clarissa turned to Tony and Dana. She looked at them, but addressed her hand-held recorder. "Except for the possible rape, this looks like a professional hit." She shut off the recorder and took a deep breath.

"Want a Red Bull?" Dana asked.

"I'll let you know."

"Dr. Hunter!" One of the techs taking samples from the hole poked his head up. "I've got bone fragments here but they look funny."

The tech held up four pieces of bone in his palm.

"Two of those are teeth," Clarissa said.

"Teeth?" Dana asked.

"I think I know what happened to their faces." Tony looked back at the bodies. "You said this resembled a professional hit? The fingers were cut off the women to prevent fingerprinting and their faces are missing,"

"To prevent any dental record matches," Clarissa said.

"What did he bash their faces in with? A shovel? A rock?" Dana asked.

"No. Something blunt, something he would have control over." Tony thought about it for a minute then said, "Sledgehammer." His theory hung in the night air.

"Jesus," Dana whispered.

The bodies were loaded into the van when Clarissa gave the okay. Tony and Dana decided to find a hotel and maybe get some sleep.

It was after three in the morning when Tony finally got around to texting Carter and briefly saying there were three dead bodies matching—sort of—the description of Vinnie, his sister, and the stripper. Tony put that he'd call later because he and Dana needed sleep. They got a hotel way off the strip and went to their separate rooms.

Without even taking off her shoes, Dana dropped face first onto the bed and fell asleep.

Tony changed his clothes and propped himself up on the headboard. He thought back over what they'd seen and wondered what Michael and Kamielle were involved in. Those three victims had died horrible deaths and, if Michael was right, Patrick had ordered the hit. If they could get a positive ID on Vinnie and link him to working for Patrick, then maybe they would have something to go on.

Agent Lange had gotten Vinnie's rap sheet and his next of kin. The stripper wasn't hard to track down since she'd been missing from work. The names they had were: Vincent James Dexter; Sophia Marie Dexter, his sister; and Camille Lois Marshall, aka, stripper Camille Lovelace.

Hopefully, the autopsy to be performed later in the morning would give them what they needed to know.

THE SUN WAS RISING over the mountains Wednesday morning when Michael pulled the Tahoe up to the gate at the dirt road driveway of the ranch. Kamielle slept soundly in the passenger seat. He didn't want her to miss the entrance to his childhood home so when he got back in from opening the gate, he shut his door a little harder than usual.

She stirred and stretched as much as she could in her seat. Rubbing her eyes, she smiled sleepily. His heart beat a little faster and he leaned over to kiss her.

"We're here."

All traces of sleep left her face and she sat up straighter to peer out the windshield. "We're here? We're at your ranch?"

"Yeah, baby."

"I'm so happy we're finally here!" She looked at the rising sun. "It's beautiful."

"Yeah, it really is." His voice was full of pride as he drove through the gate. "I'm leaving the gate open so the boys will know we're here."

"Boys?"

"The hired hands. Julie refers to them as 'the boys' and Jon and I started doing the same."

"What does she call you and Jon?"

He laughed. "Nothing that can be repeated in good company."

"That doesn't surprise me." She looked out over the rolling hills. "It looks like it goes on forever." She could see cattle grazing in the distance, but still no sign of any buildings.

"It takes a few minutes to get to the ranch house. We own almost three-thousand acres. Mom and dad started with around two-hundred and Jon and I buy up every piece we can get when it becomes available. Most of the people in the area support us because that means it won't be turned into housing developments."

They came over a small hill and down below them the valley opened up into Michael, Jon, and Julie's pride and joy. Two large barns and a corral were east of the houses.

"The small, square building is the bunk house." Michael

pointed. "The middle-sized A-frame house is the one we all grew up in and it's where Jon and I stay when we're here. The mansion-looking house is Julie's. She designed it and Jon and I paid for it."

While it did look like a mansion, it was still a cabin. There were huge windows, a wraparound deck, and it was made of logs. It looked like it should grace the cover of an architecture magazine.

"It's absolutely beautiful," she said.

"Yeah and it cost a pretty penny. Every time Julie starts ragging on Jon and me about starting a family or moving back, we remind her how much her house cost and she shuts up." He chuckled. "It does have its appeal though. You know, the whole place? I always feel a peace come over me when I drive into the valley."

She sighed. "I can't let you bring someone as evil as Thomas here."

Michael pulled the Tahoe next to the A-frame house. He pointed to the west where a small forest of trees began at the edge of a field. "Over there is a hunting cabin. That's where Thomas thinks we live. This place is in Julie and her husband's name and no one, not even Thomas, can trace Julie as Jon's or my sister. Jon and I have set the trap for there, while you'll be safe here."

"What do you mean 'safe here'? I'm not letting you do this without me." She got out of the SUV and he followed.

"I will not put you in harm's way. This man is dangerous and evil." He marched in front of the rig and grabbed her by the hand. "I just found you and I'm not going to lose you."

She was temporarily stunned by his words until his hand flexed on hers. "You think I don't know he's dangerous? I almost died because of him. You need me to help. You can't just throw cuffs on him and expect him to confess to all his evil deeds!" She ripped her arm away and moved to drop down on the front steps of the house.

He sat next to her. "We talked about this. Jon and I have video and audio surveillance set up. We get Thomas on tape admitting he tried to kill you, killed Shelby, and he ordered the hits on Vinnie, his sister, and the stripper. We get Marcos to admit he killed the FBI agent and the other witness and it's all over."

"And how exactly do you expect to get them to confess? He's not stupid. He's not just going to tell you all that while you sit down for drinks. This isn't a movie!"

"All bad guys like to brag," Michael said. He was pleading. He didn't know how they were going to get Thomas to admit everything; he just didn't want to tell her that. Jon was the expert at getting people to confess.

"Listen to me, Michael. Thomas will say it all to me. He'll want to see me upset. If he thinks he's got me 'captured' and it's all over, he'll boast just like you said. But, he's not going to say it to you."

Part of Michael knew she was right. Part of him didn't want her anywhere near Thomas. He put his head in his hands, rubbing his temples. "Can we discuss this when we've had some sleep, please?"

"There isn't anything to discuss."

They were interrupted by the sound of a truck. Someone was hanging out the passenger window and waving a cowboy hat. "Boss, boss, you're here!"

The truck roared to a stop next to the Tahoe and two middle aged men jumped out and sprinted toward the stairs.

"Jason, Terry, good to see you guys." They all shook hands. "This is my girlfriend, Kamielle. I wanted to show her the ranch."

"Ma'am," Jason and Terry said together.

"You see, guys, this is our first big trip together and we really want to be alone. So I'm giving all you boys the week off with pay."

Jason and Terry looked at each other. "You sure you got everything under control alone?"

"You bet. I've done it before. We'll be fine."

"Okay, boss," Jason finally said. "We'll do this morning's chores and set everything up for feeding tonight."

"Great. Kamielle and I want some alone time and you guys deserve a little vacation. We've been driving for over twenty-four hours to get here. We'll probably have some breakfast and go to sleep. Let the other guys know what's going on."

"That shouldn't be a problem, boss. They're riding fence and working on the tractors. General repair stuff."

"Okay, then, it's settled. You don't have to wake me when you head out." Everyone shook hands again.

Michael grabbed their bags and walked to the cabin. "Are you still mad at me?" He glanced at her as he pushed open the door.

"Yes. No. I don't know. I want to be mad at you, but I also know you're being my knight."

She looked at him then turned to survey the living room. It opened into the kitchen and dining room, half-walls giving the appearance of separate rooms. There were some family photos along with western style artwork.

"That hallway goes to the master bedroom and bath and the stairs go up to two bedrooms and a bathroom."

"Which room are we sleeping in?"

"The master."

"Does the master bath have a shower or a tub?"

"Both. Jon and I remodeled it a few years ago."

"How big is the bed?" She ran her hands over his chest.

"King. We also bought a new bed. Neither of us could

stand the thought of sleeping in our parents' old bed."

"Have you ever brought another woman here?"

"Not since we remodeled. Crystal and I used to stay in Jon's and my old room."

She turned and went down the small hall, pushing open the bedroom door. The room was all wood, including the bed frame. She'd have time to admire that later. She turned to make sure Michael had followed. He had. She pulled her shirt over her head and moved her hands to the snaps of her shorts.

"You're trying to distract me from our argument."

"We'll talk about that later. Right now I want to make love to you. I want to feel you inside me and forget the real reason we're here."

He swooped down on her. "The real reason we're here is because I wanted you to see my home and meet my family. Don't think there is any other reason." He pulled off her bra and laid her down on the bed.

Her hands went to the snaps of his jeans and she kissed him.

"Shower, bath, or bed?" He asked between nips to her lips, chin, and neck.

"I don't care. Make me forget everything but you."

The urgency swallowed them whole. Neither one knew what was driving their rapid need besides the fact tomorrow was going to change their lives.

Clothing slid to the floor. He lifted her to pull back the covers. "I forget everything when I'm with you."

"That's what love is, Michael."

"Love?" He settled himself over her and kissed her deeply. "Are you in love with me?" He rubbed against her, keeping himself from the place she wanted him most.

"I don't know. Are you in love with me?" She arched her back to get him to move, but he wouldn't.

"You've had me tied in knots since the day I met you."

"Tied in knots isn't love." She anchored her heels onto his butt and pulled for all she was worth. He started to slip inside, breath hissing between his teeth.

"Every time I slide inside you, it feels stronger than the last. If this isn't love, then we should be about worked out of each other's systems, don't you think?"

"I don't know what love is." She pulled again and he slid in as far as he could go.

"Admit you love me," he said. "Admit you've never felt this way about anyone before in your life. Admit. You. Love. Me." His last sentence was punctuated by the thrust of his hips on every word.

She exploded around him and the little tremors almost pushed him over the edge.

"Admit you love me!" he said again against her neck.

"I can't!" she sobbed.

"Why?" He stopped, holding himself above her.

"Because if I admit I love you, something will go wrong. I'll lose you!" She was angry at the world. Happiness was being dangled in front of her and she didn't think she would be able to keep it.

"I love you, Princess. I love you and you're not going to lose me." He thrust in and out of her, taking her anger and using it to make her feel how real he was.

She screamed as another orgasm ripped through her body. The tears mixed with sweat and Michael rained kisses over her face. When his own release came, he collapsed on top of her, mumbling his love into her hair.

She was finally hopeful she'd found happiness. All they had to do was catch her murdering husband and they could live happily ever after.

Yeah. What was happily ever after?

Chapter 16

Stewart Martin was duct taped to a metal chair. If he tried to move, the chair would start to fold and the tape would pull on his skin more. He was going through drug withdrawals and hadn't eaten or really slept. Stewart tried to wrap his mind around what was going on. *He* had made Stewart take off his clothes and sit on the cold, metal chair. Stewart had begged to be able to leave his underwear on and *he* had laughed at that.

Stewart realized it didn't matter now. *He* had come in at the end of every evening and turned on the hose to wash away the filth and stink.

"Where is she?" *He* would yell. "Where is my precious Kamielle?"

Stewart would always answer with the same thing: "I don't know!"

It was the beginning of the fifth day. At the end of each day he was hosed off. Stewart started drifting. Was he a kid again? Was he in Mother's basement? She only kept him for five days and then it would be Justin's turn. Justin had always gone second to save Stewart her wrath. Mother worked herself into more of a self-righteous frenzy the longer the days.

He opened the door to the basement and walked down the rickety steps. That's right, mother was dead, she couldn't hurt anyone anymore. *He* untaped Stewart's hands from the seat of the chair and re-taped them to a tabletop.

Stewart asked again, "Why are you doing this to me? I don't know where she is!"

"You tried to hurt her," *he* said. "You tried to make her impure with your body."

"I'm sorry," Stewart cried, "If I had known she was yours, I wouldn't have touched her. Why didn't you tell me?"

He put duct tape over Stewart's mouth and more tape on Stewart's fingers to spread them out evenly. Then pulled out his knife. His new knife.

That bitch, Kamielle, had somehow made him drop his best knife when she attacked him. She had slept with the FBI Agent and was no longer pure. She had to be sent to her absolution to ask for forgiveness and be cleansed by God. She was so evil not even *he* could send her to God. The Devil had welled up inside her and helped her cut him with his own knife. He'd hated to use the gun but didn't have a choice. And she hadn't died! Now she was with the FBI and he couldn't find her.

The files he'd taken from the police station didn't give much information. There were some wonderful pictures of whores who had been sent to their absolution, though. He'd spent hours looking at the pictures and taking his pleasure from the deaths of those whores. Again.

He took his knife and placed it above Stewart's taped fingers, bringing it down quickly. Stewart's pointer and middle finger of his right hand flew from the table with the force of the blow, blood spurting.

Stewart's eyes were wide with shock and betrayal as tears ran down his face and over the duct tape covering his mouth. Stewart began to shake and *he* began to laugh.

"You cannot handle the pain of God, Stewart. Your drugs and alcohol and sex have made you weak! You are not worthy of His love!" *He* brought the knife down again and all that was left of Stewart's right hand was his thumb. *He* picked up one of Stewart's fingers and held it to his nose. Then he held it near Stewart's. Stewart tried to recoil.

"Do you see what untainted flesh smells like? Now that this appendage is no longer connected to your body it's pure!"

Stewart began to panic even more. He was trying with everything he had to escape. His body was weak from capture and the more he struggled, the more blood pumped out onto the table from his four missing fingers.

"Let me help you go to God." *He* brought the knife down on Stewart's left wrist. Stewart's arm came free, waving back and forth, blood shooting over the table, the floor, and both men.

Stewart's screams were muffled by the tape as he struggled. *He* stood back and watched Stewart bleed out.

"I will find out where Kamielle went and I will send her to God."

MICHAEL DIDN'T SLEEP past noon, but Kamielle slept until three. Her emotional breakdown from the morning along with the stress of everything had definitely taken its toll. Michael expected Jon to show any time and was busy drawing a sketch of the hunting cabin when she walked out of the bedroom. Her eyes were red and her nose was pink as though she'd woken up and started crying again.

"I didn't mean to make you so upset," Michael said.

"It's a good kind of upset, if that makes any sense," she said, offering a weak smile.

"When it comes to women, strangely enough, it does." He stood and opened his arms. She walked into them and began to sob again.

"Shh, baby, everything's going to be alright."

"No it's not. Not until Thomas and Marcos are in jail or dead. I've been awake for a while and thinking about it. You're going to use me to catch them." She began her argument from that morning.

"She's right, you know." The voice seemed to come from nowhere and Kamielle jumped in Michael's arms.

Jon Carter stood at the kitchen door looking as deadly as Kamielle expected him to. What she hadn't expected was how much he would look like Michael. She'd made him into some kind of savior-demon in her mind with all the stories Michael had told her.

Jon was maybe an inch taller and had the same color eyes and hair. His shoulders were broader and he was bigger. He took up the door to the kitchen.

"Don't scare her, Jon, she's been through enough."

"I've stood here long enough to know me appearing in a door isn't going to scare her. I don't know many women who would offer themselves as bait for Thomas Patrick and Marcos Ramirez." Jon came through the door and dropped a green army-looking duffel bag on the floor.

"Mikey, love looks good on you." Jon held out his hand and pulled Michael into a half hug.

"Don't say the 'L-word', it freaks her out."

"Then I'll just keep saying it and let her get used to the idea. My darling Kamielle, I'm Jon. The better looking and more evil brother." He smiled.

"Very nice to meet you, Jon. I don't know if I can give you the vote of better looking, though."

"I'll take one of the two, love, and be just as happy. Everyone knows I'm the more evil brother."

She held out her hand. Jon looked her over from head to toe then pulled her into a tight hug. Taken temporarily off guard, she stood for a moment then wrapped her arms around his middle.

He whispered into her hair, "Neither one of us will let anything happen to you. I promise."

It was strange. The man emitted a soothing nature. It was like the Carter brothers had magical calming powers. At least on her.

"Since when have you become so touchy-feely? Julie's kids are the only ones you ever hug." Michael pulled Kami from Jon's arms and put her behind him.

"Jealous, little bro?" Jon grinned wickedly and Kami poked her head around Michael.

"He's just trying to reassure me," she said.

"I know, I know. He's also yanking my chain for the fun of it." Michael frowned at Jon then pulled Kami in front of him, wrapping his arms around her.

"You had me convinced he was such a bad-ass, I didn't know what to expect," she said.

"Oh, I am a bad-ass, love. I'll show you just how bad later. Right now we need to outline our plan for tomorrow morning because Thomas and Marcos fly in at seven a.m."

All the air left Kami's lungs in a rush. Michael pulled her closer and rested his chin on her head. She melted back against him, closing her eyes.

"You're going to be fine," Michael said.

"I believe you. I believe both of you." She looked at Jon and he winked.

The plan seemed complex to Kami, but Jon and Michael kept reassuring her it wasn't. The three of them drove to the hunting cabin so she would understand some of what they were talking about.

The cabin was set up like a studio apartment. It had a full bed and a set of bunk beds. There was a kitchen/dining room area and a small bathroom. Everything had originally run on a generator, but Jon had connected power a few years back. He said he stayed in enough places without power when he was working and wanted to be fairly comfortable at home, even when hunting.

Jon had boxes of remarkable equipment. There were goggles, helmets, gloves, clothing, and objects that looked like guns yet different. Kami felt like she was back in a spy movie.

This sent Michael and Jon into a discussion about more interesting 'spy toys' they could design. She learned they made gadgets and sold them. It was how they'd been able to spend so much money on the ranch.

"So you guys are like, what, super spies?" She looked back and forth between the two while they sat at the table.

"All the better to keep you safe, love," Jon said.

"Speaking of keeping people safe," Michael said, "Tony called this morning. The official autopsy showed all three victims died from a gunshot wound to the back of the head. Because we had possible names, they were able to match the three bodies with DNA.

"Camille Marshall had been missing for three weeks. She didn't have any family. Vincent and Sophia Dexter were siblings. Sophia was reported missing two weeks ago from New Jersey. She has a daughter who is in her twenties and the daughter's lucky she's not dead, too. Looked to me like Thomas and Marcos were covering their tracks. The daughter said she only saw her Uncle Vinnie a few times a year, but he sent money to her mom every month."

"So why were they all killed?" Kamielle asked.

"Tony, Dana, and I have an idea, but we won't know unless Thomas or Marcos tell us."

"Will you tell me?"

Michael glanced to Jon then back to Kami. "Only if you promise not to take any kind of blame."

"I'm finally realizing Thomas is the bad guy in these situations, not me." She shrugged.

Michael nodded. "The stripper's name was Camille, spelled differently than yours. She had blonde hair. We think Vinnie thought it was you. Her body showed signs of rape and they found a match by comparing it to Vinnie's DNA."

"So he screwed up a job and Thomas killed him and his sister?"

"Well, Thomas had them killed. I doubt he dirtied his hands." Michael watched her closely.

"But why kill the stripper?"

Jon cut in. "It only makes sense. You don't leave witnesses to crimes."

"Now I see why you get the vote for scarier brother." She watched him out of the corner of her eyes.

Jon shrugged. "I'm all about the job and always will be."

"Okay, enough of this. Tell me once more how we're going to execute this plan." Kamielle squared her shoulders and took a deep breath. She was getting the lingo down.

"From that corner," Jon pointed, "you can see the whole room. There's a camera."

She looked yet couldn't see anything. It wasn't a security camera like in a store.

Jon continued. "There are two different chips set up, one on each side of the room. They're for audio. We'll have Thomas and Marcos on video and audio hopefully confessing to every crime they've committed. I have yet to meet a criminal who didn't like to brag a little bit."

Michael took her hand. "We're going to spend tonight as normal as possible at our house. Tomorrow morning you and I are going to come back here and play house."

"Play house?" she asked.

"Jon laid a trail to this being my cabin and the main ranch is under a different name. They shouldn't even go near the other houses. Even if they do, there won't be anyone there. That's why I sent the hired help away for the week."

"Okay, so what does 'play house' mean?"

"We're going to act like this is where we're staying. We'll leave the curtains open, play cards, make breakfast, and act like we don't have a care in the world." He ran his thumb back and forth over her fingers.

"Where will you be?" she asked Jon.

"I'm going to be watching the outside of the cabin so we'll know when they show up. After a few hours, they'll figure out you're alone and Michael's going to leave."

"You're going to leave?" Panic edged her voice.

"No. I'm going to act like I'm driving to town but I'm going to get off the road and hike back here to keep you safe. We figure they'll come in as soon as you're alone."

"Then what do I do?" she asked.

"Exactly what you've been saying. Get them to talk. Make him tell you about the car accident and the heroin. Get Marcos to talk about the stripper, Vinnie, and his sister. See if they'll say anything about the attack from your house or the FBI agent and witness who were killed.

"As soon as they decide they're leaving with you, Jon and I kick their asses. Then we call the FBI to pick them up. Easy, neat, and clean." Michael rubbed the back of his neck.

"Easy, neat, and clean," she repeated.

"I'm going to leave you with a weapon so you'll feel protected."

"Where exactly are you going to be?"

"Remember my secret basement in the safe house?" Michael winked.

"I'll never forget that safe house basement."

Jon cleared his throat.

"Well, Jon and I made one here, first, to perfect the idea. We're going to be right underneath you."

"What kind of weapon are you giving me?"

"A gun and a knife. Have you ever shot a gun?" Michael asked.

"Yes. But it's been years."

"This one is a small pistol, a .38 snub nose revolver. You should be able to put it in your pocket. I want you to hide the knife somewhere in the room. Maybe under the chair cushion or under one of the mattresses." Michael chose a small pistol off the table of weapons.

"Can I go shoot a few times?" she asked, eyeing the gun.

"A woman after my own heart." Jon pretended to swoon. "Let's go plink in the yard while Michael watches on the outside surveillance cameras."

"Why are you taking her?" Michael demanded.

"Because I want to." Jon took her hand and pulled her out of the cabin.

Michael mumbled under his breath about annoying older brothers and went to the panel that hid the basement. He went down the steps and sat at the monitors. There wasn't any sound with the outside cameras, but the images were crystal clear.

Kami watched Jon set up pinecones on some rocks. "You're different than I expected."

"Same here, love." He walked back to her. "I figured you were some whining woman who had my brother wrapped around her finger. I really liked Crystal, and I don't want to speak ill of the dead, but she was high-maintenance. Michael did everything for her. I don't think she knew how to cook and she never drove the car. She made him happy, but I don't think she was right for him."

She eyed him cautiously. "Do you always say what's on your mind?"

"Always. There's no point in wasting time beating around the bush."

"I appreciate people who are straight-forward." She stared at the pistol. "I don't think I'm right for him."

"How can you possibly say that?" he asked.

"He met me by hitting me with his car. I didn't tell him the truth for the longest time, and I don't have anything close to a normal life." It all came tumbling out and she almost dropped the pistol when she put one hand over her mouth. She whispered, "Can he hear us?"

"No. Outside just has video surveillance, not audio."

"Oh, thank goodness!"

Jon glanced toward the cabin. "You haven't told him any of this?"

"We haven't had a lot of time to talk about the future. We've been a little busy keeping me alive." She laughed without humor.

Jon put his arm around her shoulders, taking the pistol from her trembling hands. She rested her head in the crook of his shoulder.

"Do you love my brother, Kamielle?"

She was silent for a few heartbeats then looked at the side of his face. "I really think I do. I don't know when it happened. I wondered if it was just lust or if it was the situation, but I really think I love him. I've never felt this way about anyone."

He tightened his hold in a hug of support. "Then don't give up on that. Tomorrow night you'll be your own woman. Not a fugitive from a lunatic husband, not a witness in protective custody. If you still feel the same, then you know it's going to stay."

"You and your brother should be relationship counselors." She squeezed her arm around his waist then stepped from his embrace. "Teach me to shoot something so we can get to this blissful Thursday night you're teasing me with."

They started with Jon taking a few shots and blowing the pinecones to pieces. He stood behind Kami when it was her turn and had her take a two-handed stance with her legs braced shoulder-width apart.

"The most important thing to try and remember is you don't want to flinch when you're expecting the shot. When you flinch, you tense up and tend to jerk your arms then you miss. Just squeeze the trigger gently, don't pull on it."

She fired and, of course, missed.

He turned her body so she was facing a tree twenty feet away. "Let's think about tomorrow. If you're going to need to shoot at someone, it'll be close range and he'll be about the width of the trunk of that tree. You're not aiming to kill, that's my job. You're aiming to hurt and scare. Shoot the tree and pretend it's a person."

Kami didn't balk as he expected. Jon felt her take a deep breath and release it. He felt her take another breath, and as she exhaled, she squeezed off a round. It hit the tree to the right side, bark flying in all directions.

"I did it!" She spun around with the gun in her hand and Jon ducked, taking it from her before she realized what had happened.

"Whoa, love. Don't ever spin around and aim a gun at someone unless you plan to shoot them."

Her hand flew to cover her mouth. "Oh! I'm so sorry! Are you okay?"

Michael laughed from behind them. "That was great! I wish I had a video camera. Jon, your face was priceless."

Jon glared at Michael then walked to the porch with the pistol. "She's yours, buddy, good luck not getting shot."

"Hey! I heard that!" she yelled.

He gave her a finger wave as he walked into the cabin.

Michael couldn't be shown up by his brother so he turned and shot one of the pine cones on the rock. It blew to smithereens just like the two Jon had shot.

"Okay, so you two are expert marksmen, I get it. Quit showing off and let me shoot." She fired off a round and hit the left side of the tree this time. She clicked the safety back, lowered her arm to her side, and faced Michael.

"Good job remembering to put on the safety and lower your weapon. You also did great hitting your target. Last time was to the right, this time was to the left, try for the middle."

He reloaded the pistol and handed it back to her.

"Why can't I wear earplugs or those headphone thingies?" she asked.

"Because if you really have to shoot at someone, they're not going to wait while you grab earplugs. Now, turn around, relax, and shoot."

She turned, taking her stance. A few deep breaths later she flipped the safety and fired two shots back to back into the tree.

Michael nodded. "Great job. Take two more."

She hit the tree both times. She wouldn't be winning any awards, but she'd scare the shit out of whoever tried to hurt her. Michael was fine with that.

She lowered the gun to her side and turned back to Michael. "Okay. Now what are we going to do?"

"How would you like to tour the ranch? If you're really nice to me, I'll show you the barn." He wiggled his eyebrows.

"The barn, huh? In the movies, doesn't the sexy cowboy

take the girl to the barn so they can fool around in the hay stack?"

"I'm going to have to get you better suited to country living, Princess. We don't have hay stacks. We have hay bales. But, yes, the sexy cowboy does take his girl to roll in the hay." He pulled her to his side, put the pistol in the back of his jeans, and they walked toward the Tahoe.

"Shouldn't we leave Jon the rig?" She looked back toward the cabin.

"Nope. He can walk." Michael waved over his shoulder to the camera Jon was watching.

In the basement, Jon flipped off the screen. "Yeah, piss off, baby bro. Just rub it in you have an amazing woman and I have nothing."

Jon mumbled to himself a little more then realized he'd never cared about having a woman in his life. Having a woman meant having a weakness. If an enemy found a weakness, they used it.

Part of the reason no one knew anything about Jon was because he kept to himself. He didn't make friends, he didn't date women. He did his job and moved on. He had sex, in fact, he had lots of it. Every country offered its share of clubs full of women who were out to score. When he had a need, he took care of it. It worked.

At least it had worked until he'd walked onto the back porch and seen Michael with the sweetest woman in the world cradled in his arms. Jon didn't wax poetic. Hell, he didn't even believe in happy endings. But the situation Michael had described to him resembled a fairy tale complete with princess, villains, and a knight in shining armor. Michael was Kamielle's knight and Jon had no doubt they would live happily ever after. The villains in this story didn't stand a chance when Michael and Jon were working together.

WEDNESDAY NIGHT CAME MUCH TOO FAST for Kami's peace of mind. The only good thing was Michael had shown her the difference between hay stacks and hay bales for about two hours in the barn. He'd even had a blanket to keep the hay from scratching their skin.

He'd given her a tour of Julie's house and she commented more than once how she'd like to have one just like it. Michael started forming a plan in his mind to have Julie design a house for them. He didn't mention it to her, though. He wanted to give her a little more time to get used to him and his ideas about the future.

The sun had set and Kami and Michael were alone in the ranch house. Jon had chosen to stay in the hunting cabin so the two could be alone. He'd eaten dinner with them, though. They'd gone over the plan one last time and Jon had disappeared into the darkness.

Kami was washing the dishes and Michael sat at the table drinking a beer. He'd offered to help, but she'd insisted on cleaning up.

With her back to him, she said, "It's going to be over by this time tomorrow, right?"

"That's the plan." He went to her.

She rinsed the last of the silverware. While she dried her hands on the towel, she turned. "What happens when this is over?"

"One thing at a time, Princess. I don't want you thinking past tomorrow. When they're arrested, we'll go from there. The only thing you need to worry about is keeping calm and safe."

They walked to the bedroom and silently got ready for bed. A heavy weight seemed to press around the room and not let them forget something could go terribly wrong tomorrow.

He pulled her in for a kiss. They tumbled to the bed, falling into a frenzy. It took him a few steadying breaths before he could slow them down.

"Tonight's about being safe and in love. Let me show you."

She surrendered to all he had to offer and cried silently in his arms afterward. He kissed away her tears and pulled her close.

"Try to sleep. Tomorrow's going to be a long day."

Eventually her breathing evened out. His last thought was he would take care of her tomorrow no matter what.

Even if he had to give his own life.

Chapter 17

Thomas detested flying commercially. The airport in Chicago had been deplorable, dealing with crying children and security. It was so much easier when you walked to the tarmac with your own jet waiting. You could load up the people and weapons you wanted. Luckily they had weapons and a car waiting for them when they arrived.

Thomas already had Delores checking into private flights back. There would be no way to bring an unconscious woman home on a regular airline. Money would buy him what he needed.

By the time they were in the car, it was after eight a.m. The man delivering the car was an associate of a contact from Idaho. The car had tinted windows and the man had checked Marcos's ID then handed over the keys. The trunk had weapons just as Thomas requested. It also had heroin for Thomas and Kamielle to use later.

Thomas spread the satellite photos on the back seat and looked at the top of the small cabin. There was a ranch to the east with five structures. He pushed those photos aside and studied the lone cabin, imagining all the ways he would make Kamielle pay for the trouble she'd caused.

He decided he'd even tell her about his plan for his heir so she'd know she'd be having his baby and nothing was going to happen to his unborn son this time around. Maybe he'd tell her about the car accident so she'd feel blame for the death of Shelby and the first baby. He'd also let her know it was her fault Vinnie, his sister, and the stripper were dead. If she hadn't run, none of them would have lost their lives. It was going to be perfect to watch her face and see her pain. That is what would make her go without a fight.

The drive to the first dirt road took almost an hour. Marcos parked the car and opened the trunk. Thomas rolled down all the windows and watched while Marcos concealed two pistols and knives. He put a water bottle, spotting scope, and binoculars in a small backpack.

"You are not to touch her or the FBI agent and you are not to let them see you." Thomas wiped imaginary lint from the front of his shirt.

Marcos fantasized for a few seconds about blowing his head off. "Yes, sir."

"I want you back here as soon as possible so I can go with you to get her."

Marcos walked into the trees. He was getting tired of working for this man. Patrick let too much emotion invade his professional life. His drug and sex addiction was getting worse and impairing his business decisions.

Marcos began planning. He could set up the business dealings in South America then take Thomas down. When they landed at the private airstrip, there could be a shooting accident. The armies were always attacking air strips and vehicle convoys. Thomas would die and Marcos could continue the empire. But first, he'd finish this so Thomas would get his mind back in the business game where it needed to be. There was also the added bonus of fucking the luscious Kamielle.

Marcos double-timed it to the cabin in less than twenty minutes. He found a secluded spot and set up the spotting scope. He spent ten minutes looking at the perimeter of the house. There was a small building behind the cabin. It looked like a shed for yard tools. There was a red Tahoe parked by the cabin. There didn't seem to be many footprints on the ground and Marcos was grateful for their stupidity in thinking they were safe. He smiled at the thought of the last time he had taken care of an FBI agent and witness.

He held his breath briefly when he saw the back of a slender, red-haired woman come into view. She stood at a sink and was talking over her shoulder. This should be her, but Thomas said she was blonde.

A man walked up and wrapped his arms around her, kissing her neck. Marcos pulled his head back from the scope then smiled and leaned back down. This was too good. She was fucking the FBI agent. Thomas would be enraged and Marcos figured he'd be able to torture the agent a little just for fun. Thomas would want the man and Kamielle to suffer. Maybe Marcos would be able to have more fun than he originally planned.

He watched for a few more minutes as they sat down at the table to play a card game. Marcos took that opportunity to scout the other ranch. He spent half an hour making sure the other place was empty. No one moved in any of the houses and the animals seemed docile. There wasn't even a dog to raise a ruckus, just farm animals.

When Marcos was satisfied everything was clear, he went back to the car. Thomas was pacing impatiently when he cleared the trees.

"What the hell took you so long?"

Marcos told Thomas about the other ranch being empty and the FBI agent and Kamielle being alone.

They walked back to the cabin. This time much slower than Marcos had made it the first time. There was no way Thomas could jog in his Italian loafers and Armani suit. At least he'd had the sense to leave his jacket in the car and roll up the sleeves of his dress shirt. He didn't know how to move stealthily through the trees. They wouldn't have been able to sneak up on anyone.

Marcos took Thomas to the cabin and handed him binoculars.

"She changed her hair. That won't do at all. We'll need to get it blonde as soon as we get—" he stopped as Kamielle and Michael walked to the porch.

Michael pulled her into his arms and kissed her. She wrapped her legs around his body and he turned to push her against the house. Thomas vibrated with rage, knuckles white as he gripped the binoculars. A growl of fury and understanding bubbled from his throat. Marcos had to keep from smiling. It was a small revenge, but it was sweet.

"I'll kill him. How dare he touch my wife!" Thomas let the binoculars drop away and looked at Marcos. "I want you to shoot him right now. Just shoot him in the leg and then we're going in there."

Marcos pulled his gun just as Michael started to talk.

"You sure you want Chinese food? It'll take me two hours just to drive to the nearest restaurant, wait for the order, and get back." Michael walked to the Tahoe.

"Wait," Thomas hissed. "This may work out better."

Michael took off down the driveway in a cloud of dust.

Thomas and Marcos watched Kamielle go back inside as Michael drove away. She left the front door open.

The men waited five minutes, then started to the cabin. There were no sounds except the occasional chirp of a bird and the buzzing of bugs. When they reached the porch, Marcos paused. If someone was going to intercept them to protect the woman, it would happen now. They stepped on the porch, trying to make sure the creaking of the boards wouldn't give them away. Kamielle had the refrigerator door open with her head poked inside.

"Hello, Kamielle."

Thomas's voice sent chills down Kami's spine. She turned from the fridge and looked into the cold eyes of the man she thought she'd once loved.

"I don't like your hair like this. We'll have to change it when we get home." He walked toward her and she dropped the can of Pepsi in her hand.

He reached out and picked up a section of her hair then let it fall. Looking into his lifeless eyes, Kami realized he was crazy. Completely and utterly insane. He talked like they were just going to hop in his car and drive away. He talked like he hadn't tried to kill her.

"You've been a bad girl, Kamielle. Running away from me. I've told the world you're dead so that means you can't show up somewhere alive. I'm going to have to keep you with me at all times. Are you ready to go home?"

Kami looked past Thomas at Marcos. He held up a gun and smiled with wicked intent.

"We have a little walk to the car, so I think we'll just sit and wait for a moment. Your FBI agent will wonder where you are when he gets back. Maybe we should wait for him?"

Before she could figure out what Thomas meant, he back-handed her. Her face shot to the side and she tasted blood.

"That's for running away from me!" he yelled. Then he struck the other side of her face. "That's for fucking the FBI agent!" He grabbed her shoulders and dragged her to one of the chairs at the table. "You did, didn't you? Fuck him? We watched you kiss him on the porch. You have become a whore!" He hit her again.

In the basement, Jon stood rigidly, staring at the screen, listening to the conversation going on above his head. Why hadn't it crossed his mind they would physically hurt her? It's what he would do. When you want someone to realize their mistakes, you make them feel pain, physically and emotionally. A door opened behind Jon and Michael walked in through a tunnel that connected from a shed behind the cabin.

As soon as he saw Kamielle sitting in the chair with blood on her face he clenched his hands. "What the hell are they doing?"

"They're going to wait for you to come back with dinner," Jon said calmly. "As much as I don't want to sit here and watch them beat her, he hasn't said much incriminating."

"I don't give a shit." Michael pulled his pistol and checked the clip.

Jon snaked out a hand, grabbing Michael's arm. "They aren't going to kill her. Give it a few more minutes."

Michael stared at him. "Nothing has ever come between us, Jon. If they hurt her any more, I'm never going to forgive you for not letting me go up there."

Jon looked back at the screen. Marcos had decided to frisk Kamielle and he found the .38 in her pocket.

"They're just going to smack her around a little bit, Mikey. It won't be fun to watch, but it's not going to kill her." Jon hoped he wasn't going to be proven a liar.

"Kamielle," Thomas said with a hint of sadness in his voice, "did you plan on shooting me?"

"I didn't even... I didn't know you were here." She wiped some blood from her lip.

"Why do you need a gun?"

"The FBI is trying to keep me safe. I was attacked at my home in—" she stopped.

"In Oakland. Don't think I haven't known where you were."

It was a stretch of the truth, but she didn't need to know that. It was because of her hospital stay and need for a safe house that Nathan Jorgensen had been able to find her.

"You sent that man to kill me, didn't you?"

"Now, my dear, I don't want you dead. You can't have my baby if you're dead. You know you're going to have my baby, don't you?"

Thomas sat. Marcos shut and locked the front door then pulled the curtains on the two windows.

"I figured as much," she whispered.

Thomas hit the side of her face again. "Look at me when I'm talking to you!" he yelled.

She lifted her eyes. While she was scared, she was also furious. She tried to hide it, pretending to wipe away tears.

"Why did you kill Shelby?" she asked.

"Oh, darling, do you mean that horrible car accident?" Thomas shrugged his shoulders.

"It wasn't an accident. I heard you talking outside my hospital room. I heard you say someone had messed up the brake job. I tried to stop the car and the brakes wouldn't work!" Her tears were real now.

"You were a meddling bitch!" Thomas yelled. "You wanted to know where our extra money was coming from. You weren't satisfying me anymore, either. You'd outlived your usefulness!" He stood. "Then you killed my baby!"

"You killed the baby!" She jumped up, swinging her arms at his chest. "You killed *my* baby!"

Thomas grabbed her arms roughly and shoved her down in the chair. "My baby, Kamielle! You're going to have my baby then die like you were supposed to a year ago." He pulled a syringe from his pocket.

"You wanted to know what was making us so much money? Well now you're going to know first hand. Heroin is a wonderful drug, my dear. It relaxes your body and mind. It allows you to be free of the confines of the world. You're going to love it."

Thomas took the cap off the syringe and in the basement Michael and Jon both moved to the stairs. They'd gotten some of a confession and neither of them were willing to let her be injected with the drug.

When they cleared the stairs and Michael threw open the closet door, Marcos and Thomas were both caught off guard. Kamielle grabbed the syringe from Thomas's hand, shoved it at his body, and dove under the table.

Shots fired.

Thomas's screams of pain echoed through the cabin and he fell next to the table. Kamielle stared numbly at his body writhing on the floor. He had a bullet wound in his knee, but his face was what she was looking at. The syringe was embedded in his left eye. She hadn't looked where she was shoving her hand. She had just used it as a weapon and hit the floor.

There had only been two shots fired. Was Marcos dead? Thomas continued to scream in agony as Michael walked to the table.

"Kamielle, honey, are you okay? I've got my gun on Thomas. Come out."

She crawled away from Thomas and scooted out on the other side of the table.

Thomas pulled the syringe out of his eye and was mumbling. His words were unintelligible, but it was clear he was cursing Kamielle, the FBI, and Marcos. Before they could take the syringe from him, he pushed it into his thigh.

"Shit," Michael said.

Michael pulled the syringe out of Thomas's leg, putting it on the table. His face was a bloody mess, his knee had been practically shot out, and now he had drugged himself.

Jon took the gun from Marcos. "You going to give me any trouble?"

"I don't like Patrick anyway. How about if I walk out of here and you never see me again?" Marcos held his hands up in a peaceful gesture.

Jon put the gun on the table, never taking his eyes or gun off Marcos. "Do you have any more weapons?"

"No. Patrick is stupid. He thought we'd come in here, kill that one," he lifted his chin to Michael, "take the woman and leave."

"You mean kind of like the last FBI agent you killed and the last woman you kidnapped. Wait, she died, too, didn't she?" Jon said.

"Will you let me go if I tell you what you want?"

"Tell me and I'll decide if it's worth your freedom."

"I was sent to the safe house by a leak in the Chicago FBI office. His name is Nathan Jorgensen." Marcos paused to see if they would deny a leak in their precious FBI.

"Interesting," Jon said. "I remember Nathan. Weasely little man. Pissed his pants when he realized I was going to kill him."

Marcos's eyes widened in surprise.

Jon continued. "Since I already knew about the leak, you're going to need to give me more than that."

Marcos smiled. "You had Nathan feed us the information? That's how you knew we'd be here."

"Shut up, you stupid Mexican," Thomas said.

"Do you see why I do not like him? I am not even from Mexico, I am from South America."

"Touching. Tell me something worthwhile," Jon said.

"Thomas had me kill Vinnie and his sister. He also had me kill a woman Vinnie thought was her." He pointed at Kami.

"I said shut up!" Thomas whined from the floor. He was covering his eye with one hand and had rolled to his side in something resembling the fetal position. It was hard to do when one of his legs wasn't working right.

"I left their bodies in the desert of Las Vegas. And, yes, I also killed one of your FBI agents and the woman who was in the safe house. That was on Thomas's bidding as well. I wasn't supposed to kill the woman. I was supposed to kidnap her. When I realized it was not Kamielle, I had to dispose of the mistake."

"Why didn't Thomas kill you for your mistake like he did Vinnie?" Jon asked.

"I am the best man Thomas has. He will not kill me."

"You see," Michael said, "that right there is why we can't let you go."

Marcos looked at Jon. "You killed Nathan Jorgensen. Surely you will not let the FBI man arrest me."

"Oh, oops, forgot to tell you. I'm Jon Carter. I'm Michael's brother and I work for the CIA. There's no way I can let scum like you loose on the streets."

Marcos glared and reached for one of the pockets on his cargo pants.

"Oh, no you don't. You lied to me, didn't you? You have another weapon." Jon waved his gun at Marcos and Marcos raised his arms, lacing his hands behind his head.

Jon leaned in and took the gun from the pocket. "I suggest you don't make any sudden moves."

As Jon reached to frisk him, Marcos brought his hands

down on Jon's head in a two handed swing. Jon's gun clattered to the floor. He used his downward momentum to rush at Marcos and hit him squarely in the chest with the top of his shoulder.

Marcos fell backward with Jon on top. In a flurry of hands, Marcos swung at Jon and punched him in the nose. Jon punched him back and Marcos's head bounced on the floor with the force of the hit. They grappled. Jon dove for Marcos again and they crashed through the wooden front door, landing on the porch in a heap of broken wood and flailing arms and legs.

Kami ran for the door and saw the sun glint off something shiny.

"Jon, he has a knife!" she yelled as Marcos sliced upward and cut Jon on the right side of his face.

At her frantic scream Michael ran to the door and leveled his gun at the two men squirming on the porch. Marcos was on the bottom and Jon's large body blocked any kind of clear shot.

"Jon, roll off him so I can shoot!" Michael shifted, looking for an opportunity.

Blood poured from the cut on Jon's face. Suddenly, he grunted in pain and his body tensed.

Jon felt the knife push into his stomach then Michael was there pulling him away. He used all his strength to pull himself out of his brother's arms at the same time he pulled the knife from his gut.

"You son of a bitch!" he yelled and plunged the knife into Marcos's chest.

Marcos stared up at Jon in wide-eyed shock. Jon pulled the knife out and shoved it back in two inches to the right.

By the time Michael got his grip back on Jon the porch was covered in blood. Marcos's sightless eyes were wide and the knife handle was all that poked out of his body. The blade was at least seven inches long and Jon had pinned the man to the porch.

Jon pulled off his shirt and pushed the wadded material against his abdomen. "God damn fucking son of a bitch stabbed me." His voice was a mix of pain and utter disbelief. He looked at Michael. "Next time our plan involves getting the bad guys to confess, we're frisking them, tying them to a chair, then letting them talk their little heads off. Shit!"

The cut wasn't as deep as it could have been, considering the length of the blade, but it still hurt like hell.

Michael helped Jon to his feet. Jon grabbed his gun and checked Marcos's pulse. You never left a body lying on the ground unless you knew it was dead. About the time that thought crossed his mind, they heard Kamielle scream.

The brothers barreled through the door.

Thomas had managed to pull himself into one of the kitchen chairs. He was covered in blood and he had Kami kneeling on the floor in front of him. The gun Jon had taken from Marcos was in Thomas's hand.

"Fuck. I never set a gun down without unloading it. Today's my day to do everything wrong." Jon was talking to himself as Michael moved farther into the room with his gun pointed at Thomas.

"Let her go, Patrick. We have you and Marcos on tape confessing to crimes, and there's nowhere for you to go."

As soon as he said it, Michael realized his mistake. What was killing Kamielle if Thomas thought he was going to go to jail or die?

"Then another death won't matter, will it?"

In the split second it took Thomas to glance at Kamielle, Jon and Michael both fired. Kamielle screamed and dove forward as Thomas's body rocketed backward in the chair. He crashed to the floor with twin holes in his forehead.

Kami stayed on the floor until Michael came to her. He knelt and put his hand on her shoulder. "You're safe, baby. Both of them are dead. It's over."

She pulled herself up and lunged against him. They fell back with the force of her momentum. "You said it was going to be easy, neat, and clean."

"Yeah, you did," Jon echoed from above them.

Kami looked up and saw Jon's face and stomach. "You're hurt." She looked at Michael. "Are you hurt, too?"

"No. There are five people in this cabin and I'm the only one not bleeding." He stood and pulled her up.

She walked to Jon and tried to wipe the blood from his right eye, making him hiss in pain.

Michael stepped over Thomas's body. He grabbed a roll of paper towels from the counter and two icepacks from the freezer.

The three of them walked outside, stepping over Marcos's body to get off the porch. They went to the Tahoe and Michael administered simple first aid to Kami then Jon. Jon wouldn't let Michael look at his 'cuts', as he called them, until Kami had an icepack on her already bruising face.

When Michael went to help Jon, he had mopped the blood from his own eye. "That's gonna leave a mark." He examined his sliced-open eyebrow in the mirror.

Michael waved his arm at the wounds. "You need stitches. On your face and stomach."

"It's no big deal. I've had worse." Jon shrugged and turned to Kamielle who was in the back seat. "I'm so sorry."

"What are you sorry for? You guys saved my life."

"I promised we'd keep you safe. You got hurt."

She shook her head. "I'm fine. You got more hurt than I did."

Michael looked back and forth between the two of them.

"You're both hurt, you're both not fine. We're going to call the FBI and have them send a clean up crew. We're going to get the video and audio surveillance handed over so no one will question what happened here today. And we're going to the hospital. In fact, we're going to the hospital first. I'll make phone calls while we drive." Michael glared at both of them and shut Kamielle's door. Then he waited for Jon to pull his legs inside and shut his door, too.

Michael got in the driver's seat. He turned and looked at Kamielle. "I love you, Princess. You're going to get used to it." He looked over at Jon. "I love you, too, and you better tell me you're not this careless in the field. I'm not burying you early, do you understand me?"

Jon glared at his brother. "I'm not this careless in the field. It's the reason I never work with people I care about. You distract me from what's important." Jon looked at his stomach. "Damn it to hell anyway. I'm going to Russia in a few weeks. At least there I won't care who gets hurt."

Kami sat speechless in the backseat. Halfway to the hospital she found her voice. "It's really over, isn't it?"

Michael looked at her in his rear view mirror. "We'll have to answer some questions and explain what happened, but yes, it's all over."

"Thank you, Michael."

"Don't thank me. When the police and the FBI are finally gone, you're going to have to deal with me."

"I think I'll be able to handle it." She smiled and blew him a kiss in the mirror.

Chapter 18

Thursday wasn't the blissful night Jon had convinced Kami she'd have. The FBI and state police arrived at the cabin within hours of Michael's call. They secured the crime scene, reviewed the audio and video surveillance, and dealt with the fact that Thomas Patrick was a very bad man. Not to mention a very dead man.

His psychotic ramblings had only answered a few questions. But now that the FBI would have access to his personal files, contacts, and secretaries, many other mysteries would finally be solved.

Jon had been kept in the hospital overnight because of the possibility of infection in the cut on his stomach. There wasn't any muscle or tissue damage, but he needed fifteen stitches. The cut above his eye needed five.

On Friday, Tony and Dana arrived at the ranch. Introductions were made, then Tony and Dana pulled Michael aside to discuss the prostitute serial killer case. Kami spent time fussing over Jon and making sure he was comfortable. She insisted he take the master bedroom so he wouldn't have to use the stairs and he told her he was going to get soft if she kept babying him.

By Saturday, the Feds were finally done at the ranch. The

five of them spent all weekend repairing the cabin. By Sunday night, everyone was exhausted, but parts of the cabin looked brand new. It was a job well done and they had bonded over the hard work and stories of Jon and Michael's childhood and Michael and Tony's college days.

MONDAY MORNING, Michael surprised Kami by cooking a huge breakfast in honor of her birthday. She was only twenty-seven, but felt like she'd already lived a lifetime and a half. They sat around the table discussing what everyone was going to do now.

"You know, when the Director realized the deaths in Las Vegas had nothing to do with the serial killer case, he wanted me to come back." Tony took a drink of coffee.

Michael saluted Tony with his mug. "Luckily I'd called him to say I needed assistance in Montana. He wasn't happy when he found out I was here. He almost shit Twinkies when I handed him Patrick and an FBI leak on a silver platter."

Michael and Kami looked at Jon.

"What? Patrick got rid of the leak. I may have doctored my discussion about Agent Jorgensen on the audio before it was handed over." Jon smiled.

Tony raised an eyebrow.

Jon said, "I could tell you but I'd have to kill you."

They all burst out laughing and Dana almost choked on her coffee.

Michael took Kami's hand. "Do you want to go out tonight for your birthday?"

"Actually, I'd rather stay in. Is that okay?" The ranch was peaceful and she wasn't ready to go out into the world.

"No, that's fine. I was just thinking when I took Jon to the airport we could go out."

"I have a better idea," Dana said. "I'm dying to do something. How about if you give Tony and me the name of a happening club or bar. That will let you two have a peaceful evening alone here for your birthday."

"Sounds good," Michael said. "And I'll take Jon to the airport so I can get groceries."

Jon's flight left for Virginia that afternoon.

Kami watched him put his duffel bag by the door. "How did you get here?"

"I flew."

"How did you get to the ranch?"

"That's classified." He glanced at Michael and smiled.

"Will you just tell her," Michael said. "If you don't, she's going to be pestering me."

"Michael has a buddy who flies helicopters. He picked me up from a flight that landed in Colorado and brought me in."

"Why didn't we hear the helicopter?" Kami asked.

"I have this ranch buried in paperwork and don't trust anyone to know where it is. He dropped me a few miles south at a clearing and I hiked in."

Kami shook her head and chuckled. "You live such a strange life."

"Don't I know it, love." He took her hand. "Mikey, Kamielle and I are going for a quick walk before we leave. Stay in the house."

Kami laughed on her way out the door.

"I have an answering service. I want you to have the number if you ever need anything. Anything at all." Jon gave her the number and she saved it into her cell phone.

"Mikey loves you, Kamielle."

"I know that."

"Put the poor guy out of his misery and just tell him you love him, too." Jon looked back at the house. Michael was watching them through the window.

She nodded. "I will. Tonight."

Jon looked back at her, gently touching her face. "If Mikey pisses you off or does you wrong, I'll come back and kick his ass. Then we'll run away together, okay?" He smiled.

"Sure." She laughed and hugged him. When she stepped back, she took both of his hands in hers. "Jon, thank you. I don't know what would have happened if you hadn't been here."

"You and Mikey would have been just fine." Jon dropped her hands and turned toward the house. "Okay, little bro, quit hovering by the door and get out here. Grab my bag, would ya?"

Michael came out with the duffel and Tahoe keys. "Was he trying to get you to run away with him?" he asked.

"Only if you treat me bad." She put her arm around Michael's waist.

"Well, then, you won't ever be running away." He threw the bag at Jon and pulled her into a tight hug. "I'll probably be gone about three hours."

"That's okay. I'll enjoy the silence."

Michael turned toward the house and yelled, "Medina! Petty! Let's go! I'll have you follow me to the first stoplight! You know where to go after that."

Tony came out looking as cool and sexy as always. He had on slacks, dress shoes, and a short-sleeved dress shirt. Dana appeared a few minutes later and all the guys stared.

"What? Is my hair messed up?" She put her hand up self-consciously.

"No, Dana, you look beautiful," Kami said. "The poor guys aren't used to seeing a woman fixed up. I'm always covered in bruises and you've been wearing jeans."

Dana looked like a totally different person. She'd put her

hair in a clip and dark tendrils framed her face. She'd borrowed some make-up from Kami and done a basic job. The dress was black with red roses. It was tight at her chest and hung loose after that, ending a good five inches above her knees. Tiny black buttons went the length of the front and the top three buttons were open revealing cleavage Tony hadn't known was there.

"Wow. I'll have to beat the guys off with a stick. Are you bringing your gun?" Tony stood staring.

"No. I wouldn't have anywhere to conceal it." She laughed and twirled on the porch.

"Why do you two get to hang out with hot women and I have to go back to work?" Jon asked.

"Because we're cooler than you," Tony said.

"And better looking than you," Michael added.

Jon glared. "If you ladies get tired of these yahoos, just look me up." He waved to Dana and blew a kiss to Kamielle.

"See you around, Carter," Tony called to him.

Jon put his duffel in the Tahoe and walked back to Tony. "Thanks for having Michael's back when I can't be here, Medina."

"Always," Tony said.

Tony and Dana went to Tony's truck.

"Happy Birthday, Kamielle," Dana called. "Enjoy your quiet evening."

"Thank you, Dana."

"Don't wait up for us!" Tony said. He was pretty sure he remembered how to get to the first stoplight. He drove off and honked.

Michael pulled Kamielle into a hug. "I'll be back as soon as I can, okay? Just relax and think about the fact we'll be alone soon."

"I won't be able to think about anything else." She stood on her tiptoes and kissed him hard. "Hurry back."

Michael and Jon got in the Tahoe.

"You're one lucky son of a bitch. You know that, right?" Jon said.

"Yeah. Now I just have to convince her to stay."

Jon didn't say anything until they were on the pavement of the main highway. "You going to ask her to marry you?"

Michael almost ran off the road.

"You love her, don't you?" Jon grabbed the dash but acted like they hadn't almost crashed.

"Sometimes it's like you're a mind reader." Michael glanced at him. "I was going to stop at Harrison Jeweler's and pick out a diamond ring. Is that insane?" Michael asked.

"No. Ever since Crystal, mom, and dad died, you and I have been talking about how short life is. We work jobs that could take us away tomorrow. I used to think it would be dumb to try and start a normal life. But what if you don't die young, you know? What if you live to be a hundred? I don't want you to be alone." Jon stared at the passing trees.

"What about you? What if you live to be a hundred?"

"There's no way I'm going to live that long and you know it. I run around the shit-holes of the world and I'm going to die in one of them. I came to peace with that a long time ago; you should, too. The fact I screwed up so badly on Thursday proves I work better without distractions." Jon looked at Michael. "You've shown me it's okay to care about people a little more, though. You and Tony work well together. You brought in Dana and that's something I never would have done. I could do some things a little different."

Michael glanced over at his brother then back to the road. "What about fall in love? Think you could do that?"

"There'd have to be a really tough woman to put up with my obnoxious ass and I think you already bagged her."

They rode the rest of the way to the airport talking about

new equipment to design and ideas for Christmas presents for Julie's family.

As they pulled up at the airport, Jon said, "If she hasn't agreed to marry you by the end of summer, I'll come back and talk some sense into her."

"I hope it won't come to that. Thanks for everything. Thanks for dropping whatever you were doing to help me."

"Always. Family comes first." Jon grabbed his duffel, waved goodbye, and disappeared into the airport.

Michael drove to the grocery store and parked. He sat for almost five full minutes before pulling back out and driving to the jewelry store.

He walked around a few minutes before finding the ring he could picture on Kamielle's hand. The words 'Princess Cut' jumped out at him. He chuckled.

It was a two carat princess-cut diamond solitaire on a platinum band.

His purchase tucked safely in his pocket, Michael went back to the grocery store. He bought the food he needed, a bouquet of flowers, and a bottle of wine.

He whistled as he drove home. He knew they had a lot of decisions to make and Kamielle still needed to get her life back. He honestly didn't care if they were engaged for five years as long as she admitted she loved him and agreed to get married some time.

Back at the ranch, Kami cleaned up the dishes, swept and vacuumed the floor, and started a load of laundry. All her homemaker tasks complete, she took a shower. Her comment about the boys always seeing her with bruises reminded her she hadn't really shown Michael her good side. He'd seen her every other way there was, though.

She took extra time to primp, lotion, perfume, and then chose a casual outfit. She dried and curled her hair, putting on a little makeup. It was as she was spraying on one last shot of perfume that she heard the front door open.

She ran to the living room and stopped dead in her tracks. Michael was not the one at the door. She found herself looking into the last face she ever would have expected to see.

She stared in disbelief. "What? Why?"

"I saw Agent Carter on the news with the FBI and the state police. It was quite a report. It seems you had a little trouble with your husband, Kamielle." He walked in and shut the door.

"I don't understand," she said.

"You will."

"To half of a job well done." Tony raised his wine glass and toasted with Dana. They sat across from each other at a small table in the back of Diamond Lil's Bar. They had decided on drinks and dinner first and then they would go to the club with the dancing. Dana wasn't sure what kind of music the place would have, but right now she was glad to not be stuck in Tony's truck or dealing with murderers.

"The other half of the job will not be discussed tonight," Dana said. "I'm tired of thinking of serial killers."

"Agreed."

The bar had a jukebox and they had to lean close to hold any kind of conversation. Tony noticed the delicacy of Dana's skin and the dark brown of her eyes. How had he ever thought she was plain? And now, her mouth didn't look too big for her face, it looked full and sexy.

"What do you want to eat?" he asked.

"I think I'm just going to have the club sandwich. What about you?" She smiled and Tony noticed a dimple in her right cheek.

"I was thinking of having a burger."

They ate and listened to the music.

When their bill was paid, Tony led Dana outside. "Are you up for dancing?"

"I'd love to!"

They walked a few blocks to a place named Moose's. Since it was Monday, the place wasn't that busy. They found a booth right away and Tony ordered a bottle of wine. After a glass each, a song came on Dana wanted to dance to.

The song had an up-tempo beat and she grabbed Tony by the hand, dragging him on the floor. They shimmied and shook and Dana laughed when Tony spun her around. He spun her again so she was facing away from him and they ended up doing a little bump and grind as the song ended.

They went back to the table and Dana almost drank an entire glass of wine to quench her thirst.

"You're a great dancer," she said.

"I like to go out on the weekends. Dancing is a good way to relieve stress. You're not too bad yourself." He winked.

"I used to go out dancing all the time. Then I started dating this guy who didn't like to. I haven't been dancing since we got together."

"So. Are you still dating this guy?" Tony tried to sound like he didn't care one way or another.

"No. Remember when you came to work last week and I told you I was having a bad couple of days? Well, we'd just broken up. He's a cop. It's too hard to date someone you work with, you know?"

"I've never dated anyone in law enforcement."

"You haven't?" she said.

"Nope. I don't like work to overlap with my personal life. I have to say it's been nice to hang out with you and have something in common. This has been fun these last few days. You know, when you take out the part with Thomas, Marcos, and the serial killer."

She laughed and looked into his eyes. In her experience, guys who looked like him never fell for girls like her. She was plain and simple, he was exciting.

Tony pulled her back to the dance floor when a slow song came on. She started out with six or so inches between them and as the song went on, her body moved closer to his. By the time the song ended, she was plastered from knee to chest against him and not ready to pull apart.

Since not that many people were in the place, most of the couples only danced during a slow song. In order to keep people on the floor, the DJ played another one.

Tony pulled her tighter against him and put his mouth by her ear. "You look beautiful tonight, Dana."

"Thank you. Does that mean I didn't look beautiful before?"

"No, you've always looked beautiful. I just thought we'd come far enough in our relationship I could compliment you like this."

They danced through the second song and Dana began to think they were coming close to crossing a line between professional and personal. They were obviously beyond most professional relationships.

She'd been stuck in a car with him for most of a week and they'd lived at the Carter ranch for the weekend. They'd laughed and gotten to know each other better. This was another subtle shift. People who worked together didn't slow dance like this. They also didn't enjoy the feel of each other's bodies.

When the song was over and a fast song started, Dana excused herself to the restroom. Tony watched her walk away, enjoying the sway of her hips, and caught himself almost following her. Being around Michael and Kamielle had made him miss the company of a good woman.

What the hell, he'd give it a shot. Dana was pretty and seemed to like him. Maybe they'd get along in the sheets as well as they did working together. He slipped the DJ a twenty and asked him to play two slow songs in a row again.

When she returned from the restroom, he refilled their wine glasses.

"Do you think both of us should drink anymore? One of us needs to drive back to the ranch." She sipped her wine.

"By the time we're ready to leave, I'll be fine. If for some reason I'm not, we'll get a hotel room."

Her eyes opened wider and she took another drink.

The DJ played the first of the slow songs and Tony took his opportunity. "Come on. I like dancing with you."

He pulled her close. The song was over much too soon, but the DJ did his job. When the music segued right into a second slow song, Dana sighed into Tony's shoulder.

He pulled his head back just a little and she raised her head to look at him. Taking the advantage, Tony lowered his lips to hers. The kiss was light and gentle.

"Tony?"

"Don't think tonight. Let's just see where this goes."

This time he kissed her harder. He angled his head and traced his tongue along the seam of her lips. She opened her mouth and sucked lightly on his tongue. The kiss took on a mind of its own after that. They forgot about dancing and Dana wrapped her arms around Tony's neck. He put his hands on her hips and spread his fingers down over her butt.

Tony's pocket vibrated and they jumped apart as though they'd been shocked. Their bodies had been so close together Dana had felt the vibration, too.

"Shit," Tony mumbled as he pulled the phone out. It was a text from Shawn Doyle in the FBI forensics lab.

Tony looked at Dana. She seemed a little shell shocked and Tony imagined his face mirrored hers.

Tony rubbed a hand down his face. "It's the forensics lab. I had them get back on the knife used to attack Kamielle in hopes we could pin one more attempted murder on Patrick."

"Um, good thinking." How the hell could the man string together coherent sentences? Dana felt like her brain was fried from that kiss.

"I better see what he's got." Tony stood awkwardly.

"Yeah. It could be important." She looked everywhere but at him.

He walked to the edge of the dance floor with his phone. Dana followed on complete autopilot.

"What have you got for us?" Tony plugged one ear. "Just a minute, I can't hear anything."

He dropped a fifty on the table and signaled the waitress. Taking Dana's hand, they went out the front door. She stared at their joined fingers and abruptly let go once they were outside.

"I'm going to put you on speaker phone so Officer Petty can hear what you have to say."

The voice came over the speaker, "I finally got a chance to do some DNA searches on the knife from the Kamielle Johnson attack. It got pushed down on the priority list since you left town. Sorry 'bout that. I came up with some really interesting information, though. You owe me big time, Medina." Shawn laughed. "Maybe I'll make you take me out on one of your wining, dining, and dancing dates. You know all the hot chicks and always manage to score on those."

Dana gasped and Tony looked at her like a deer caught in the headlights.

"It wasn't like that with you, Dana, I swear."

"What?" Shawn asked.

Tony looked at his phone then at Dana. "I swear."

When she didn't respond, Tony closed his eyes. "Just get to the point, Shawn."

"Okay, okay, sheesh. I can tell you don't want to share your black book. Anyway, the knife had trace blood from five different sources. Four were female: Kamielle Johnson, Karen McKay, Jessi Andrews, and Shyla Marx. The fifth was from an unknown male."

"Jesus. You just named three of the prostitute serial killer victims."

"It gets better. The unknown male has DNA markers in common with Stewart Martin. As soon as I saw that, I sent some boys to find him. He's dead. They found him duct-taped to a chair with his fingers cut off his right hand. His entire left hand was cut off. It was still duct taped to the table. He bled out. There were pictures of the dead prosti-tutes taped all over his walls. The techs said they're our pictures."

Dana and Tony stared at each other. The kiss was forgot-ten. Tony's black book was forgotten. All that mattered was the killer had DNA markers in common with Stewart Martin.

Tony took the cell off speakerphone. "Shawn, I need you to transfer me to the Director now." He grabbed Dana's hand, dragging her to the truck.

When he was connected to the director, Tony said, "Sir, I need you to get some men on Justin Martin. He's a lawyer and he's Stewart Martin's brother. I have good reason to believe he's the prostitute serial killer and he's trying to kill Kamielle Johnson, Kamielle Patrick. Whatever her name is."

Dana pulled out her cell. "I'm calling my captain."

They both relayed the information they had then hung up to wait for a call from either the FBI or the Oakland PD about the whereabouts of Justin Martin.

"Why did he set his sights on Kamielle? His M.O. is prostitutes on the full moon. She's not a prostitute and it was after the full moon when he attacked her." Tony couldn't figure out why Kamielle was a target.

"His brother was her next door neighbor. Maybe he got infatuated with her. Karen wasn't a prostitute."

"She used to be. She'd been clean for over two years, but she'd been involved in some really bad stuff."

"Okay," Dana paused to gather her thoughts. "Let's say he became infatuated with Kamielle. He attacks her, it doesn't go as expected, so he's been looking for her so he can finish the job. You don't think he can possibly know where she is, do you?" Dana sounded horrified at the thought.

"He's a lawyer. He has access to private and privileged information. It's how he got my files from your department. No one looks twice at a lawyer going through files. Jon laid a trail for Patrick to follow. Justin Martin could find the same trail."

"We have to call the house. Michael would be back from town by now, wouldn't he?" Dana stared at Tony.

"Unless he ran any other errands. He was going to the store and I don't know how long that would take."

Tony tried to call Michael's cell. It said he was unavailable. Damn it. He tried the house next and the phone just rang. Tony gave Dana the number for the house. They both kept redialing, hoping someone would answer.

Tony finally got through to Michael ten minutes later.

"Is Kamielle with you?"

"No, I'm just pulling into the driveway. Why?"

"Do you have your gun with you?"

"Of course," Michael said.

"Listen and don't freak out." Tony tried to tell the main parts as quickly as possible so Michael would get the gist of the problem.

He heard Michael yell Kamielle's name six or seven times.

"She's not here!" Michael's voice broke. "The coffee table is overturned and there's a picture of Stewart pinned to it with a knife. He's taped to a chair and dead. Justin wrote me a message."

"What does it say?" Tony almost didn't want to know.

"It says, 'Kamielle's mine and you're next'."

Chapter 19

Kamielle woke in the back of a moving vehicle. She had the mother of all headaches and her limbs felt like they were being poked with millions of pins and needles. Not only was she tied, but there was a gag in her mouth and something over her eyes.

Her shock at seeing Stewart's brother, the lawyer, still hadn't gone away. Why had he kidnapped her? She'd only met him that one time with Michael and didn't understand what he was doing.

She was lying on her side with her hands and feet tied behind her back. Her ankles and wrists felt like they were connected and her heels were almost touching her butt. She took deep, even breaths to keep her head from spinning and listened closely to what was going on around her. Gripping the ties connecting her ankles and wrists, she loosened the pressure on her joints. The rope was digging into her skin and she knew she was bleeding.

Thomas and Marcos are dead. What's going on? Did Thomas hire this guy? Where's Michael? She rubbed the side of her head against the floor of the vehicle, trying to push the blindfold off. It was slow going, and now she had rug burns on her cheek, but eventually she was able to free one eye.

She was in some kind of van. Her head throbbed from the effort, but she managed to see there were no windows on the sides and the back door windows had something over them. The floor, walls, and ceiling of the van were carpeted. The lawyer was whistling along to a song on the radio. Whistling. Who was in a good mood when they'd kidnapped someone? Freaks. That's who.

Kamielle tried to make sense of why Stewart's brother had taken her. Hell, she couldn't even remember the man's name. She replayed the moment in the house when the lawyer had lunged at her. She'd tried to move out of the way but tripped over the coffee table. It had broken under her weight when she fell. He'd stabbed a knife next to her head then grabbed her by the hair, yanking her up. The last thing she remembered was walking toward the front door and trying to run outside. He'd hit her on the head with something. Her head chose that minute to throb and remind her.

They drove for what felt like endless miles. She had no idea what time it was, although the sun was still out. Somehow Michael had to find her. He should have been back to the ranch at any time. But how in the world could he know where she was? Or who had her?

"I know you're awake. You can quit trying to pretend you're not. I heard you move and," he looked at her in his rear view mirror, "I can see you've pulled off part of your blindfold."

"Whaf hu u wan?"

He laughed. "What do I want? Oh, I want you, my darling. I also want to see Carter's face when he finds your dead body."

"Whyf?"

"Because he kept getting in the way. I have so many lovely things to show you and tell you first."

There was a loud noise and the van careened to the right. The force sent Kamielle rolling. The good news was her blindfold slipped the rest of the way off. The bad news was she slammed against the wall and there was horrible pain in her right wrist. It was a good thing her hands were practically numb because it kept the pain from being more severe. She grunted and yelled into the gag as the lawyer slowed the van.

"Damn it!" he yelled. Then looking toward the sky he said, "How can I do Your bidding if You keep giving me such hard obstacles?" Finally, he lowered his head and mumbled, "The Lord helps those who help themselves."

Justin got out of the van and looked at the front driver's side tire. It had blown out, leaving little pieces littered on the road. He'd had the van for two years and only took it out when he went hunting on the full moon, so the tires weren't that worn. It didn't matter now. He had a damn tire to change.

He looked up and down the highway. There wasn't a sound coming from any direction. He opened the back doors of the van and Kamielle squinted against the light. He unhooked the spare tire and pulled out the jack and tire iron.

"This will just take a minute, my dear, and we'll be on our way."

"Uck u!"

"Such language. We'll have to discuss that along with your whoring ways."

He slammed the doors and began to jack up the front of the van. He changed the tire and was tightening the lug nuts when he heard a car in the distance. The first wave of fear crashed through him when a Montana Highway Patrol car crested the small hill just behind him.

The car slowed, turned on its lights, and pulled behind the van. The officer stepped out of the car, nodding his head to Justin. "Looks like you got yourself a flat there, sir."

Well no shit, Sherlock. "Yes, sir. But I have it all under control now. I'll just get this tire loaded and be on my way." Justin gripped the tire iron in his right hand.

"Well, how about if I help you? No sense in getting your dress clothes any dirtier."

Justin looked down. There was gravel and dirt embedded in the knees of his slacks and a slash of grease across the front of his white dress shirt.

"Well, seeing as I'm already dirty, that won't be a problem, Officer."

"Nonsense. It's been a slow day. I'm here to serve."

Kamielle heard the voices and had been trying to yell. Despite the pain, she started slamming any part of her body that would reach against the side of the van. The patrolman heard the muffled noises, but before he could pull his weapon and ask what was going on, Justin Martin was swinging a tire iron at his face.

MICHAEL, Tony, and Dana stood in the Kalispell Sheriff's office. It had been over an hour since Michael had arrived at the ranch to the note from Justin Martin. They didn't have an accurate timetable for how long Kamielle had been missing. Assuming the worst, Michael and Sheriff Cline chose three hours. If Martin drove sixty mph, they were looking at a search radius of just under two hundred miles. That was a lot of ground to cover.

"We need something, a lead, anything," Michael said.

Dana was pacing the small office and her movements were being watched by every man in the room. Tony found himself suddenly jealous.

"We've got an APB for Justin Martin out over three states: Montana, Wyoming, and Idaho," Tony said.

"Yeah, but we don't know what he's driving or if he's disguised himself in any way." Michael said.

This was worse than when Crystal had died. He hadn't known she'd been the target of a killer. Standing in the office twiddling his damn thumbs was driving him crazy. Kamielle could be hurt or—

"Let's think about this from our normal point of view. Put it out of your mind for a minute who we're looking for," Tony said. "He isn't going to be disguised. He practically left his calling card for you by using the picture of his brother. He also carved your name into Karen's chest. This has become personal for him and he's going to want some kind of showdown. There's also the fact we've already requested a list of all vehicles registered in his and Stewart's names to give us some possible vehicle leads. We're doing something."

"Well, it's not enough!" Michael yelled.

Sheriff Cline cut in, "I've got a call on line two I think you're going to want to hear. It may have something to do with what's going on." He put the phone on speaker.

"Sir, I found a Highway Patrol car on the side of the road about forty miles from town. It's bad."

"Tell us," Sheriff Cline said.

"The patrolman's been beaten with a tire iron, sir. He's barely alive. The medics are on their way, but I don't know if he's going to make it."

"I want you to get in his car and upload the video on his camera. I never thought I'd say this, but thank God for technology."

"I'll do that as soon as the medics have him secure, sir. I can't just let him lay on the road alone."

Michael wanted to scream at the officer to upload the

footage now. Dana noticed his increased tension and walked over to pull him away from the phone.

"I know you want him to do it now, but that's one of our own lying in a pool of blood, Michael. He deserves a few minutes of our time." Dana rubbed his arm.

He pulled back. "You think I don't know that? Hell, this may not even be because of Justin Martin. But it's something, damn it! At least it's something to rule out or something to follow! I hate this!"

Five minutes later, Michael, Dana, and Tony were hovered behind the chair of Sheriff Cline's desk. Cline was on his computer accessing the camera footage from the car. They scanned through miles of driving until they saw the car come up on a van pulled over on the side of the road. The images were grainy, black and white, and there was no sound, but what transpired was clear.

The officer got out, gestured to the tire, and then the back of the van. The man changing the tire stood and Michael sucked in a breath. "That's Justin Martin."

The officer reached for the back handle of the van and Justin swung the tire iron at his head. Dana turned away but Michael, Tony, and Cline watched Justin hit the officer seven times. Justin raised his face and arms, holding the bloody tire iron to the sky, yelling.

He ripped open the door to the van and they all saw her. Kamielle was on her side, tied up and gagged. Michael cursed repeatedly and started stalking the room. He pulled at his hair then went back to the computer.

Justin was waving his arms and pointing behind him while Kamielle lay there. He threw the tire iron at her, slammed the doors, and got in the van. It sped away and was eventually out of sight.

"If he so much as harms one hair on her head, I'll kill the son of a—"

"We have a road to canvas." Tony took off out the door with Dana and Michael right behind him.

The Sheriff's department split into teams of two and had four cars behind Tony's truck. They drove until they found the scene of the attack. There were three other Montana Highway Patrol cars parked next to the downed officer's car.

Tony stopped. A patrolman walked up to them.

"You must be Agents Carter, Medina, and Petty. Sheriff Cline called to say you'd be by here. He tells me the guy who beat my buddy has a hostage and is a serial killer?"

Michael nodded. "Listen, I grew up around here. There are four farms you can get to off this road over the next ten miles. Any of them empty that you know about?"

"Well, one's for sale about four miles that way." The patrolman pointed down the road. "Think he'd be dumb enough to stop there? That'd be like waving a flag."

Tony turned to look at Dana in the back seat. "I think the attack on the patrolman rattled him; it wasn't part of the plan. Right now he'll just be looking for a place to go and wait for Michael with Kamielle."

Dana nodded. "I agree. He's not thinking straight right now. That's going to make his decisions poor, but it's also going to make him more dangerous."

Michael looked back and forth between the two. "You're the profiling experts." He looked at the patrolman. "We're going to sneak up to the place for sale and check it out. Have your guys stay in contact with the Sheriff's Department. Thanks, again."

Tony drove until he saw the For Sale sign. He turned onto the road and Michael unbuckled his seat belt, pulling out his pistol.

"Stop and drop me off just as the farm comes into view. Don't let them go roaring up there. Set a perimeter sweep and check the barns first. I'm going to the house."

"You can't just run in there half-cocked. You have to play this by the book," Tony said.

"Screw 'by the book'. I almost lost her to this sick fuck a month ago. A few days ago I almost lost her again. I'm going in there and finding her." Michael opened the door.

When the truck was almost stopped, he jumped out. He took off at a dead run to a small building near the house.

The place seemed deserted. He watched for a few minutes and didn't see any movement. If they were here, he didn't want Kamielle with Martin a second longer than she had to be.

Screaming ripped through the air. All the hair on Michael's neck stood up then, abruptly, the shrieking stopped.

"Fuck this." Michael started running across the field. He was beyond trying to be stealthy and careful.

Justin hauled Kamielle to the back of the van by jerking on the rope connecting her arms and legs. She cried in pain as it pulled her shoulders back and yanked on her wrist. When she was at the back of the van and prepared to fall on the ground, Justin cut the rope and the pressure on her joints lessened. Her whole body ached and she was sure her wrist was broken. Every movement shot fire up her arm and brought tears to her eyes.

"We're going to have ourselves a little fun. Don't try anything stupid. I'd hate to have to hurt you early."

Kamielle let her body go limp as Justin tried to pull her from the van. His name had come to her when he'd been screaming at her about how she'd killed a cop. Where was the cool and composed lawyer she'd met? The man was insane. Maybe even more insane than Thomas, and that was saying something.

"Ake off uh ghag."

"May as well, there's no one to hear you scream but me and I like it when they scream." Justin pointed to an ice chest. "I should get a motor home. It would be so much easier to travel with my treasures if I had a refrigerator."

Kamielle had no idea what he was talking about and at the moment, she didn't care.

"Sit up so I can remove your gag."

She tried to roll to a sitting position, but her muscles weren't cooperating. Justin became impatient and yanked. Of course he grabbed the right arm, and the rope pulled on her broken wrist. She moaned in pain. It was the wrong thing to do. If possible, he looked even more insane.

"Do you think it hurts now? Wait until we play with my knife again. I owe you."

He unbuttoned his shirt and pulled it open. Kamielle stared at a healing cut on the right side of his chest. She turned away.

When the gag was off, she moved her jaw back and forth, swallowing. "What do you mean 'I owe you'? I don't understand what this is about, Justin."

"Oh, goody, you do remember my name. But you really don't know why you're here?"

She looked around. They were parked in some kind of shed. No, barn. It was too big to be a shed. There was a hay loft with no hay and some stalls for animals. Late afternoon sun filtered through the cracks in the boards to illuminate the dust floating in the air.

"No, I don't know why we're here."

"I want you to kiss my scars."

She recoiled. "What? No!"

Justin grabbed her head, pushing her face into his chest. The smell of him and the pain of her body were too much. She bit down and he yelled. His fist smashed into the side of her face and she fell back crushing her hands into the small of her back.

"You bitch! Let me show you what happens to bitches who don't know their place in life. Let me show you what happens to whores!"

Justin opened the lid of the ice chest, pulling out a jar of some kind of food. It looked like meat, little sausages.

As Kamielle's vision cleared, she realized she was looking at fingers. A jar of fingers. This time she did throw up. Justin stood at the back of the van laughing.

Then he did the unthinkable. He dumped the fingers all over Kamielle's face and upper body. She started screaming. Justin hit her twice. She threw up again.

"Don't get vomit on my women! They've been cleansed. Can you smell their purity? You'll be pure soon."

He pulled a knife and slit open the front of her shirt. She rolled away, trying to get the fingers to fall off her skin.

He trailed the knife between her breasts. "I remember these tits. So nice and pretty. How are your scars?"

He sliced the fabric holding the cups of her bra together. He traced the tip of the knife over the thin scars. Everything clicked into place. It still didn't make any sense, but she knew who he was.

"You're the prostitute serial killer. You're the one who attacked me. Why?"

"Don't call me a killer! I'm not a killer! Do you know what blood looks like in the moonlight? It's thick and black. The moonlight shows blood for what it really is. It has to be cleansed. I sent those women to God to be cleansed. Mother taught me to praise God."

He started rambling about being tied to a chair in a basement, but Kamielle was only catching every other word.

He pushed harder with the tip of the knife while tracing her scars. She cried out and he hit her in the face. She cried out again and he hit her in the stomach.

"I'm going to cut you. I'm going to make you bleed. I'm going to fuck you in a pool of your own blood. Then I'm going to carve Carter's name in your chest just like I did in Karen's. He's been too close for too long. Don't worry, though, you won't be dead.

"I'm going to take your ring finger so you can never get married and I'm going to take your ear so you won't be able to hear. Women don't listen anyway. Why do you need ears? I might just leave you alive. See if Carter still wants your body after I've used it."

Justin put the knife to his mouth and licked. He held it to Kamielle's mouth. "Taste."

She clamped her lips shut and shook her head.

"I'm tired of you not doing what I want. I think it's time to take your finger."

He rolled her over to get to her hands, but she tightened her fingers as much as she could. It hurt to make fists, though if she could save her fingers, she'd deal with the pain.

After trying to maneuver her, Justin finally cut her wrists apart and retied them in front of her. The rough treatment of her right wrist was excruciating.

Justin looked at it. "I think you broke it, dear."

"Don't call me 'dear'," she hissed at him. He slapped her and she fell sideways.

"I'm tired of psychotic men trying to kill me."

He leaned over to get at her hand and Kamielle shored up

every bit of strength she had left. Spinning on her hip, she threw her bound feet at Justin's head. He slammed the knife down on her hand and flew back from the van as her feet connected. She heard wood breaking and wondered if he'd crashed through the floor somehow.

She heard gunshots.

The barn was silent for a few heartbeats before yelling broke through the haze.

"Kamielle! Kamielle! Where are you? Talk to me!"

"Michael." Her voice wasn't loud enough.

She tried to sit up and couldn't. She looked down and saw the knife poking up from her hand. There was blood all over.

"Michael," she said a little louder.

He came rushing to the back of the van and looked at her. Her shirt and bra hung off her arms, her chest was a mass of cuts and blood, and her hands were bleeding.

"Oh, baby." He pulled out his own knife and cut the ropes around her ankles. "What happened? Why did Martin fall on the ground?"

She looked at him with wide eyes. "I kicked him in the head."

"Oh, Princess. You just keep surprising me." He tried to laugh and it came out strangled. "I thought I was going to find your body."

"I thought you were, too." She sat up with his help and they both stared at her hands.

Her right wrist was swollen. Her left hand had a knife sticking out of it.

"I'm going to cut your wrists free first and go from there, okay?"

About that time Tony, Dana, and two cops came running into the barn with their weapons drawn. When they saw Martin on the ground with a bullet in his forehead and Michael standing with Kami at the back of the van, they lowered their guns.

Michael helped Kamielle scoot to the edge of the van and he pulled the pieces of her shirt over her chest.

"I need a medic, now!" he yelled over his shoulder. "Tony, Dana, get over here and help me."

The ropes fell from Kamielle's wrists, but she left her hands held together, afraid to move too much.

Dana cursed when she saw the knife. Tony pulled his shirt over his head and gently set in on Kamielle's knee. He lowered the hand with the knife onto it.

"Michael's going to pull out the knife and I'm going to wrap my shirt over the wound, okay?" He stared into Kamielle's eyes and his gut clenched when he saw her bruised and bleeding face along with the tears.

She nodded her head. Dana walked to her other side and braced Kamielle's right arm so she wouldn't jar her wrist. Michael pulled the knife out causing her to scream in pain. Her head dropped forward onto his chest.

"I know, baby, I know. I'm so sorry."

She tried to relax. "Remember the day you met me? The day you hit me with your car? I had dubbed that my worst day ever. I'd like to change it to my birthday being the worst day ever. Can we legally change my birthday? Because I don't think I can handle another June 14th and live through it."

Michael stroked her shoulders. "I'll do whatever you want me to, Princess."

The ambulance pulled up twenty minutes later. They loaded Kamielle into the back and Michael got in with her. Thomas and Marcos were dead. Stewart and Justin were dead. There shouldn't be another living soul out to get her.

"I knew you were trouble the first time I laid eyes on you."

He wanted to hold her hand, but both were injured. He settled for smoothing the hair back from her forehead.

She met his eyes. "I got all dressed up for you tonight. I even put on makeup. I realized my crack to Dana about you only seeing me in bruises was true. Now here I am again." She started to cry.

"I love you no matter what you look like, baby."

"I know. I love you, too."

He stopped stroking her hair. "Did they give you pain meds?"

"Not yet, why?"

"You just admitted you loved me and I was wondering if you were under the influence of drugs." He tried to smile, but couldn't.

"I'm under the influence of having my life flash before my eyes too many times. I don't want to be alone, Michael. I want to be happy. With you. I don't know if it will be happily ever after, but I know we'll do what we can."

Michael leaned down and kissed her. "I bought you a present for your birthday. This wasn't how I planned to give it to you."

"Do you want to wait until I'm not in the hospital? Or maybe until I have use of at least one of my hands so I can thank you?" She smiled through her tears. It was going to be alright.

He stood as much as he could in the ambulance and pulled a velvet box from his pocket. He knelt next to her.

"I know this is soon. But we know so much about each other and we've been through more together than most people ever will. I can see myself falling asleep beside you every night and waking up next to you every morning. I'll give you happily ever after, Princess. I will. Let me." He flipped open the ring box.

Kamielle sobbed and looked into his eyes. "I love you so much, Michael."

"Is that a yes? I didn't hear yes."

"Yes! Yes! Yes!"

The ambulance crew, police, Tony, and Dana cheered.

"This is beautiful, but I think we need to get Kami to the hospital." Dana had tears in her eyes.

"You're right." Michael looked at Tony. "I'm riding with her. Will you meet me there?"

"You bet."

Two medics got in the front of the ambulance and one got in the back to set up an IV drip. He waited for it to get going then injected a pain killer into the stream.

"Before I am under the influence of drugs, I want to tell you again I love you. It feels good to say it out loud." Her eyes started to drift shut. "I love you, Michael."

"I love you, too. But don't forget who said it first."

Chapter 20

After two days in the hospital, Kamielle got to go home. 'Home' was the ranch. Jon had flown back to Montana as soon as he'd gotten the voice mails from Michael.

Julie, her husband Bob, and the kids were home at the end of the week. They were happily surprised to have Michael and Jon home and even more surprised when they got the story involving all that had gone on in their absence. Julie complained they never let her know what was going on in their lives and Bob thanked the men for that.

Kamielle's right wrist was broken and she needed a cast for at least six weeks. Her left hand was a mess. The knife had missed all major arteries because the blade was small, but it had shattered a few smaller bones and caused some muscle and nerve damage. The doctor told her with some physical therapy she should be able to make a loose fist yet may never be able to clench her hand again. She was just happy to have a hand at all and couldn't wait for the swelling to go down enough so she could wear her 'Princess Ring' as Michael called it.

When the weekend came, Dana and Tony finally admitted

they needed to get back to California. There had been a few awkward moments when they'd found themselves alone together. He'd tried to talk to her about the kiss but she'd raised her hand to stop him.

"I get it, Tony. I was available and we were celebrating. I'm sorry your plan to dance me out of my clothes didn't work. The sex probably would have been fabulous." It didn't take a genius to tell she was pissed.

Tony caught her Saturday making a plane reservation.

"Do you want me to drive you to the airport?"

"No. Julie has to go to town and said she'd drop me off."

Dana was gone Sunday morning and Tony was left feeling like he'd somehow made the biggest mistake of his life but didn't know what.

Between the Thomas Patrick and Justin Martin incidents, Tony and Michael had spent the entire week doing paperwork and making phone calls. They finally had everything wrapped up and were able to put closure to the prostitute serial killer case. It hadn't ended well, but it was over. Tony drove off Monday morning.

Jon stayed a few days after Tony. He was leaving for Russia in September. The op had been pushed back because one of the people they were supposed to meet up with had gone to Asia.

The only plus to the timetable change was now Jon could spend some time with Elana Miller and see if she had any kind of skill in the field. He figured he was going to have to teach her some hand-to-hand combat and how to act. Every time he thought of Elana, though, all he could picture was that damn spandex suit. Hopefully, they'd be out of Russia by the end of September.

The hired hands came back to work and when July rolled

around, everything was back to normal at the ranch. On the 4th of July, Julie and the kids decided to make it Kami's new birthday. They said what better way to celebrate than with fireworks and a BBQ.

The death of Thomas Patrick and the fact Kamielle was alive had rocked the east coast. All his holdings tied to the illegal businesses had been seized. He had many legitimate business dealings, though. With the help of an accountant, Kamielle sold off all the businesses and properties that had been left to her in Thomas's will. He'd never changed it, stupid man.

She donated almost all the millions to different charities. She kept some money for herself since she didn't know what the future really held. Besides, she could give it away to more charities later.

At the end of July, Michael took Kami to get her cast off. Instead of driving her back to the ranch, he headed south out of town and they ended up north of Flathead Lake in the town of Somers.

"I thought we'd have a picnic."

He pulled a blanket out of the truck and the picnic basket it had been hiding. Since they weren't driving back to California any time soon, Michael had returned the Tahoe to the rental company at the airport. They were driving around in one of the ranch trucks. It wasn't as comfy as the Tahoe and Kamielle mentioned more than once she wanted to go into town and test drive SUVs.

Michael spread the blanket on the grass and helped her sit down. He rubbed her hands and looked at the scars covering them.

"My hands are ugly now." She glanced at their linked fingers.

"No they're not."

"I know what would make my left hand look better." She smiled and wiggled her fingers.

Michael laughed. "You're stealing my thunder, babe."

He pulled out the diamond ring. Kneeling next to her, he slipped it on. Then he kissed each finger and her palm. He treated the right hand to the same attention.

"We have a lot to discuss," he said.

They'd spent the last month and a half living day to day. They hadn't talked about the future, California, or anything of major importance.

"When do you have to go back to work?"

She knew he'd been on the phone with Tony about every other day discussing 'things'. She didn't want to know about his work with the VCTF; she'd dealt with enough violent crimes.

"Well, that's one of the things we need to talk about. You said you'd marry me. Where do you want to live?"

She looked around. There were families picnicking, sailboats on the water, and the sounds of summer fun. She looked to the sky and knew why Montana had the nickname of 'The Big Sky State'.

"I love it here."

"So do I. Want to stay here forever?" he asked.

She looked momentarily stunned. "I can't ask you to give up your job!"

"You're not asking me to. I've been thinking about leaving the VCTF for a while. I'm tired of spending my days in the minds of killers and other horrible people. The FBI doesn't have an office in this state but the Highway Patrol said they'd make an opening for me to be a liaison. I could work cases with them, be home every night with you, and not have to work violent crimes as a daily job anymore." He studied her face.

"Please, only make these changes if they're for you, not just for me."

"Well you see, Princess, it's not just 'me' anymore. It's 'us'. I want to be home with you every night. I don't want to go on cases that take me away for weeks at a time looking at death and worse."

She wiped away a happy tear. "Okay."

"That's it? Okay?" He looked at her skeptically.

"Right now I'm content being with you and that's enough." She kissed him and pulled him down to lay beside her on the blanket.

"Now, let's talk about a wedding." Michael grinned.

"I want simple."

"How about simple and quick?" he asked.

"What do you have in mind?"

"Well, it seems we have some things to take care of in California. I have a house to sell, we have belongings to get packed and shipped up here, and you have a demon cat Tony refuses to take care of any longer."

Kamielle sat up. "How could I have forgotten about Simon? My poor kitty! Is he okay?"

Michael pulled her back down. "Yeah. Tony had someone watching his place while he was here. Watering the plants and taking care of your cat. Simon trashed his house, by the way. I think it's hilarious."

"Why didn't you tell me sooner?"

"You had more important things to worry about".

"So, we fly to California and take care of everything?" She relaxed as Michael stroked his hands up and down her arms.

"I thought we'd fly to Las Vegas first. If you want simple and quick, what do you say we get married in Sin City?" He wiggled his eyebrows.

"I think that would be perfect." She leaned over and kissed him again. "I need to tell you something."

"What's wrong?"

"Nothing's really wrong. I had Julie take me to the clinic last week while you were out working on the ranch."

"Why?"

"I wanted to see an ob-gyn."

"Are you pregnant?"

"No. But I talked to her about my miscarriage and had her do some tests. Remember how I told you my doctor in Chicago said I may not be able to have kids?" She lowered her head.

Michael pushed her chin back up so she'd meet his eyes. "You want to have babies, don't you?"

"I want to have babies with you." She burst out crying.

"It's okay, honey, we'll have babies."

"Well, the doctor said I might be able to. She asked how long I'd been trying to get pregnant and I told her I wasn't actually trying, but we'd been having a lot of sex without birth control."

He grinned. "Yes, we sure have."

"She told me to give it a few months and helped me determine when I'm ovulating and stuff like that."

"I don't know what that means, but, okay."

"She said if we don't conceive naturally by the end of this year, we can look at medical ways to help me get pregnant."

"If that's what you want, baby, that's what we'll do. Does this mean we have to make love every single day?"

"What do you mean 'have to'? Don't you mean 'get to'?" She laughed.

"I think everything is going to be just fine, Princess."

"I do, too."

Michael leaned in and whispered against her lips, "I love you."

"I love you, too. And don't worry, I won't forget who said it first."

They lay on the blanket watching the end of the sailboat races. A light breeze blew, birds chirped, children laughed. Life didn't get much more perfect.

Maybe there was such a thing as happily ever after.

A Note From The Author

Thank you so much for picking up your copy of *Outrunning the Hunter*. I want you to know that without you, this adventure would not exist and I appreciate you more than I can say. You matter to me as a reader! As an independent author, your reviews of my stories matter too. I depend on the honest reviews readers like you leave on Amazon (just scan the QR code below) and Goodreads. Other readers use your insights when choosing what to read and will appreciate hearing your opinions of my book. I, of course, would love to hear from you as well. Please leave a review to let me know what you think.

Wishing you all the best,
Kyona

Acknowledgments

I couldn't have done any of this without my families, given or chosen, who have been part of my life and made me who I am.

A very special thank you to those who read my drafts and encouraged me. Carla, Erin, Jordana, Brandy, Twyla, Kate, Kelly, Jan, Charlotte, Jordan, Suzy, Kayla, and Eunice: Thank you for your honesty, support, and love.

To the teachers who shaped my life as educators and colleagues: You are amazing and don't ever let anyone tell you differently!

For my mom and dad, Twyla and Fred. No matter what, you always wanted what was best for me. I love you both, always.

I took a lot of liberties with procedures and locations – please excuse (and enjoy) my overactive imagination. Any mistakes are my own.

Acknowledgments 2012 – Charity and Clyde, thank you for helping to make this story even better and letting me share it with the world. Thank you Kara and Jo! I don't know what I'd do without you. Kara your extra hours and love of this story made it great.

About the Author

 As a teacher, Kyona is always writing stories and reading books for work and fun. Reading gives people an opportunity to relax and escape the pressures of everyday life. She lives in Eastern Washington with her loving husband and crazy dogs.

Life is short; enjoy it any way you can.

Also by Kyona Jiles